Memoirs Aren't Fairytales

A Story of Addiction

Marni Mann

Booktrope Editions
Seattle WA 2011

Cover Design by Greg Simanson

Edited by Rachel Brookhart

This is a work of fiction. Names, characters, places, brands, media, and incidents are either the product of the author's imagination or are used fictitiously. Any resemblance to similarly named places or to persons living or deceased is unintentional.

Print ISBN 978-1-935961-29-1

EPUB ISBN 978-1-62015-033-7

DISCOUNTS OR CUSTOMIZED EDITIONS MAY BE AVAILABLE FOR EDUCATIONAL AND OTHER GROUPS BASED ON BULK PURCHASE.

For further information please contact info@booktrope.com

Library of Congress Control Number: 2011961145

ACKNOWLEDGMENTS

From the conception of my novel to its birth, you've stood by my side, Mom. Your endless support and advice gave this book the love it needed. When I had doubt, you never stopped believing. Dad, I never would have made it here if you hadn't listened to my rants. My P, Nicole Vander Clay, you caught me before I fell. Your words brought me to the place I needed to be. Nina Kesner, your excitement was and always will be a force that drives me to reach further. Jen Howard, I will never be able to thank you for everything you've done. Your guidance and wisdom made this novel shine. Jane Ryder, you always made me smile; your support will never be forgotten. Jody Ruth, my partner-in-crime, your voice kept me going when I thought I couldn't take another step. Melissa Roske, you pushed me to find the right words. Your feedback made them sparkle. Katy Truscott, Kathy Dieringer, Junying Kirk, and Pat Mann, I couldn't have done this without your love and support. To the crew, Erin Burke, Mike Lucido, Katie and Dan Kinnetz, thanks for the inspiration and amusement. Never say never, right? Rachel Brookhart, I appreciate all your hard work and commitment. Greg Simanson, thanks for bringing life to my novel. Krista Basham, thank you for being the best manager I could ever ask for. This journey wouldn't be the same without you, and I'm honored to have you along for the ride. Katherine Sears and Ken Shear, thank you for giving me a chance and for believing in me. Tess Hardwick, you made this all possible and I will be forever grateful. Big hugs, my friend. Codi and Bella, you have my heart. And Brian, my dreams are all possible because of you. Don't ever stop holding my hand. I love you.

DEDICATION

To Susan, my light.

We were moving to Boston into a studio apartment in Chinatown, and all he needed from me was half the security deposit and a yes. I gave him both.

I didn't know what our apartment looked like. I'd never been to Chinatown before, and I didn't care. We were approaching the Tobin Bridge, and for the first time since I'd moved back in with my parents, I felt free.

At the start of the bridge, my hands grabbed the support bar on the door. Eric's hands were on ten and two, his knuckles white. It was like we were strapped in a cart, riding up to the peak of a rollercoaster. The skyline of Boston was in front of us, and somewhere in the middle of all those tall buildings was the place we were going to call home.

Eric shouted over the music, "We did it, Nicole! We're here!"

All four windows were open, and I leaned my head against the back of the seat. My eyes closed. Wind was rushing through the car, filling it with the smell of smog and fish from the Mystic River.

A clothes hanger was tickling the side of my ear and pulling out strands of my ponytail every time we went over a bump. The metal was cold, and as it touched my hair, it reminded me of my mom's cool hands, brushing the hair out of my face and tucking it behind my ear when she put me to bed as a child.

My hands let go of the bar and I put my arms up in the air, feeling the breeze swish between my fingers. "Hell yeah, we did," I said.

Our apartment was on the third floor, and we were the only tenants in the building who spoke English. Below us lived the owners of the Chinese restaurant downstairs, and above us were their parents—both sets and a few dogs. Our place was small, about the size of two dorm rooms. The fridge rattled and the oven worked, but the burners didn't. The bathroom was tiny, and the shower never had any hot water.

We were roughing it like we were on a camping trip, but without our parents nagging us to clean up the tent. Our air mattress was a twin, and we wobbled off the edges during the night. It didn't matter if our feet touched or if our arms crossed because we myself. Especially since the homeless man at the corner had harassed me. It had happened late at night, when I was walking to the train to visit Eric at work. The man came up behind me, wrapped his arms around my chest and cupped my boobs. I screamed, and his fingers squeezed my nipples. I tried to wiggle out of his grip, but couldn't. He was too strong and so much bigger than me. A woman ran over and hit him over the head with her purse, knocking him to the ground. After the boob incident, Eric said he'd get me a job at the club once a cocktail waitress position opened up. But until then, he'd support us.

On the nights Eric worked, loneliness would transform into paranoia, and every creak in the ceiling made me jump. For eight straight hours, I'd smoke weed and pace the room, checking the door every few minutes to make sure it was locked. So instead of being by myself, I'd hang with my neighbors at the Chinese restaurant downstairs who would liquor me up with scorpion bowls. When I was drunk, sleep came quickly, but it was always interrupted by nightmares. The nightmares had started when I'd moved back into my parents' house, and the same dream replayed in my head every night. The dreams seemed so real, I was scared to close my eyes again.

One night, I smoked a few bowls before I went to bed. I normally never mixed smoking and heavy drinking, but I was just so tired. All I wanted was a full eight hours of sleep. My screams woke me up. My body was shaking and I was sweating. The blanket underneath me was wet. I sat up, crossed my legs and wrapped my arms around my stomach, swaying back and forth. That was when I felt the pool of water under me. Even during college when I drank myself sick, I had never peed the bed.

I didn't want Eric to know about my accident, so I put the blanket in the shower and poured shampoo all over it. The pee had soaked through the blanket and into the velvet pillow top of the air mattress. I wiped the bed as best as I could and sprayed it with his cologne.

When Eric got home, I was in the bathroom, crouched between the toilet and sink.

"You okay?" he asked. He rocked me with one arm and lit a joint with his other.

I shook my head. "My dream, it felt so real," I said and hit the joint.

This nightmare was different than the one I usually had. I'd woken up in the woods on top of a mound of snow, and there was a burning and stabbing pain between my legs.

He looked over at the shower and at the sopping blanket covered in shampoo bubbles. "Did you get sick?"

I took another hit and turned my head, blowing the smoke into the shower. At some point, I shrugged my shoulders.

He helped me out of the bathroom and piled all our clothes on the floor.

"What are you doing?" I asked.

He took our pillows and put them at the top of the pile. "Making the bed," he said.

We sat on our new bed, and he lit a second joint since I'd sucked down the first. When it was smoked to the roach clip, we lay back and passed out.

In the morning, he called his manager and asked to be assigned to the door so I could go to work with him. He thought he could cure my nightmares by spending every minute with me and being next to me when I went to bed. It didn't help, but I did start going to work with him. With my book of word searches and his CD player, I'd park myself on a bench by the front of the club.

Jimmy, the owner of the club, asked Eric if he'd work a security gig for a Fourth of July bash at his house in Cape Cod. He offered Eric a hotel room and five hundred bucks for the night. I still didn't have a job—no waitressing spots had opened up yet—and we really needed the money. Eric said he'd do it, and that afternoon he took me to Goodwill and bought me a dress for the party. Jimmy told him not to bring any friends or a date, but somehow Eric would get me in.

The morning of the party, we filled the rabbit with gas and set off for the Cape. We hit so much traffic we had to drive straight to Jimmy's so Eric wouldn't be late for the pre-party meeting. He changed in the car, and after I dropped him off, I drove to the hotel. The room was in Eric's name, but I told the front desk clerk I was Eric's wife and he gave me a key.

I had three hours to get ready for the party so I filled the big Jacuzzi tub and soaked, letting the jets massage me. I washed my hair with the little bottles of shampoo and conditioner and lathered up with shower gel that smelled like honey. I felt like I was at a spa.

I took my time painting my face, making sure my blush was blended with my concealer and my eyelids were smoky with dark shadow. Before I left, I ironed my dress and smoked a bowl.

At the end of Jimmy's long driveway was a valet parking sign. All the cars pulling up were expensive looking. The rabbit would tag me as a party crasher, so I parked it a few streets away and walked up the side of the driveway, through the trees. Eric was working the front door with a clipboard in hand and had told me earlier to walk up behind a couple and pretend I was their daughter. I followed an older couple to the front door, and once Eric checked their names off the list, I was inside.

The house was a palace, with stone pillars in the entryway, staircases on both sides of the room, and tall windows that ran along the back, overlooking Jimmy's private beach. Behind the house, was a big white tent where appetizers were being passed around by waiters in tuxedos. Paper lanterns and candles lit up the tent, and twinkle lights flickered from the surrounding trees.

I waited in line at one of the bars and ordered a glass of champagne. I downed it, and the bartender topped off my glass before I stepped away. There was an empty table at the far end of the tent, by the beach, and I sat down to watch the ocean. I hoped no one would show up to claim this seat.

"Are you a friend of Jimmy's?"

A man with gray hair and glasses, dressed in a white suit sat next to me.

"Yes—" I said and stopped. I had only met Jimmy once. "I know him through a mutual friend."

"Are you here alone?" He held his hand out for me to shake. "Bernie," he said.

"Nicole, and I'm here with a friend."

Should I have told him my real name? For all I knew, Bernie could be Jimmy's brother, and if I got busted, Eric could lose his job.

"Is your friend male or female?" he asked. He eyed me up and down.

"Aren't I a little young for you, Bernie?"

If I wasn't at Eric's boss' house, I would have told him to fuck off. I didn't date men who were old enough to be my grandfather.

He put his hand on my shoulder and laughed. "My son is here and he's single," he said. "Stay here and I'll go get him."

The band had started playing and the dance floor filled up. I wasn't much of a dancer unless I was really drunk, but I was into food, and dinner was arriving at the tables. In front of me, a waiter placed a thick steak, garlic mashed potatoes, and some type of vegetable that didn't look familiar. The tuna noodle casseroles Eric and I had been eating were like mystery meat slop in comparison.

Bernie returned to my side. "Nicole, meet Jefferson, my son." Jefferson had at least ten years on me. And like his father, he wore glasses and combed his frizzy hair to the side.

Jefferson sat to my left and after shaking my hand, he dove into his plate. While we ate, he asked where I was from and what I did for a living. I said I was a first grade teacher, living in a loft in the South End of the city with a Boston terrier named Pork Chop.

That was the life I'd always hoped for anyway. And it felt good to say it, instead of telling him I was an unemployed college dropout.

My champagne buzz had peaked, but it'd soon be gone from all the food. I had a joint in my purse I was saving for when Eric got off work, but the party could last all night and into the morning so I decided not to wait for him. But I had to lose Jefferson first.

Just as I was about to excuse myself to the bathroom, he pulled out an orange bottle of prescription pills and washed one down with his beer.

"Am I giving you headache?" I asked.

"Adderall," he said and shook the bottle. The pills rattled inside.

Adderall mixed with a couple hits of strong bud had always given me a wicked good buzz. In college, my roommate and I used the two to cure our hangovers.

I held out my hand.

"You want one?" he asked.

"Oh yeah."

Since my champagne glass was empty, he handed me his beer, and I washed down the pill.

"You want to sm—"

"I want to show you something," he said. "Come with me."

Wherever we were going, we'd have to smoke when we got there.

We stopped at the bar to refill our glasses and walked up the lawn to the house. My feet were tired and sore from wearing heels, but the champagne was helping to numb them.

Inside, couples were sitting on couches and standing in groups talking. Jefferson held my arm, pulling me around the crowds.

The house was a maze of hallways and rooms, and everything was white: the couches and pictures, the sculptures, even the wood floors.

After several turns, Jefferson stopped in front of a closed door. "Are you ready for some fun?"

He looked like one of the guys in the computer class I took in college. And if he was anything like them, I figured we had different definitions of fun.

There was a number pad next to the door. He pressed some buttons and the door slid open. The walls inside the room were covered in little glass tiles that sparkled in the candlelight, and the ceiling was mirrored. A swimming pool took up most of the room, and the lining was so dark the water was black. At least twenty people, men and women, were in the pool, floating in the deep end and standing in the shallow water. All of them were naked. And if they weren't hooking up, touching and kissing, they were watching.

"Come on," Jefferson said. He stepped into the room, loosening his tie and unbuttoning his shirt.

Skinny-dipping? At Eric's boss' house? I wasn't into it. Jefferson wasn't attractive and neither were any of the men in the pool.

"Real sexy crowd, huh?" Eric whispered in my ear.

I hadn't moved from the doorway.

"I bet that guy in the corner is really turning you on."

The man Eric was referring to had thick black hair covering his back and a belly the size of Santa's.

I punched his arm, and we both laughed.

"How did you get back here?" Eric asked.

"That guy," I said and pointed at Jefferson. Jefferson had his pants off and was pulling down his whitey tighties. "He said he wanted to show me something."

"Sick fuck," Eric said. "Let's go, the fireworks are about to start, and Jimmy gave me a thirty-minute break to get some grub."

I waved goodbye to Jefferson, but he was climbing down the steps to the shallow end. His ass was so white it was practically shining.

Eric took me out a back door, and we walked down to the beach, sitting in a spot away from the other guests. I lit the joint and took a drag. When I coughed, I handed it to him.

"Whitey tighties gave me an Adderall," I said.

Eric exhaled a cloud of smoke and then looked at me. "Damn, lucky you."

"Sorry I couldn't score you one too. Take some extra hits so you can catch up."

The fireworks shot into the dark sky and exploded into bursts of color. The noise they let off was so loud I couldn't hear anything else. But there wasn't anything else to hear. Eric was taking pulls off the joint, and my brain was silent. Adderall and weed was a nice mix of calm, and the fireworks were little puffs of beautiful.

After the grand finale, a firework in the shape of the flag, the beach cleared. The band was playing a slow song, and the waves were washing over my feet.

"This is perfect," I said.

"Shit, I'm glad we escaped Bangor."

I agreed. And it didn't matter that we were broke and slept on an air mattress with only tuna and noodles in our bellies. I had everything I needed.

CHAPTER TWO

A group of servers from Lucy's, the bar next door, came to Eric's club one night. They told Eric they were out celebrating because they were going abroad for the semester. I was on the bench out front, and Eric called me over. The girls said I should apply for one of their open positions. I did, and the manager, Mark, put me on for six nights a week with Sundays off. Eric had the same schedule. It was perfect.

With my tips and our hourly wages, we could expand into different food groups and go back to buying half ounces of weed, instead of dime bags. We pooled our money and kept it in a pickle jar in the freezer. If there were something we wanted to buy, like a new pair of sneakers or a coffeemaker, we'd check with the other one first.

My co-workers asked all kinds of questions about Eric and me, if we were dating, if we hooked up, and if not, were we related? I didn't know why they cared so much. It was like they had never seen a guy and girl be friends without benefits. I asked them, if Eric were a girl would they think I was a lesbian? That shut them up.

Eric was a good-looking guy. He was tall and meaty with sea-green eyes and a pile of auburn curls. But hooking up with him would be like hooking up with my brother Michael. Eric protected me, even though he couldn't stop me from having nightmares. I was there for him too, in an I'll-take-care-of-you-like-your-mom-did sort of way. And that's just what I did the night we scored some free mushrooms. Eric couldn't stand the taste of shrooms. Neither could I, really, so I broke them up into small pieces and coated them with butter so they'd slide down his throat.

We both had the night off, and we were going to the club to celebrate Craig's, one of the bouncers, birthday. Since shrooms took an hour to kick in, we smoked a bowl and left before we were too distracted with visuals to go anywhere.

At the club, there was a line all the way around the building, but we walked to the front and didn't have to pay the cover. The bash was on the second floor in the VIP lounge, and tons of people had come to party. Besides the bouncers and Casey, a cocktail waitress we'd smoked with before, I didn't know anyone. Casey was also celebrating, and she put Eric and me on her tab. She'd graduated from Northeastern University and just gotten a job at a marketing agency, so this was her last week working at the club.

I sat with Casey on one of the couches, sipped a vodka and Red Bull, and smoked a cigarette. When the cherry at the end of my cig started flickering like a sparkler and the bits of sparkles turned into shapes, I knew the shrooms had set in. Eric was tripping too. He was standing against the wall in the corner of the room, staring at his hands and moving them in circles in the air.

The lights in the ceiling changed to a dark pink. Everything around me went warm like a fire was heating it. The lights above the DJ booth changed to green and yellow, red and blue. The colors danced through the smoke-filled room.

"Come on, girl, let's dance," Casey said.

She pulled me to my feet and moved me through the crowd.

The warmth of her hand made me want to see her face. "Casey," I said.

She turned around, standing only inches away. "What's up?"

She was so pretty. Her eyes were giant emeralds, and her skin was creamy and swirled like soft serve on a cone.

"Nothing, I..."

"I need a potty break first, then we're going to dance," she said.

I watched my feet as we walked to the bathroom. My shoes moved over the floor and left black footprints whenever I lifted to step. People swished past me, blob-like and wavy, and then Casey opened a door and pulled me inside. The stalls looked like long hallways, and the neon overhead light turned everything green. Even my hands were green. I went to the sink to wash it off.

The soap was purple, and rainbow bubbles floated into my face. Was my face green too?

I looked up at the mirror. I had green skin with thick red veins popping out of my cheeks and purple lips.

I touched my forehead.

Did I really look like this?

"Nicole, you ready?" Casey asked.

She stood next to me, looking in the same mirror as me. But she didn't look like a monster.

She looped her arm through mine and brought me to the dance floor. Strobe lights flashed, making the room black and then white. The faces around me were skeletons.

The music felt like a massage. The beat went through my body, vibrating all the sensitive parts. I swung my arms over my head and watched the trails of colors that swirled as they moved. I grinded my hips against Casey's. She danced behind me and in front, and I tried to keep her pace.

The eyes and teeth around us sparkled like icicles in the sun.

"I need a drink," Casey said.

I didn't know how long we'd been dancing. It seemed like only minutes, but I was thirsty too.

Back in the VIP room, Eric was on couch, holding an ice cube and staring at it. I sat next to him, watching his hand fill with dark blue water.

"Did you bring any weed?" I asked. Smoking intensified the high.

"No, you?"

I checked my purse, but found only a few roaches, and we didn't have a bowl to smoke them in.

Casey sat beside me. Her lips went around the straw and glowed like she was sucking on a light bulb.

"Casey," Eric said. "Do you have any bud?"

"I do, but it's at my apartment," she said.

We had some at our apartment too, but our place was too far to walk.

"It's last call," Casey said. "You guys want to leave and go smoke?"

We'd been here for four hours? Time had really slowed down.

"Let's go to our place," Eric said.

"I'm parked in the lot behind the club," Casey said.

Eric and I had taken the train. With Casey driving, we could save the six bucks in train fare and buy some munchies. I was really hungry, or maybe I just wanted to chew something.

I got in the passenger seat, and Eric climbed into the back and leaned forward so his head was between my shoulder and Casey's. She stalled twice before we got out of the lot, and the car jerked each time, sending my head into the dash.

"Do you see the spiders?" Eric asked.

The taillights on the car ahead were red daddy longlegs with big black eyes.

"That's too creepy," I said.

I had a fear of spiders. Snakes also.

"What did you guys take tonight?" Casey asked.

Nothing around me was normal. I couldn't believe it had taken her this long to notice. Maybe she was too drunk.

"Shrooms," Eric said.

She told us about the last time she'd tripped. She said she'd felt like she'd peed her pants, but every time she checked her panties, they were dry.

My underwear did feel a little wet. I felt the crotch of my jeans and it was dry. They still felt wet. I had to get my mind off my underwear.

When we got back to our apartment, Eric rolled a blunt. Casey flipped on the TV and found a station that was playing music and danced around the room.

When the blunt was down to a roach, Eric said he wanted to take a shower and went into the bathroom. I wanted to take one too. Warm blue water and colorful soapy bubbles sounded fun. I'd have to wait until he got out.

I sat on the floor, and Casey danced around me. She lifted my long hair off my back and held it like horse reins.

"Your hair smells like cookies," she said.

She dropped my hair, and her fingers went to my scalp, scratching and rubbing the tender spots. My hands were in front of me, writing in the air with my fingers.

"You know, I've always had a thing for you, Nicole."

I hadn't known her all that long and had only hung out with her a couple times, but she was cool. Pretty girls like Casey weren't usually nice. But she was.

"Are you into all that?"

"Into what?" I asked.

She sat in front of me, and her hands touched my cheeks. Her lips went to mine, and I tasted the blue cocktail she'd been drinking at the club. Her tongue slid in and caressed, twirled and poked mine.

"Girls," she said after she pulled away.

My underwear was wet again.

I'd never been with a girl. I found them beautiful, but they didn't have that spicy smell and rough edge like guys did, and those were the things that turned me on. But there was something about Casey that felt safe. Safe like when I was around Eric.

She held the bottom of my shirt and stared into my eyes. The emeralds were now sapphires. My shirt came up and over my head. She unhooked my bra, and the straps dropped off my shoulders.

And then her lips were on my nipples, tugging them with her teeth and flicking them with her tongue. It was incredible. I didn't know if I'd feel the same way sober, looking down at a head of long, blond hair and painted fingernails, and be turned on like I was. Still, it felt incredible.

My nipples became sore, and I gently pushed her away. She smiled, her teeth star-like, and arched her back. Her shirt was silk and melted into my fingers. I lifted it off and flung it onto the air mattress.

At the club, her skin had swirled like soft serve, but now it flickered like fire. Red and orange flames shot from her stomach to her chest. My cold tongue started at the base of the fire, tasting her sweetness, and it warmed as I got closer to the tips of the flames.

She moaned.

Her nipples were smoldering rocks.

Although I'd never been here before, I knew what I liked. I wanted to give her the same safeness she made me feel.

I tickled and teased her boobs with my fingers. My mouth moved away from hers and landed on her neck, the spot where it dipped to her shoulder. Using a small chunk of my hair, I traced the circle around her nipple.

She got on her knees and pushed my back to the floor, taking off my jeans and underwear.

Her fire had spread into me.

She knew where to touch me. The spot at the very top that wanted to be rubbed with just the pad of her finger. She didn't push too hard or soft, and she didn't tug or tap. She circled, and the faster her finger moved, the louder I got.

Her mouth focused on my nipples. But she was softer than before, sucking just enough to give my body everything it needed to build.

I gripped her hair and pulled. My moaning turned into a scream. And then my body rippled like an avalanche. I exhaled as the calm swept over me.

"That was…"

She kissed me. "Amazing," she said.

I was able to let go and have an amazing orgasm, like when I used my own fingers, but a girl getting me off was so weird.

The water from the shower turned off, and the curtain screeched when Eric slid it open.

"We should probably get dressed before he comes out," she said.

She helped me put on my bra, and I helped with hers, and she told me she had to go. We hugged and kissed at the door, and when she walked down the hall, she left a trail of rainbows behind her.

Eric came out of the bathroom and asked where Casey was. I told him she had to go.

"Damn," he said. "I like having her around, I wish she wasn't leaving the club."

I liked having her around too. Actually, I wanted to hang out with her more. But only for the same reason I liked hanging out with Eric. I didn't need friends to get me off. My fingers were just fine.

The girls I worked with weren't fun and adventurous like Casey. They were catty and made fun of overweight customers, and when they didn't get a good tip they'd re-run the credit card and tack on an extra percent or two. And then I met Renee. She looked like a rock 'n' roll groupie. Her voice was raspy, her hair was dreaded in sections, and she had piercings in her nose, lip, and tongue. With her smudged makeup, unmatched clothes and short attention span, she seemed constantly hungover even though she said she rarely drank. She was the bartender, and during our breaks we'd go out back and smoke together. She had the dankest weed and didn't mind smoking me up as long as I didn't tell the other servers I was high or who I got the pot from.

She was a no-frills, no-bullshit stoner, and quickly we became pals. Her apartment had a real bed, a couch, and dishes in the cabinets. Her most prized possession was a two-foot glass bong named Baby, and many nights after work Baby got us so fucked up Eric and I had to crash there.

Renee became our go-to for weed. We'd been buying it from Eric's co-worker, but he was unreliable and expensive, and the herb tasted like dirt. Every payday, we gave Renee sixty bucks. She'd go to her dealer's house and come back with a half-ounce of the whitest, stickiest bud we'd ever seen. We used to get some sick shit in Bangor because lots of people grew it. This weed was different, hydro grown, and after a bowl you could barely remember your name. She referred to her dealer as Jesus. I was pretty sure she wasn't religious, but weed, she said, was her bread and wine, and Jesus was her savior.

Her secret lasted until the end of winter. Renee went back home to New Jersey for two weeks to visit her parents, and when she returned we noticed a change in her. At first the change was slight. She had loads of energy and never stopped talking. Then she started to lose weight. She was never fat to begin with, but the thickness on her arms, thighs, and stomach were disappearing. I watched her eat dinner at the bar and munch on snacks after we smoked. I also noticed her frequent trips to the bathroom. That meant one thing, she had to be bulimic.

One night after a few hits from Baby, Eric and I confronted her. She laughed when I said the word, bulimic, like I was crazy, and then asked if we wanted to meet Jesus. It was odd how she shifted the conversation and suddenly wanted to introduce us after months of keeping him a secret. Maybe she was tired of being the middleman, or maybe Renee wanted to share the blessing with us. Maybe Jesus could recite a prayer that would stop me from having nightmares.

We took the train to Jesus' house on a Saturday night when we all got out of work. I was telling Eric about the tips I'd made when out of nowhere, he nudged me and signaled me to look up. Towering over my seat was a man, his legs inches from my knees. I didn't know how long he'd been standing there or how I hadn't noticed him before. He was dressed like the homeless, bundled in layers with a stained jacket. His eyes were closed, his mouth open, and his back was slowly bending forward, so his face was getting closer to mine. Eric kicked his shin, and the guy straightened his back and opened his eyes for a second. His pupils were the size of a grain of sand.

When the man started to take his second nosedive, someone on the train yelled, "Methadone saves lives," and all the other passengers laughed.

Eric stood up and said, "Get the hell away from us."

The guy stumbled toward the door, held onto a side railing, and continued to bend forward like he had done when he was in front of me.

I had heard of methadone. Bangor had a methadone clinic, and some oxy-head acquaintances from high school were rumored to be enrolled.

"What's he on?" I asked Renee.

"Heroin." She said it like she'd seen the effects of the drug hundreds of times before.

I couldn't take my eyes off his face. He was young, close to my age or a few years older, although the wrinkles on his forehead and the dirt and scruff on his cheeks made it hard to tell. I found it strange that he didn't flinch when that person yelled or when everyone was laughing at him. If anything, his expression was peaceful like heroin had deafened him.

Watching him reminded me of the first time I tried ecstasy and the emotional numbness that came with it. The most devastating thing could have been said to me, like Michael had died, and it wouldn't have sunk in when I was tripping on that shit. Was that the kind of high he was feeling? If it was, I envied him.

Jesus' townhouse was different than the dealers I bought from back at home. Bangor pot-pushers sold to support their habit and lived in duplexes that weren't in the nicest part of town. This place was in a decent neighborhood, fancy electronics and leather couches furnished the living room, and there was a fish tank that took up almost an entire wall.

There were four men sitting on the couch, playing a video game on the giant TV. We stood in a line by the door, pressed against the wall, and listened to them yell. My attention shifted to the staircase when a guy appeared at the top of them.

"That's Jesus," Renee whispered.

His head was shaved and covered with tattoos of spider webs and skulls. The tattoos carried down and wrapped around his bulging biceps and forearms. He stopped on the middle step and made eye contact with Renee. She moved to the steps and we followed behind her.

When all three of us were upstairs and standing outside a closed door, Jesus unlocked the five padlocks drilled into the doorframe. By the way he patted Eric and me down and flashed the gun holstered in the waist of his jeans, I thought we were entering the cash room of an underground casino. But it was like any normal bedroom with clothes dumped in the corners and a bed by the window. Once the door was locked behind us, we were told to stand in front of it. Jesus stood a few feet from us and his eyes shifted between Eric and me.

Eric said his name and stuck his hand out. Jesus reached forward with a closed fist, and Eric quickly balled his hand and pounded Jesus' knuckles.

"Que," he said.

So Jesus wasn't his real name.

"I'm Nicole," I said.

Que nodded at me.

"What are you guys looking for?"

"A half-ounce of green," Eric said.

There was a padlocked wooden cabinet next to Que's bed, and when he swung the door open, I was shocked by what was inside. The dealers back home kept a small stash of weed, an ounce or two, and on occasion Vicodin or ecstasy pills. This was like a fucking pharmacy.

The top shelf was filled with a shopping bag of weed. The bag was clear, and the buds were the size of corn on the cob. The second shelf was pills. Rows of pill bottles were filed along the sides and back wall, and sandwich bags of white powder were in the middle. There was a metal pan on the bottom shelf holding wax-paper packets stamped with emblems.

Que took out the shopping bag and used a digital scale to weigh out a half ounce. Eric placed our money in Que's hand and pocketed the weed. Renee was next, but she didn't say what she wanted. Que just reached into the cabinet and pulled out two sandwich bags from the middle of the second shelf. They exchanged what was in their hands and he walked us out to the hallway.

"Can we start buying from you?" Eric asked. "Without having to bring Renee?"

Que wrote his phone number on a napkin and gave it to me. "Call first and just the two of you, no one else, ever," he said.

We took the train back to Renee's place. Eric packed Baby with bud while Renee dumped some powder onto her glass table. She spread out three lines, rolled up a dollar bill, and gave it to me. I'd snorted coke a handful of times when I was in college, but I was always drunk, so I didn't feel it. Coke wasn't the only drug I'd tried. My roommate, Katy, and I experimented with pain pills and ecstasy, and tripped on shrooms and acid. But mostly, it was weed, and we wouldn't start our homework without smoking something first.

But sitting in front of Renee's coffee table, I was sober. The coke shot through the bill, into my nose, and straight to my brain. I took a hit from Baby, and the smoke expanded in my lungs and came out of my mouth like a chimney.

My jaw was swinging like a pendulum. My lips were moving like propellers on a speedboat. I felt good. Too good. And I had more energy than I knew what to do with.

The three of us went out for a walk, and I found myself talking to the men I passed on the street. I hadn't done that in the year I'd lived in Boston. I'd always kept my head down whenever I was outside to avoid stares. But I was looking up and making eye contact. I even smiled and flirted a little. I jumped in puddles of slush, and the snow and dirt hit the front of my legs. I thought, I'm never going to wash these jeans again. I would keep them as a reminder of this night, just like the battle scar I had under my chin from my last night at college.

I felt cloudy and sore when I woke up Monday morning. I didn't know when I had gone to bed or how long I slept, but I knew I didn't have any nightmares. My stomach was gurgling. We hadn't eaten since Saturday night.

Eric was curled up on the other side of Renee's couch, and I shook him awake. He opened his eyes, and I nodded my head towards the coffee table. Renee was sitting next to the table, separating the last of the blow. Eric looked back at me. His eyes gleamed, and his front teeth bit his lower lip. The last time I had seen that look was when we were driving over the Tobin Bridge.

Why not, I didn't have to be at work until five. I felt pretty fucking lucky, because not everyone had the chance to find Jesus.

CHAPTER THREE

Snorting coke was like being connected to a pair of jumper cables. Once that cane was up my nose, my battery ran perfectly. I flipped my tables faster than the other servers by delivering my own food and sold add-ons like appetizers and pitchers instead of mugs of beer. If the bar had been open twenty-four hours a day, I would have worked straight and never gone home. My boss Mark was loving me too. He told me almost every day I was his favorite because I was making him so much money.

It was like Que had written me a prescription that said, "Every hour, blow one line of coke on an empty stomach. Mix the drug with alcohol as needed. Don't try to sleep. You won't be able to operate machinery without laughing."

The best part of it all was my nightmares were gone. Since coke kept me from sleeping, I couldn't dream about what those bastards had done to me. And how they dirtied my insides without even wearing a condom.

I'd come a long way since the month I'd lived on my parents' couch. And I'd changed without the help of a therapist. My parents had nagged me that whole month to enroll in Bangor's community college, to go to work with my dad at the *Bangor Daily News*, and to meet with a therapist. My parents didn't get it. I wanted to be left alone. I didn't want to talk. I didn't want to listen. And I sure as hell didn't want to meet with a stranger who held a notebook and wrote as I talked, pretending like they cared or understood.

Eric got it though. Bangor was only twenty minutes away from the University of Maine. So he picked a city where, besides Michael, I wouldn't know anyone and no one would have heard about what happened to me.

I'd promised my parents before I left that I'd call them every night. I'd kept my promise, and recently they said they had noticed a change in my voice. They said I sounded happy. I was right, leaving Bangor had been the best thing for me.

Confidence flowed through me. I traded my baggy clothes for booty shorts and belly shirts and strutted around the bar like I was working at Hooters. I was that girl I'd been in college.

Phone numbers found their way into my apron, and men openly flirted. I'd kid right back too, like the night when five college guys sat in my section for happy hour. They called me beautiful and gave me all kinds of compliments like how my eyes were sexy and my smile was a tease. I told them I'd keep the rounds coming if they took extra special care of me. They said they would, and they'd make sure I was left satisfied.

One of the guys in their group was really cute. He was a little bigger than Eric and wearing a Boston College football t-shirt. I'd busted him checking me out when I was working my other tables. I liked the big linebacker type with messy hair and a baby face and hoped he'd stick around after closing, so we could get a beer.

At last call, I stopped by their table to drop off their last round and Boston College grabbed my arm, pulling me against his chest. "Will you come home with me?"

"I don't get off for a while," I said. "We have a meeting—"

"Fuck the meeting, I want you."

His hand moved to my ass, and he squeezed one of my cheeks.

"I'll think about it," I said and tried to pull away, but he clamped down even harder.

"What's there to think about?" he asked. He placed my hand on his crotch. His dick was hard, and it was longer than my fingers. "We all want you."

"All?"

He nodded at each of the guys around the table.

I didn't have a chance to respond because a pair of hands clutched me from behind and pushed me out of the way.

"What the fuck?" Mark shouted at BC. "Apologize to her."

The five guys rose from the table and circled around Mark.

"Did you hear what I said? Apologize to her. Now."

I backed away a few feet and watched the guys puff out their chests and clench their fists like they were getting ready to fight. Mark was tall, but standing next to these guys, he looked like a horse jockey.

"She's a fucking whore," BC said. "Look at how she's dressed."

All the other servers dressed like me, wearing shorts and tank tops. Why did my clothes make me a whore? And a whore would be having a lot more sex than I was. The last time a guy had touched me had been over a year ago—Casey fingering me didn't count as sex—and getting raped didn't count as sleeping with someone.

Mark swung at BC, and everyone attacked at once. Mark was at the bottom of the pileup and the five guys were on top of him, wrestling and kicking. The fight didn't last long because Big Dan, the bouncer who worked the front door, came running into the dining room. He pulled the guys off the floor by their collars and told them to get out before he called the cops.

Mark stood up and came right over to me. "You okay?" he asked. His lip was bleeding, and there was a scratch under his eye.

"Yeah, I…"

"They didn't leave you a tip," he said and pulled out his wallet. He took out a wad of bills and handed it to me. "Take this."

"You don't have—"

"And don't worry about closing up," he said. "Just go home for the night."

My closing duties would take me at least an hour to finish, and there was a bag of coke in my apron just waiting to be snorted.

"See you tomorrow," he said and he walked towards his office. I said thanks, but I didn't think he heard me.

Renee was standing behind the bar, staring at me. With everyone watching, I didn't want to go over and tell her what happened. She had told me we needed to keep our friendship a secret from our co-workers. We kept our distance at work.

I flashed Mark's money and mouthed, "party at my house." She had this odd smirk on her face. I thought she'd be excited I'd gotten a handout from Mark, but it didn't appear that way. Of course, later that night after we re-upped from Que, she was blowing lines of cane with a big 'ol grin on her mug.

The next morning, Casey pulled up just as Eric and I were walking out of our apartment building. We hadn't seen her since that night we'd tripped on shrooms at the club. We'd called her a few times, and she'd called us back, but we were never able to catch each other.

She rolled down her window. "What're you guys doing today?"

"We were just about to run an errand," Eric said.

"You want to go get a tattoo?"

We didn't have the money for a tattoo. Plus, Que had told us to be at his house in twenty minutes.

"Can't, we're broke," I said.

"I'll pay," she said and smiled.

"You go," Eric whispered. "And I'll go to Que's."

I had always wanted a tattoo.

Her eyes bounced from Eric to me. "So..."

"Nicole will go, but I've got something I have to do," Eric said.

I got in the car and asked about her new job. She said she was designing online ads for a big law firm and buying something called media space.

I hadn't touched a computer since college. My email inbox was probably full, if it hadn't already been shut off from not using it.

"Do you like working in an office?" I asked.

"I get to design and that's all I've ever wanted to do, but my cubicle is kind of small."

Casey had gone to school for marketing and was now living her dream. I'd have to go back to school to become a teacher, but never wanted to step foot on another college campus.

She asked about Eric and some of the other bouncers. I guess she hadn't kept in touch with anyone. I filled her in on all the gossip Eric had told me about his co-workers, which kept us from talking about our hookup. I wasn't sure how I was going to tell her it was a one-time thing, and I really just wanted to be her friend. Luckily, I didn't have to. The shop wasn't too far from my place, and once she parked, we both got out of the car.

The walls inside the tattoo parlor were decorated with thousands of pictures of all the tats they'd done. They even covered the ceiling. Casey had brought a drawing she'd done herself. It was intertwining lines that formed a circle with three names in the middle.

"My family," she said when I asked who the names were.

I didn't know what design I wanted. My family was in my heart, but it seemed a little strange to put them on my skin too. I didn't like Chinese symbols or tribal bands. Casey suggested a butterfly or flower, but those were too girly for me. I decided to get the skyline of Boston inked on my foot. A symbol of how far I'd come since moving here.

"Who wants to go first?" Austin, the tattoo guy, asked.

"You go," Casey said.

I got on the dentist-like chair, and Austin drew on my foot with a marker. After I approved the placement and design, he took the tattoo gun out of its plastic bag. He inserted a new needle into the tip and dipped the head into a cup of black ink.

Casey held my hand, but she didn't have to. It wasn't painful, more like an annoying scratch that wouldn't go away.

"I want to put in a few details, is that okay?" Austin asked.

"Do whatever you want," I said, taking in all the pictures on the ceiling.

Eric had a tattoo, and so did a lot of my friends in college. But their tattoos weren't like these. These were pieces of art.

"All done," Austin said after a while.

Around the skyline, he had put yellow, blue, and pink swirls. They were like the bursts of beautiful I saw on the beach in Cape Cod. A needle had inked this special memory. A story. And now I'd never forget it.

Casey got into the chair, and I watched the needle. The names popped in a rich red, the circle black and shadowed with yellow. She winced and complained and said how she couldn't believe how brave I'd been.

I wasn't brave. The needle just didn't hurt.

Austin covered her tat with a bandage, like he'd done for me, and Casey drove me back to my apartment. She parked in front and turned off the engine.

"Can I come up?" she asked.

I only had an hour before work and I still needed to shower and get ready.

"I have to leave soon."

"That's fine," she said. "I'll just give Eric a quick hug and take off."

When we got inside, Eric was in the kitchen separating the coke into two bags. On the other side of the counter were a rolled-up bill and two lines he'd chopped up. I left Casey at the door and snorted both lines. When I looked up, she was pale.

"Is the tattoo hurting you?" I asked. "Sit down and I'll get you some water."

"I don't need water, I'm fine," she said. "Was that coke you just snorted?"

"Yeah—"

"Why do you have so much of it?" She pointed at the two bags in front of Eric.

Eric told her one bag was for me and the other was for him.

"This is too much for me," she said. She turned around and opened the door.

I caught her before she got through the doorway.

"It's not a big deal," I said.

"It is."

"Casey—"

"I thought you were like me, Nicole, but you're not."

She ripped my hands off her arms and ran down the hall.

I looked at Eric, and he smiled and cut a line for each of us to snort.

CHAPTER FOUR

My daisy dukes and tight tanks were getting me bigger tips, and I was picking up all double shifts, but we still never had enough cash. We never had enough of anything, really. There wasn't enough food in the fridge or money to pay the rent and electric bill, and there was never enough blow to snort.

Our landlord would bang on our door at the first of each month, threatening to evict us if we didn't get caught up. He came early in the morning, and Eric and I would hide in the bathroom. We'd play a game of how many lines we could get up our noses before he stopped knocking and left us alone. Usually it took about six. But in the third month, I only had enough time to do two before I heard what sounded like a bulldozer clawing through the kitchen wall. I checked, and the walls were intact, but the front door was being rammed with something hard. Both the deadbolt and chain were locked, so the wood splintered in the middle, and our landlord came plowing through the gap. He had a crowbar in his hand and aimed it like a gun, flashing it in our faces. Spit was flying from his mouth as he yelled about the rent we owed. All I could do was laugh. I mean, the guy looked like Homer Simpson, with his bald head and rippling pot belly.

I put my hands in the air and backed away from the crowbar to find my purse. I emptied my wallet, handing Homer all the money I had. It was a fist full of change. "Will this buy us one more night?"

He pocketed my change. "I want you punks out of my building. Get your shit and get the fuck out right now."

I stuffed my two backpacks full, but there was still so much to pack. We didn't have any boxes. We were out of trash bags except for the one in the kitchen filled with garbage. I turned the trash bag upside down, dumping all the rubbish onto the floor. Homer yelled at me for making such a mess, but he wasn't giving me much of a choice. The trash bag smelled like stale milk and moldy Chinese food. I didn't have time to soak up the liquid or wipe off the chunks of food that were stuck to the bottom of the bag. I threw in everything I could.

I did a final sweep of the room. We were leaving behind the lamp and coffeemaker, towels, plates, silverware and the air mattress. I asked Homer if we could have more time to move. His response came out in a paragraph, and it wasn't in English. I guess the answer was no, and whatever else he said was just some bullshit. Besides the rent, we were good tenants.

Eric hoisted the TV into his arms, I carried the backpacks and trash bag, and we left the building with Homer and his fucking crowbar tailing us. The rabbit had been impounded for unpaid parking tickets, and Eric was out of cash too. We had to hoof it to Renee's.

The top of the trash bag ripped, and Eric's CD player smashed into pieces. We weren't even halfway to her place yet. Clothes fell all over the sidewalk, and a pair of underwear soaked with something nasty flopped onto my shoe.

Eric set the TV down on a bench and put his hands on his hips. "You've gotta be fucking kidding me."

I flung the underwear over to him, and it landed on his shoulder.

"Real nice," he said, throwing my panties on the ground.

I started to scoop all our stuff into a pile but stopped and looked over at him. He was just standing there, rubbing his temples. "Can you help me out?" I asked.

We clumped everything together in a big mound and stared at it like somehow, miraculously, it would walk itself to Renee's.

"We need another bag," I said.

"No shit, genius. Fuck, wait here."

He went into a few stores and came back empty handed. "Call Renee and tell her to pick us up in a taxi," he said.

When she pulled up to the street corner where we were sitting, she couldn't stop laughing. I glanced over at Eric, squatting on top of the TV with his pants and shirts in a ball under his feet, and lost it.

He did too. We didn't care that the people passing us were gawking. This shit was funny. The only person who didn't find it funny was the cab driver. He charged us extra because our clothes stunk up his backseat.

Things were easier with all of us living together. We spent less money on trains since Renee lived close to our jobs and we didn't have to divvy up the coke. And now that the rent and utilities were divided three ways, we had no problem affording them. But like with everything else, things changed by the second month. The more money we made, the more coke we bought. The more we snorted, the more we wanted. We decided to cut what was less important. We stopped buying weed and only ate at the bar because the food there was free.

We were paying our bills, but always late. We got letters in the mail from our utility companies telling us they were going to disconnect service. Eric pawned his TV and CD collection to pay the electric bill. The cable company started calling Renee's cell a few times a day, leaving long and threatening messages. She got so fed up with screening her calls, she pretended to be her mother and told the collector Renee was dead. That was the last time she heard from them. To pay our rent, Renee sold the stuff in her apartment. She even hocked Baby, but we were still behind. Once we paid our overdue balances, the next month's bills came in.

Soon her apartment was bare except for the bed, couch and a few dishes. Our electric was shut off, and our rent was three weeks late. It was time to come up with a plan. We couldn't deal coke because we didn't know enough people. We couldn't get second jobs since we were already working double shifts, so we decided to hit up our parents.

Renee didn't have any luck with hers. I guess she'd been sucking them dry for a while. Eric's parents sent him two hundred and told him to make it last because they couldn't afford to send any more for at least a month. He cashed the check and we went straight to Que's. But two hundred dollars worth of coke only lasted a little over a day.

When I called home, Dad answered the phone. I told him we'd been kicked out of our apartment because the building was getting renovated and we had to move in with a friend. He didn't think that was a bad break. I told him we'd lost a month's rent when we moved, and he suggested to pick up some overtime.

I needed a different approach. What would make him open his wallet for me?

"But Daddy, I don't have enough money for food and I'm starving."

"Michael told us you'd lost a lot of weight," he said. "Oh sweetheart, why didn't you ask me sooner?"

I was still going to Michael's place, but instead of every week, I went every other.

I'd been using coke for about four months, and at first, the weight had come off slowly. It wasn't until we gave up weed and binging on munchies, and we stopped buying food that the weight had really started to shed. I'd already lost at least thirty-five pounds.

My dad agreed to deposit fifty dollars into my account every Friday. Fifty dollars a week was a joke. I needed around eighty dollars a day. Between the three of us, we had a two hundred and fifty dollar a day habit.

It was time to talk to Que.

Renee got called into work, so Eric and I went to his house without her. All we had was the twenty bucks Michael had given me the night before. It wasn't even enough to buy three Percs.

"Que, I'm jonesing," Eric said. We were sitting on the bed, and Que was slouched in the chair by his desk. Since our first visit, we'd been promoted from standing against the door to lounging on his bed.

"What can you do for a twenty-spot?" Eric asked.

Que's hand hovered around the middle of the cabinet and then landed on the third shelf. Coke and weed weren't the only drugs we had bought from him. We'd dropped hits of ecstasy and snorted Percs when he was out of coke. But up until today, we'd never graduated to the third shelf. Renee told me that shelf was reserved for junkies. By the way she said the word junkie, it sounded like that was someone honorable.

He grabbed one of the packets and held it out to us. It looked all professional with its perfect, wax-paper wrapping and stamped emblem.

"What is it?" Eric asked.

"Heroin," Que said.

I wondered why he kept it on the bottom shelf of his cabinet. Wasn't heroin like the king of drugs?

"How much does it cost?" I asked.

"Each bag is a nick or a bundle of ten bags for fifty."

Damn this shit was cheap. And the packet was fat too.

"We snort it?" Eric asked.

"Snort it, freebase it, slam it. Same as coke," Que said.

Eric's face turned red. He must have felt embarrassed for asking. I would have asked too if he hadn't. Eric knew as much about drugs as I did, which was nothing compared to what Renee knew. She taught us about coke and opioids, how to cut them into a fine powder and how to snort them in a hurry without a straw or a dollar bill.

We had planned to suggest doing runs for Que, like a delivery service where he could pay us in coke. We hadn't talked about subbing heroin instead.

"It's good?" Eric asked.

I already knew it was good. The image of that homeless guy nodding out on the train was stuck in my brain.

"You want a taste?" Que asked.

"Hell yeah," I said and looked at Eric. He nodded and smiled. "We both do."

Que grabbed a water bottle and a lighter. His hands were moving so fast I couldn't keep up with what he was doing. He handed Eric a glass pipe that looked like one of those test tubes we used in chemistry class, but both ends were open. In front of Eric, Que held a piece of tin foil that he'd smeared with the cooked-up mix.

"When you see smoke, suck it through the pipe," Que said.

The smoke burned off the foil in thin, squiggly lines. Eric sucked, and when his lungs were full, he held it in until he coughed. When he exhaled, his eyes closed. His back leaned towards the bed.

I asked him how he felt. He didn't say a word. His only movement was his fingers releasing the pipe so it dropped onto the bed.

Que held the foil for me, and I followed the smoke with the end of the pipe. The taste was an odd mix, sweet like kid vitamins and bitter like vinegar, and it burned my lungs. I felt it, slowly, at the tip of each limb and then a rush up to my head. The rush wasn't anything like coke. This, well, this was euphoric—tingles and sparks and melting—like I was being swallowed by a cloud of cotton and the sun was wrapping its rays around me like a blanket. I could feel my chin falling towards my chest, my back hunching forward. My body was acting on its own, and my mind was empty, like all my memories had been erased. There was scenery behind my lids. Aqua colored water and powdery sand that extended for miles. The beach looked familiar. Maybe it was Ogunquit Beach, where my parents had brought us as kids, or Nantasket Beach, where my grandparents lived in the summers when they were still alive.

I didn't know how long I was like that—asleep or awake or totally fucking out of it—but when I came back, Eric and Que were staring at me.

"What do you think?" Eric asked.

"Give us four bags."

I was never going back to coke. I wanted more heroin. And I wanted it now.

We needed tin foil, so on the way home we stopped in an alleyway a few blocks from the mini market to count the change in my wallet. It added up to less than a dollar.

"We're at least two dollars short," I said.

"Buy a pack of gum," he said. "And I'll meet you down there." He was pointing to the corner of the street.

There were three people ahead of me in the checkout line. Out of the corner of my eye, I saw Eric walk in and go down one of the aisles. There was only one camera, aimed at the register, but there were mirrors near the ceiling in all four corners of the store.

The line moved fast. I unzipped my jacket, undid the top three buttons of my shirt and arched my back. The customer in front of me finished paying, and I reached for a pack of Juicy Fruit, setting it on the counter.

"Forty-nine cents," the cashier said, but his eyes weren't on me, they were scanning the aisles.

"Can you tell me how to get to Quincy Market?" I asked, handing him two quarters.

He looked at the change, and then his eyes slid a few inches up to my chest. "You, uh..."

While he watched, I adjusted the underwire, and my boobs popped out even more. "I'm sorry, I didn't hear what you said."

"Err, t-take the Orange Line to State Street and it's, uh, a b-block from there."

I heard Eric cough, and then the bells on the front door chimed. We were in the clear.

I told the cashier to keep the penny and thanked him for the directions. He didn't say you're welcome, but I still gave him a little shoulder shake for being so helpful.

I caught up to Eric at the end of the block. "Did you get it?" I asked.

He leaned forward and the box of foil poked out from the collar of his jacket.

"That was too easy," I said.

"You made that dude almost swallow his tongue."

"I did good?"

Eric laughed and put his arm around my shoulder. "They did good," he said, nodding towards my chest.

We rushed back to the apartment. Eric's hands were shaking so bad he dropped the keys before he got the door open. We took the stairs two at a time and already had our jackets off before getting inside. We sat on the floor by the bed, and Eric followed Que's instructions. The heroin was cooked up, and he spread it over the foil.

When I was in fifth grade, a cop came into our classroom. We were all wearing our black t-shirts with D.A.R.E across the front. We stared at the cop while he paced in front of the chalkboard, showing us poster-sized pictures of different kinds of drugs. When he got to heroin, he said it was like a terrorist. I didn't know what that meant, but I knew it was something bad. During my sophomore year at UMaine, I watched on TV the attack on the twin towers. How could that cop compare tragedy and murder to this harmless white powder? Something that made me feel this incredible shouldn't be categorized as a terrorist.

Heroin deserved the top shelf in Que's drug cabinet. It deserved the highest rank.

Coke gave me energy. Ecstasy made me dance and want to be touched. Shrooms made me hallucinate. But heroin. Shit. Heroin was kind. It didn't trip me out like acid or bring me into a dark hole like PCP. It showed me the quietness of the waves.

When the smoke came out of my mouth, I felt every muscle relax. The replay of my parents' nagging was muted. The looks of pity that flashed in my head from when I moved out of my dorm room were blurred. And the dirtiness I felt inside my crotch was wiped clean.

I heard Renee walk through the door. She dropped her purse on the floor. I felt her sit down next to me and I opened my eyes just slightly to greet her.

"Chasing the dragon, huh?" she asked.

I was chasing something. And damn it felt so fucking good.

CHAPTER FIVE

When the three of us got back to the apartment at two in the morning, all our stuff was dumped in the hallway. The bed frame was in pieces, and the mattress leaned against the wall. All our clothes were thrown in boxes piled on top of the couch cushions. We were only two months behind on rent. Shit, I thought our landlord would be more forgiving than that. He had changed the locks while we were at work and put a No Trespassing sign on our door. We tried to break in, but the door was like steel, and Eric couldn't knock it down. We needed a pick-up truck to move it all and a place to crash. With seventeen dollars, we weren't going to get very far. We filled our backpacks with as much as they'd hold and headed for the park.

I could have called Michael and asked him to put us up, but since I started basing dope three months ago, I'd only been to his place once. It was weird too, sitting there all high while my brother talked about—I don't know what. I nodded out after dinner, just so full and warm. I woke up in the guest room, tucked under the blanket with pillows surrounding my head. He had taken my sneakers off before putting me in bed, and on the dresser was a towel and toothbrush. All the lights were off in the living room and kitchen, and his bedroom door was shut. I grabbed the leftover pizza from the fridge and left. We didn't talk again for a few days, but when we did, he told me he'd planned on cooking me breakfast.

If we stayed at Michael's, we'd have to hide our smoking. And then there was the whole nodding out thing. What would I say about that? I'd have to deal with his questions too like why I didn't have a place to live. I decided Michael was for emergencies and this was a fender bender. The way I saw it, as long as I had Eric, Renee, and a bag of heroin in my pocket, everything else would work itself out.

There was a hotel near the bar that advertised rooms for nineteen a night. Eric wanted to check the place out. Renee didn't. She rested her back against a tree and pulled out a full foil and a pipe. After she took a hit, she said sleeping under the stars on H would be an adventure. I didn't disagree with her, but I sided with Eric. There weren't any cops around, but if they showed up, we couldn't afford to get arrested.

When Renee was high, she'd agree to anything, so it didn't take long for us to swing her decision. The owner of the hotel hooked us up with a week's stay for a hundred bucks. We could pay the hundred in installments as long as we gave him a little cash each day.

As we walked down the hallway to our room, I could hear moaning and yelling from the doors we passed. Flies swarmed around the flickering overhead lights. And there was a strange smell, not smoke or burning chemicals, although there was plenty of that too. The scent was like rotten peaches.

Renee passed out when we got in the room. Eric and I took the other bed and shared a foil between us. The mattress was comfortable compared to Renee's lumpy couch and the grass in the park. The room wasn't too bad either, even with the funky smell and smoky haze that made everything inside look yellowish.

We never made it back to the apartment to get the rest of our stuff. Before we smoked, we talked about borrowing Mark's truck and moving everything to the hotel. After the pipe hit our lips, our plans went to shit. We promised each other before we went to bed we wouldn't smoke the next morning until all our stuff was moved. Then a week passed. We figured by then it was too late, the landlord had probably scrapped it all anyway.

When I first started basing, I'd smoke an hour before work, and I'd be high the whole shift. Being on dope at work was like sitting in class the morning after a keg party. I had no energy and couldn't concentrate. All I wanted was to sit in front of the TV and rip cig after cig. I'd forget to check on my tables, glasses went empty and I ignored them, and requests like extra napkins and silverware never got delivered. I used the other servers to help me out. Mark had a hard time keeping employees, so there was always a new face who wanted to prove herself. I'd have her run my food and check on my tables, and I'd pretend to be too busy. By the time the waitress got sick of doing my job, she had either quit or was let go.

Soon the high was lasting only a couple hours, and the cravings would set in at work. I'd leave during my dinner break to smoke at the hotel. The thirty minutes I was given would turn into an hour, sometimes two. I'd come back to the bar prepared with an excuse like a doctor's appointment or family drama or the ATM machine had eaten my card. My excuses weren't very creative, but somehow they worked.

It didn't take long before Mark caught on to my lies. I told him one day I had food poisoning and had gone to the hospital to get checked out. He wanted proof like an invoice or a statement from my insurance company. He knew I didn't have either and chewed my ass out. I'd seen him fire other servers over stupid things like forgetting to roll the silverware in napkins and stock glasses at the end of their shift. And here I was, stumbling into the bar three hours late, and all Mark did was yell at me. He must have had a thing for brunettes with big boobs, because there was no other reason he was keeping me around.

Renee was never late to work. The way she moved behind the bar was like she was on coke again. When Mark reamed me out for being late, I asked her how she was holding it together so well, and she taught me how to be a functional smoker. It was common sense really: take just a few hits rather than basing half a bag, and pound Red Bull to give me the energy the dope took away. So instead of spending my dinner breaks nodding out in the hotel, I smoked in a bathroom stall at work. I thought I was being more responsible. I was real slick about it too. I'd blow into the toilet and flush, so the water sucked down all the smoke.

And then I got busted. Someone must have ratted me out, probably one of the prissy waitresses who was picking up my slack. It all happened so fast. I was freebasing off the foil, and the next thing I knew, Mark had pried open the stall door. Our eyes locked. His got all watery, and his hand went over his mouth like he was witnessing a car wreck or something. There wasn't anything I could say that would justify what I was doing. He saw the foil and the pipe, the bag of dope in my lap, and the stream of smoke coming from my lips.

He yanked me by the arm and pulled me out of the bathroom, dragging me through the restaurant. His grip was strong and should have hurt. The customers glared and whispered from their tables. I didn't feel the pain or the humiliation. All I could see in the back of my mind was a foil of heroin Mark flushed down the toilet, and I wanted to dive into the water and save it.

He plopped me down in a chair in his office and sat in front of me on the edge of his desk. I was expecting a lecture about how much potential I used to have and how I screwed up all the time, and blah-fucking-blah about my lies and excuses and worthlessness. If he did say any of that, I didn't hear it. I couldn't hear anything. My ears were buzzing like bees were dancing on my eardrums.

Damn, I had smoked more than I thought. I couldn't keep my eyes open. My chin was falling to my chest, and I couldn't stop it.

When my eyes were closed, I saw fields of sunflowers. When my lids fluttered open, I saw compassion and tenderness like I was Mark's sick child.

I couldn't control the nod. I couldn't tell him I wasn't sick. All I could do was follow the path of sunflowers, smell their petals, and touch their prickly stems.

"Nicole, stay with me," Mark said.

I felt the warmth of his breath and the light slaps of his hand on my face, and my eyes shot open.

Mark was no longer sitting on his desk. He was kneeling in front of me and his hands were rubbing my cheeks. "Are you okay?" he asked, his lips close to mine.

I thought, without a doubt, I was getting fired. I needed him to believe I was sorry, even if I wasn't.

"It won't happen again," I said. "I'll change, I promise."

My eyes filled and I blinked, so the tears ran down my face, a skill I'd learned in drama class at my high school. I'd stare at something without blinking until my eyes welled. Right now, that was Mark's face, and he reacted by pulling me into a hug. When he finally let me go, he put his arm around my shoulder and walked me to the employee entrance. He told me to go home and rest. I still had six hours left of my shift, and there was some big game on TV, so the tips would be good tonight. But I didn't argue with him.

Eric was sleeping when I got to our hotel room. I woke him and asked him to cook up for me. While he spread it over the foil, I told him what happened.

"You're shitting me, right?" he said.

From the look I gave him, he had to know I wasn't joking.

"He hugged you, isn't that a good sign?"

I took a long pull and held it in until I coughed. The point wasn't that he hugged me. I was pretty sure the tears had worked and I was in the clear. The point was how careful I was going to have to be. I couldn't smoke at work anymore. I couldn't go back to the hotel to smoke because I couldn't be late. I couldn't go more than five hours without smack. How was I going to make it through my shift without hitting the pipe at least once? He might as well have fired me.

"You have any dope left, my foil's short," he said.

I checked my pockets and purse. Both were empty. What had I done with the bag of dope when Mark came into the bathroom? I called Renee and asked her to look for it. She put me on hold and when she came back to the phone, she said it wasn't in any of the stalls and hung up. Mark must have swiped it when he reached for my arm.

"It was a full bag," I said.

Money was too tight. I had to get it back. "Can you distract Mark while I search his office?"

Eric reached for my pipe, and when our fingers touched his eyes scanned my face. "You sure you want to do this?"

My dope was somewhere in his office, and he kept his door unlocked. I just had to get in and out without being seen.

I looked around our hotel room. The few clothes I owned were on the floor. There was trash covering the top of the dresser. On the nightstand were burnt foils and spoons and empty packets of heroin. This was who I was now. And I needed my dope back.

We waited until midnight to go to the bar. There was a line by the front door that wrapped halfway around the block, and Big Dan was checking IDs. We went to the side entrance, and I punched my code into the lock. Once we were inside, Eric went to find Mark. Mark and Eric were bar buddies, so we figured Mark would think it was just like any other night. I just hoped Eric could keep their conversation flowing with the bar this packed.

From the employee entrance, it was a straight shot down a long hallway to Mark's office. I kept my back against the wall and looked both ways after each step. When I was halfway down the hallway, I ran the final stretch before anyone had a chance to spot me and closed the door after I got inside.

His office light was on. Had he forgotten to turn it off or was he coming right back? It didn't matter, I still had to hurry.

I sat down in his chair and scooted close to the desk. My hands were shaking like I had drunk a pot of coffee, and every few seconds my eyes darted to the door.

I couldn't find anything in the drawers but office supplies. I needed it. Where the hell was it?

I found a first aid kit, and I pulled the lid off, rummaging through all the medical stuff. My hand grazed over a pair of latex gloves, but stopped when I touched something hard and rectangular inside the glove. Through the latex, I saw the packet of heroin.

It was all there, every little speck of powder I hadn't smoked sealed inside the pouch.

There was a reason Mark hadn't flushed my dope. What was it? Did he want to try it? He did look like a partier, one of those eighties rock stars with his long hair and a dangly left earring.

A plan started to come together in my brain. Mark would need me, he just didn't know it yet. And I'd never have to worry about losing my job again.

I poured half the powder into an envelope and put that in my pocket. The rest of the dope went back in the glove, just like I found it. There was enough there to turn him on and have him coming back to me for more. I knew after a taste he'd be hooked.

I pushed the chair under the desk and backed out of the office, closing the door quietly.

"What do you think you're doing?" Mark asked from behind me.

I turned and faced him. He towered over me by at least a foot, and when I moved to the side, he moved with me.

Where the hell was Eric? He was supposed to call my cell phone if Mark headed towards his office.

"Don't worry, I left you a taste."

"That's not why I kept it." His palms landed on the door behind me. I was trapped in a Mark cage. "Let me help you."

His mouth was searching for mine. One of his hands touched my waist and lifted the bottom of my shirt. He caressed my stomach, running his fingers from my bellybutton to the wire of my bra.

"Get off me," I said, trying to wiggle his hand away.

He found my nipple and squeezed like his fingers were a pair of pliers. His lips brushed my neck.

"You want to keep your job, don't you?" He clamped my earlobe between his teeth.

I thought of that mound of powder in my pocket, how it would feel to have its smoke fill my lungs and the rush that would enter my body. Without my job, we wouldn't have enough money. Without money, my cravings would go unfulfilled, my nightmares would return, and I'd be left with nothing but the sickness of withdrawal.

"How bad do you want it?" he asked.

I wanted it worse than anything. In the back of my throat, I could still taste the hit from a few hours ago. If I could make him come real quick, I'd be able to taste it again in twenty minutes, thirty tops.

I opened my mouth and it was filled with Mark's tongue before I had the chance to respond. His lips were hungry. His saliva tasted like cigarettes and beer.

My head smacked against the door. My face got slapped with the back of a fist. There was someone hitting Mark from behind, and he turned to defend himself. I couldn't see who it was. My jaw was throbbing. My head was cloudy from hitting it against the door, and arms were flying in my direction, so I slid to the side, shielding myself from the wrestling bodies.

"What gives you the right to fucking touch her like that," Eric shouted.

Eric?

Eric landed a punch to his nose, and Mark's head jerked backwards. He fell to the ground, and Eric kicked him in the gut over and over.

"We've got to get out of here," Eric said, grabbing my hand.

I was frozen, unable to move, and my eyes wouldn't leave Mark's face. Blood was dripping from his nose, and his eyes were swelling.

What did all of this mean? Was Mark going to blame me?

Eric pulled me to his side, walking me down the hallway.

"Don't ever come back," Mark said. His voice was quiet and sharp. "Or I'll call the cops."

Who was he talking to?

I looked over my shoulder. Mark was on his knees with his hands around his stomach. The look he gave me was the answer I needed. My job here was done.

I ran back into the office.

"Where are you going?" Eric yelled.

I yanked open the desk drawer, but I pulled too hard and it came all the way out and fell to the ground. The first aid kit tumbled out, and I opened the lid, grabbing the latex glove. I shoved it in my pocket and rejoined Eric. We stopped at the end of the hallway, looking towards the bar. It was so swarmed with customers I couldn't even see Renee. I begged Eric to go get her.

"She'll be fine, I'm worried about you," he said and opened the employee entrance. He picked me up in his arms and carried me through the door.

We didn't talk on the way to the hotel or when we got inside our room. He set me on the bed and cooked up the heroin from my pocket. He even held the foil for me. His hands were trembling, and the foil was bouncing, making it difficult to get a good hit.

His eyes avoided mine, and knowing Eric, that meant he was too ashamed to look at me. I dropped the pipe, placing my hands on each side of his face. "It wasn't your fault," I said.

"If I had gotten there sooner, he wouldn't have laid a finger on you." He took the pipe and placed it between my lips.

"But nothing happened, you stopped it in time."

I wanted to tell him that his timing didn't matter because I would have done anything for him and Renee, even if that meant having sex with Mark. Eric was trying to protect me, but what happened wasn't anything like the rape. Then, I'd been drugged and double-teamed and then those fuckers left me to die, alone and freezing in the snow. Mark had given me a choice, and I was going to say yes. But the more I thought about that decision, the more I realized what it truly meant. I'd become that person who would sell my body for smack.

Now, heroin controlled my body. And since it had been violated, did it really have any value to me anymore? No. I could whore out all I wanted. I could screw ten guys for a hundred bucks. As long as dope was inside me, I didn't care if a man was too.

Eric was still holding the foil, and I sucked the smoke through the pipe as hard as I could. I couldn't get the dope in fast enough.

The taste I had dreamed of in the hallway with Mark was finally filling my lungs, and with it came total silence.

Renee was an hour late coming home. She walked through the door acting as if she'd found a purse full of cash on the sidewalk. She was smiling and all giddy, bouncing through the room like there were springs on the bottom of her shoes. Usually after work, she was bitchy and short-tempered and we had to avoid talking to her until she took her first hit.

She disappeared into the bathroom and returned with a bottle of water, taking a seat in front of me on the bed. "Guess what I got," she said.

Eric shrugged his shoulders. He was just as confused as I was. Why wasn't she saying anything about the fight? Mark would have told all the employees after the bar closed, wasn't that why she was so late coming home?

She reached inside the apron tied around her waist and pulled out three syringes bundled in plastic. "I picked them up after work, aren't they pretty?"

"How much did they cost?" I asked.

Que had a hard time getting fresh needles. They went quick and he charged a lot. We'd never been able to afford them, plus Eric had this weird thing about needles. He'd been scared of them since he was young. Que wasn't the only hook-up, though. There was also a needle exchange program, but we'd heard bad things about it like how cops would hide out around the building and arrest people for possession after they re-upped on rigs. Renee didn't want to get arrested, so she must have gotten them from Que.

"Doesn't matter, I did good tonight," she said.

"It does matter Renee, shit, I got fired."

"What are you talking about?"

"Mark didn't tell you?" Eric said.

Renee said that after she saw Mark and Eric talking at the bar, she didn't see Mark again. She had stopped by his office on her way out, but the door was locked and he didn't answer.

I told her the story, and when I got to the part where Eric found us, he took over from there. When Eric spoke, I watched Renee. Her face was like a fucking statue.

"He felt you up and stuck his tongue down your throat?" she asked.

What? There were so many other questions she could have asked, like how could you be dumb enough to lose your job, what are we going to do for money, what are we going to do when we get kicked out of the hotel? But all she cared about was Mark sticking his tongue down my throat.

She didn't wait for me to answer. She dumped the powder onto a spoon and heated it with a lighter. When all three syringes were filled, she laid them on the bed. "Who's first?"

If she didn't want to talk about our money situation, then I didn't either. Mark didn't know we lived together, so her job wasn't at risk. I had to find a way to contribute to our family and it was up to me, not her.

Eric went first. I held his hand, and while Renee found a vein and stuck it, he looked at me. I squeezed his fingers and smiled. I didn't know if he saw my grin or felt my touch because he nodded out immediately.

I'd been around needles my whole life because my dad was a diabetic. He kept a box of syringes in the pantry, and I'd watch him take his insulin every morning before school. He said if he didn't take his medicine, he would die. He used needles to keep him healthy, and the syringe in Renee's hand was about to do the same thing for me.

Renee tied her belt around my bicep and slapped my arm for a vein. "I didn't know Mark liked you...like that," she said and pricked my skin with the tip.

She pulled back on the plunger. My blood came through the chamber, looking like a head of broccoli before mixing with the clear liquid. When she pushed the heroin into my vein, she gave me a look—jealousy, maybe, with a touch of resentment. Her expression lasted about a second because my eyes closed and my head dropped.

Smoking heroin was like an appetizer. It satisfied my hunger cravings, but when you ate the same thing every day, like tuna and noodles, your taste buds wanted something more flavorful. My body got so used to smoking dope, the high was nothing like the first time I had tried it.

If basing was like an alcoholic drinking only one Bud Light, shooting heroin was like drinking a gallon of vodka. The rush was like an orgasm. The dreams were like an acid trip. Bright colors swirled together and formed scenes like in action movies. I was jumping over rooftops and parasailing over the Atlantic. The warmth that spread over my body was like the sun beating down, inches above my skin. It was magic.

I felt my stomach churn, and bile poured from my mouth. I couldn't get to the bathroom. I couldn't even move. Puke was all over the bed, and me, I think. If felt good to throw up. The heaving made my throat tingle like it was being tickled with a feather.

A second swish of sparks shot up my spine. My nose touched something soft. The blanket, maybe? The skin on the sides of my fingers turned hot. Really hot. Was my cigarette burning my flesh? I wasn't sure, and I didn't care because it felt good too.

Besides Eric and Renee, there were only two things that mattered, the dope that ran through my veins and the needle that pricked my skin. Fuck Mark and my job, and the customers who left me shitty tips. I'd find something better.

CHAPTER SIX

I'd stopped freebasing after that night when everything went down with Mark and only mainlined after that. The high from the needle was more intense than basing, and it lasted longer too. Eric based at the club, Renee snorted at the bar, and they both shot up when they were home. They called shooting up their treat after a long day on the job like it was a piece of pie or something. If that was true, I had a wicked sweet tooth.

In our family of three, we not only used our heroin differently, but we each had a separate role too. Renee did most of the drug runs because she had a thing for Que. Eric was our moneyman. He collected the cash we made each day and budgeted enough for heroin and needles. Our needles had to be replaced every few days because they got dull. We didn't share needles either. Maybe they did, but I didn't. After each shot there was leftover blood in the chamber and at the tip of the rig, and if their blood touched mine, all sorts of shit could happen. I didn't keep tabs on who they slept with, and for all I knew they could have HIV or Hep C.

Eric also rationed out the dope. We each got our own bag that would have to last us the whole day. Renee made sure it was divided the second she got home from Que's. In the past, she had accused me of using more than her, so it was better we had our own bags.

I was responsible for paying our rent. I didn't want to work, I wanted to lie in bed and shoot dope all day. But thanks to Abdul, the owner of our hotel, I had a job.

After Mark fired me, our rent was late for three weeks, and I explained to Abdul what happened—I subtracted the heroin part and added in a few exaggerated details. He walked me into his office and handed me a bucket of rags and cleaning supplies. "Scrub, scrub," he said. "I give you list, you clean rooms."

I had to take the job, we needed to maintain the budget, right? The easy stuff was washing dirty sheets and dumping trash. But damn, the other stuff like cleaning the rooms was so wrong. Hookers left their Johns' used condoms on the floor, and drunks missed the toilet when they barfed.

I found a dead body once too. I had one room left to clean and was going to rush through it because my high was wearing off. When I opened the door, this smell hit me, like huffing a bag of decayed meat and rancid lobster, and I spewed all over the carpet. I buried my nose under my shirt and tiptoed into the room. There was a naked man, his skin gray, lying face up on the bed. There was a lot of skin too, the dude was the size of a sumo wrestler. My eyes were so focused on his body, I almost didn't see the bottle of lotion in his hand or the porno playing on the TV.

The phone was on the nightstand, and I didn't want to get that close to him, so I found Abdul and told him to call 9-1-1. The rest of my day was spent in bed, sticking in the needle and dreaming about Japanese fighting fish.

The next morning, Abdul filled me in on what I missed. It took three paramedics and two firefighters to carry the guy out of the room because he was too big for a stretcher. The paramedics told Abdul they thought he died of a heart attack. That poor fucker, I thought. The last seconds of his life were spent jerking off to porn when there were plenty of hookers in the hotel he could have hired.

I was just pissed I had puked up my breakfast. Abdul fed me before my shift each morning. He'd bring in this weird concoction his wife made for dinner the night before and we'd eat it together. That was my only meal of the day, and I had wasted it on the floor of that perv's room.

Since Eric and Renee worked nights, I was spending a lot of time by myself in the room. I wasn't lonely. Heroin was there to keep me company, and I had Michael too. I was calling him a lot like I did when I'd lived in Maine. Our talks weren't long because I told him I was on my dinner break and when he asked me to come over after work, I made up an excuse. I wasn't sure why I called him so much, but there was something about his voice that gave me comfort, like when you fell off your bike as a kid and needed a hug from mom. The smack did most of the talking, telling him how good I was doing at the bar and all the things I was buying for our apartment. I didn't even consider telling him the truth. He always said how happy he was for me, and I liked the way those words sounded. And really, wasn't I doing good?

One night while I was on my way home from Que's, my cell phone rang. I answered it, thinking it was Renee or Eric calling from work to see if Que's shipment of dope had come in. Que had been dry all day, so we had nothing to shoot, and the three of us were feening. But it was Michael on the phone.

"Mom and dad are coming next weekend," he said. "Can you do brunch Saturday morning at my place?"

I no longer spoke to my parents every night, more like once a week or every other. Our conversations were short, mostly about the weather and all the other boring shit they liked to talk about, and I hadn't seen them in at least six months. The last time was when I'd met them for dinner at Michael's apartment. But that was during the coke days. Since I'd been on heroin, they had only visited once. I called them the morning we were supposed to get together and told them I was in Jersey for Renee's sister's wedding.

"Don't tell me you have plans already," Michael said.

"I have to work."

"Then get the day off, or we'll come to the bar for lunch."

Shit.

"No, no, I'll be at your house," I said and hung up.

I wished I had looked at the caller ID before answering the phone. And I wished I hadn't said yes to brunch. I didn't want my parents to see me like this, all skinny with dark circles under my eyes and blemishes on my face. But they'd be pissed if I stood them up again. They were still giving me an allowance, and if I kept avoiding them, they'd cut me off.

I spent all week trying to come up with an excuse not to go. But when I talked to my parents, they told me how excited they were to see me and how they wanted to take me shopping after breakfast. I needed clothes and toiletries, and figured the few hours I'd have to spend with them would be worth it.

The morning of the brunch I got up early. The plan was to be at Michael's by eleven, and I needed at least a few hours to put myself together and come down a little from the high before leaving. I hadn't been spending a lot of time on my appearance lately and, honestly, I was caring less and less about it. I didn't exactly wear makeup and dresses when I scrubbed toilets and wiped up vomit. But today I had to look my best.

We didn't have a lot of makeup besides Renee's concealer, black shadow, and liner. I lathered the liquid tint over my face, trying to cover my pimples and my scar. The doctor had treated the burn right after she performed the rape kit on me, and at first it was just red and puffy. It had healed into a purple, horseshoe shape. The makeup made it look almost green.

Renee's clothes fit me now, which doubled my wardrobe, but not by much. The only half-decent pants we owned were the jeans she wore to work. They were full of holes and my knees poked through, and brown stains splattered the thighs. Our shirts were tight and short, so I chose one of Eric's sweaters. It billowed around me like a garbage bag.

I was twenty minutes late getting to Michael's. I hadn't planned on getting that cranked before breakfast. The doorman let me into the building and escorted me to the elevator. The back wall was mirrored, and I stood in front of it, staring at my reflection while the elevator climbed.

My sunken cheeks and ashy complexion made me look like a poster child for one of those TV commercials where they were trying to raise money for malnourished children. My fingernails were dirty, and the ends of my hair were tangled. The makeup covered the redness of the sores, but the heads of each pimple could still be seen through the concealer. My clothes were so baggy it looked like I'd played dress-up in dad's closet.

This was a bad idea.

I pushed all the buttons to make the elevator stop, but it kept rising, and when the door opened, Michael was standing there to greet me.

"You look like shit," he said. "What, are you hungover?"

"Nice to see you too."

I followed him to the hallway. His door was already open, and my parents were standing inside. Mom grabbed me first and hauled me into a hug. "Oh I've missed you, baby," she said.

Her lips were puckered and her nose was scrunched like she got a whiff of something nasty. I hoped it wasn't me. After I showered, I realized we were out of deodorant, and the clothes I was wearing hadn't been washed in weeks, maybe even months.

"You smell so—"

"Hi, Daddy," I said, interrupting her. I threw my arms around his neck and pulled away before he could smell me too.

"Why are you so late?" Dad asked. "We were starting to get worried."

I walked past them into the kitchen and poured a cup of coffee. "The train broke down," I said over my shoulder.

We took our seats at the table. Michael had prepared quite a fancy spread. There were vases of flowers and cloth napkins, and platters of my favorite breakfast foods. Everyone filled their plates but me. I was too nervous trying so hard to act sober, and my stomach was on the verge of queasy. The smell of the eggs was making me nauseous.

"Cole, honey, aren't you going to eat something?" Mom asked. "You're so thin."

I glanced up from my empty plate. Her fork was mashing a hunk of melon, and she looked like she was about to cry.

I had two personalities. There was Nicole, who didn't believe in fake smiles and spoke without a filter. And then there was Cole, who smiled like she just got her braces off and lied to make her parents and brother proud. I couldn't hide my appearance, but I could feed them with bullshit. It was time to put my Cole face on.

"I'm just getting over the flu, and my stomach is still a little upset," I said.

Mom got up from the table and returned with a folder. "I've done some research," she said, handing it to me. The folder was filled with papers, each highlighted and covered in her handwriting. "Those are all the schools in Boston that offer teaching degrees."

I set the folder on the table and placed my napkin on top of it.

"We think it's time you go back to school," Dad said.

I stared at my empty plate. "I'm not ready yet."

"You're just going to give up?" Dad asked.

"You worked so hard for those scholarships and your GPA," Mom said.

I had worked hard to maintain a three-five GPA so I could keep my scholarships, but that was before. They didn't understand. Classes, homework, and studying weren't for me anymore.

"We want the best for you, and being a waitress isn't your best," Mom said. "Honey, if it's about what happened, then let's talk about it."

I didn't want to talk about the rape, especially with them. What was there to discuss anyway? They couldn't change the past or make me forget.

"Is that the reason you've lost so much weight?" Dad asked.

"You haven't been this skinny since you were in sixth grade," Mom said.

I guess it wasn't bad they were blaming my weight loss on the rape. That was better than being targeted as a drug addict. And their reasoning made sense because I'd never had a problem with food before. If anything, my problem was eating too much. In my teenage years, I had a large chest and was always at least fifteen pounds overweight.

My pinned eyes and heavy movements should have been a sure sign I was on a diet of heroin. But my parents wouldn't consider that. While lots of my high school friends had gotten busted with pot in their bedrooms and smoking weed in their cars during study hall, I'd never been caught. Cole had told her parents she was anti-drugs and gave them no reason to think otherwise. Even in college, they thought my partying only involved liquor.

"I've been taking really good care of myself," I said. "I watch what I eat and run a couple miles every day."

I explained how Renee ran track in high school and how she was teaching Eric and me about endurance and healthy eating. I used the running and sweating to justify my acne and the stomach flu for the last ten pounds I'd lost.

"But the flu—"

"Did Cole tell you about her promotion at work?" Michael asked, interrupting my mom.

The talks I was having with Michael at night had paid off.

I thanked him with a quick smile. I mean, my parents hadn't seen me in six months, and the rape and my weight were what they wanted to talk about?

"She's doing really good," Michael said. "Cole, tell them."

Mom propped an elbow on each side of her plate and leaned in to get closer to me. Dad reached his hand across the table and placed it over mine. They wanted to hear more. I told them I was working over sixty hours a week and how Mark was training me for management. That triggered a round of questions like how much was a manager's salary, was I getting overtime, and benefits?

My cell phone rang. The caller ID showed it was Renee. The timing couldn't have been more perfect. This would be my excuse to leave.

"Hi, Mark, what's going on," I said into the phone while the three of them continued to eat, pretending not to listen.

Renee laughed and even played along by deepening her voice. She asked how breakfast was going and I answered with an uh-huh. She said she and Eric had just gotten up and were about to celebrate their day off with a shot.

"I understand. I'll be there soon," I said and hung up.

I told my parents the bar was short staffed and Mark needed me to come in. They dropped their forks and looked at each other with raised eyebrows.

"Does Mark know we're in town and how long it's been since we've seen you?" Dad asked.

"He's running a business," I said. "And I'm about to be his manager."

"I'll pack you up some food," Michael said. He returned from the kitchen with a Tupperware container and filled it with a little bit from each platter before we all walked to the door.

"It would make your father and I feel better if you talked to a therapist," Mom said after we hugged. "It's been two years, and by the looks of it, I'm afraid you haven't dealt with it yet."

"I'm fine, really," I said.

My dad left the doorway and returned with the folder. "I love you, Cole," he said and threw his arms around me. I pulled away, and his hands landed on my biceps. "You need to put some meat on these bones."

My dad wasn't the type of man who said I love you all the time. He saved those words for special occasions like my birthday or when I went away to college. The knot that had formed in the back of my throat wasn't because he said it. It was that he was saying it to Cole, not me.

Dad handed the folder to me and closed Michael's door. I was alone in the hallway. My body felt like it was on fire, and the extinguisher it needed was tucked inside my purse. It would take me at least fifteen minutes to get back to the hotel. I didn't want to wait. I wanted to inject it now.

There was a rooftop gym with a bathroom in Michael's building. I remembered seeing it when he gave Eric and me a tour the first time we visited. I figured as long as the bathroom door locked, I'd be set.

I took the elevator to the top floor. The gym was empty, and the handle on the bathroom door had a lock. I dumped my purse on the floor and made a pile of everything I needed to cook up. The needle slid into my vein, and the chamber emptied into my bloodstream. It took only seconds before the fire was out.

A loud noise woke me up. It was a ringing sound echoing off the walls of the bathroom. It took a minute to realize it was my cell phone, and by the time I answered, the call had gone to voicemail. There was a list on the screen that showed at least ten missed calls, all from Renee.

I called her back as soon as I got outside Michael's building, and she answered before I even heard the phone ring. "Nicole, I don't know what the hell to do."

It sounded like she'd been running. She couldn't catch her breath and I heard her lungs wheeze.

"What's up?" I asked.

"We have a big fucking problem."

Had Abdul come into our room and found our heroin? Did Mark fire her?

"It's Eric, he's blue," she said. "His fucking lips are blue."

I felt everything stop. My heart wasn't beating. My muscles had stiffened and my legs halted. "What are you doing? Call 9-1-1," I said.

"I... I can't. There's drugs and shit all over the room."

"Who the fuck cares, call them right now."

"I can't," she said.

"Then I'm calling them."

"You want to get blamed for this? We're talking jail."

I was trying to piece together how we'd get blamed and if we'd go to jail, and none of it was making any sense. My brain was all mushy. But I couldn't lose Eric. Not like this.

CHAPTER SEVEN

The ride home took forever. I wanted to grab the conductor by the throat and threaten his life if he didn't get the train moving faster. It seemed like we were stopping every ten seconds to let people on or off. And then some asshole would stick their hand in the door right when it was about to close, causing another delay. I'd been guilty of doing the same thing in the past, and people would yell at me like I was screaming at them now. But today I really had somewhere to be. Eric's lips were blue.

I scrolled through my call log, and twenty-two minutes had passed from when Renee's first call came in. It used to take me twenty-two minutes to drive from my parents' house to the University of Maine. The morning after the rape, it took twenty-two minutes for the doctor to tell me the results of the tests. Time was a fucked up thing.

Before I hung up with Renee, I told her to stash the dope and call 9-1-1. She said she would. But did she? I didn't know if I believed anything she said. There was so much she hid from us. She wouldn't talk about her parents or her childhood or the reason she moved to Boston. Besides the rape—that was the one topic off limits—she knew everything about me.

Our relationship with her was one sided. Eric and I talked and she listened. The only time she had anything to say was when she didn't agree with something, like how I was smoking too many cigarettes out of our shared pack or if I wasted money taking the train when I should have been walking. She was our smack sidekick and our connection to Que. But did she have our backs? I didn't know. We'd never been in a position where we had to find out.

It hit me again—the reason I was rushing home. When I was on dope, my brain didn't loop around in circles, it was more like a maze. One minute I'd be thinking about Renee and our friendship, and then other memories would pop in like Mark and Que and college. I'd get in so deep, it was hard to remember my original thought, which was getting back to the hotel to help Eric. Renee said his lips were blue, but she was high, so maybe they were more like a dark red. Even if they were blue, Eric was going to be fine. Renee would get him on his feet and walk him around the room to get his blood pumping again. And then this awful day would be behind us.

I saw the ambulance from the sidewalk. That was a good sign, I thought. It was parked in the front of the hotel and the door to reception was propped open with a brick. Crowds of people had gathered by the ambulance. I pushed my way through them and looked inside. The ambulance was empty.

In the hallway on my way to our room, I bumped into Abdul. "Renee wanted me to hold this."

He was holding my backpack. Without opening it, I already knew what was inside. She had packed it full with all the drugs and paraphernalia, so the police wouldn't find anything if they searched our room.

"Put it in your office, I'll get it later," I said and jogged towards our room.

Renee was sitting on her bed, and there was a police officer standing next to her taking notes.

I couldn't see Eric. There was a paramedic blocking the entrance to the bathroom, and I tried slipping past him, but he stopped me and told me to take a seat on the other bed.

My whole body was shaking. I'd never even been pulled over for speeding. The last time I had spoken to a cop was at the hospital when they needed my statement about the rape.

"What's your name?" the officer asked.

I didn't know my rights. Did I have to answer? I looked at Renee for help, but she was staring at the floor. Why wouldn't she look at me?

"Nicole," I said.

"Nicole what?" the cop asked.

"Does it matter?"

"If you live in this room it does."

I decided to be straight with him. "Brown, Nicole Brown."

He asked more questions like my age, place of employment, and my relation to Eric. I answered him honestly, but I wouldn't make eye contact. I was high and I didn't know if he could tell.

"Did Eric—"

The paramedics were wheeling Eric out of the bathroom on a stretcher. There was a blanket covering his body, but I was too far away to see if it was covering his face too.

I stood up to follow them outside, and the cop said, "Sit back down, I'm not finished questioning you."

"I have to be with Eric."

"You can stop by the morgue when we're done."

The morgue? His lips were blue, but that didn't mean he was dead. When I went swimming in Moosehead Lake in the summer, my lips turned blue too. The pig didn't know what he was talking about.

"You meant the hospital, right?"

He started to answer, but Renee stopped him by putting her finger in the air. Her arm went around my shoulder and she sat next to me on my bed.

"Eric's dead," she said.

Her words were so final. The paramedics hadn't saved him? His lips were blue, but that didn't mean he was fucking dead.

"I don't believe you, no, I have to see him, I have—"

"Sit back down," the cop said. "You can see him when I'm done with you."

Questions poured from his mouth—where had I been at the time of Eric's overdose, did I know he was a heroin addict, was I one too?

I remembered seeing a movie with a little boy and a little girl. The details were vague, but I think they were running through fields of grass and the little girl said, "Dear God, make me a bird. So I could fly far. Far far away from here."

I wanted to stick a needle in my vein and turn into a bird.

The cop had said overdose. What the hell did that mean? Eric had overdosed on the same smack that was running through my veins. I was too fucked up to hear Renee's phone calls, and I was nodding while Eric's lips were turning blue. He'd taken too much.

Eric was dead.

Renee was a selfish bitch. Couldn't she have called 9-1-1 sooner? The drugs in our room didn't matter. Neither did jail or probation or whatever our punishment was.

I had needed that shot in the bathroom after seeing the way my parents looked at me. But she didn't have an excuse for not watching Eric and making sure he was okay.

I was done with her.

CHAPTER EIGHT

R enee and I gave our statements to the police. We answered all their questions about Eric, where he worked, his boss' name, the hours he worked, and his parents' phone number in Bangor. They asked us over and over if we knew about his heroin addiction and flipped the questions to try and trick us. But our answers didn't change. We didn't know Eric did heroin, we'd never seen him use and no, we definitely weren't addicts too.

The cops searched our room, and the only drugs they found was the packet of dope Eric had left in the bathroom. The cause of death was obvious, the needle was still in his arm when the paramedics arrived. They couldn't arrest us, so they took our cell phone numbers for follow-up questions and left the hotel.

"You think they'll do an autopsy?" I asked Renee when everyone cleared out.

"Probably, and the toxicology report will show how much dope he had in him."

"How long does all that take?"

"Depends, a month, maybe."

I'd be able to hold my parents off until the toxicology report. But Bangor was a tiny city, and news of an overdose would spread like herpes back home. Not to mention Eric's story would be printed in the *Bangor Daily News*. Once my parents heard the truth, I didn't know if they'd still believe my lies.

Abdul came barging into our room. "I treat you like my own child and you bring drugs into my house."

Was he fucking serious? The hotel was like a crack house, drug deals going on in the hallways and broken pipes and empty bags in almost all the rooms I cleaned. He rented rooms out by the hour and I was the bad one?

"We didn't bring shit into your house," Renee shouted. She bolted from the bed and ripped the backpack out of Abdul's hands. "Eric fucking did."

His face turned red and his teeth went into an underbite. "Get out, one hour, you get out." He slammed the door behind him.

Renee dumped the backpack onto the bed and handed me a clean needle and one of the packets of dope. "Screw that sandbox, let's get our fix in before we leave."

Damn, I wanted to get high.

We had nowhere to go. We had seven dollars left after the bundle Renee had bought that morning. And even though I was mad at her for letting Eric die, I couldn't leave her. I needed her paycheck and tips to buy heroin.

There was only one place left to go. The park.

I filled my backpack with a few of Eric's sweatshirts, and we found a bench in the park to sit on. I wanted to lie back and enjoy the quietness that was finally in my head, but I couldn't. There was something I still had to do. I picked up my phone and dialed.

Eric's mom answered the phone.

"It's Nicole," I said.

"Hi sweetheart, how's everything? Eric tells me you both are doing so well."

"I have something I need to tell you."

It was hard to talk because my mouth was so dry. A milkshake would be good. A thick chocolate shake to coat my throat and satisfy my sugar craving.

"What is it, honey?" she asked.

"Eric had an accident."

"What's the matter? Is he there? Let me talk to him."

"He's dead."

First there was swearing, one curse after another, and they came so fast it was like she had Tourette's. Then came the sobs. Her words slurred together and she wasn't making any sense. She even puked at one point because I heard her heave. I rested the phone on my chest, she was being too loud and I needed both hands to scratch. The dope was making my arms and legs itch so badly.

"Who's this?" Eric's dad asked.

"It's Nicole."

"What the hell did you say to my wife?"

"I told her Eric's dead."

The phone went silent. And then I heard a deep groan like a bullfrog would make. "How... how did it happen?"

"I thought you should hear it from me," I said. "You know, before the cops called you."

"How the fuck did it happen?"

"The police said he overdosed."

He started to cry.

"I'm sorry," I said. I didn't know if he was still on the phone or if it had dropped from his hands because I could hear both of them now.

"My son did drugs?" he asked.

"I guess so."

"You guess so? And you didn't try to get him help?

"I didn't know."

"That's bullshit, he was your best friend and you—"

"I have to go," I said and hung up.

I put the phone back in my purse and gave into the nod. It was a pretty dream too, full of birds and helicopters.

That was the first night I ever slept outside. I'd camped a lot when I was younger, but I had a tent and sleeping bag. This was Renee and me on a bench in the cold April air. We didn't have a fire to keep us warm or s'mores. We wrapped ourselves in Eric's sweaters and kept our bodies fed with heroin. The sky was full of stars, and the trees whistled as the wind blew past their leaves. The twinkling lights from the surrounding buildings were beautiful.

Renee's shoulder was my pillow, and a squirrel was eating an acorn not too far from my feet. The park was so comfortable. I didn't have to clean hotel rooms anymore to pay my rent. Renee's job at the bar would supply us with plenty of dope, and with Eric gone, we'd have even more to shoot. Eric had watched over me, but so far, I was doing fine on my own, and Renee wasn't going anywhere without me.

I had everything I needed. And what I didn't have, like a bed or clean towels or TV, I could easily do without.

After we did our morning shot in a McDonald's bathroom, I called an old friend from Bangor. Tim was a real Dead Head, long beard, lots of tie-dye and always smelled like patchouli. He was a drummer in a few local bands and heard all the gossip. I told him about Eric, and he didn't sound surprised, but that was the pot talking. Tim had one tone and that was stoned. I asked him to keep his ears open for any news on Eric's funeral, and he promised to call when he heard something.

Renee called Mark an hour before her shift started. She told him she couldn't come in because she'd been throwing up all morning. She wasn't lying either, she'd puked all over the bench and we had to find somewhere else to sit. I asked if she was coming down with the flu, and she said she must have eaten something bad. We hadn't eaten since Eric died, so I didn't know what she was talking about. Mark told her to feel better and he'd see her tomorrow.

Since Renee wasn't going into work, we'd have to find another way to make money. She was pretty good at stealing, and there were pawnshops on every corner that bought almost anything you had to sell. And if I had to give a blowjob to get my fix in, I'd do that too.

She'd been trying Que since we woke up, but he hadn't answered. Que had this thing about calling before you went to his house. I guess he didn't want more than one deal going on at the same time. The shitty thing was he didn't always answer. Sometimes Renee would try him for hours before she got through. She didn't leave a message or send him a text. When it came to dealers, you just didn't do that.

We were pretty sick too. Our last shot had been about fifteen hours ago, and I'd barfed up the milkshake and fries I ate for dinner. This was the first time I'd been dope sick. I couldn't stop shaking, my muscles ached, and I had the sweats and chills.

I'd been telling her all day that waiting for Que was a waste of time because we didn't even have enough money for a dime bag. What we needed was to leave the park and stand by a store and panhandle, then go to Roxbury and buy some dope from a pusher on the street. She kept telling me to lay off, that Que would help us out once she got in touch with him, and he'd also let us stay at his house. I didn't know why she was so sure Que would hook us up, but I was too sick to keep arguing.

It was after midnight when Que finally answered and told us to come over. When we got there, he and his brother Raul were smoking a blunt and listening to music in the living room. Renee sat next to Que on the couch and they started whispering. Raul patted the cushion beside him, and I took a seat along with the blunt he passed me. The weed was settling my stomach, but later when it wore off, I was going to be sick again. Heroin was the only thing that would make me right. Renee really needed to hurry this shit up.

I handed her the blunt and she hit it hard, blowing out a cloud of smoke. Before she took her second hit, she told the guys about Eric. The brothers said something in Spanish I couldn't understand.

"You'll hook us up, won't you?" Renee asked and she whispered something else in Que's ear. I thought she nibbled on his lobe too.

"Real good, boo," Que said.

They took us upstairs and Que cooked up four bags for Renee and me to split. I could taste the heroin before it was even in my body, and my mouth watered for its flavor. We sat on the floor and used our own rigs, tying off with our belts while the brothers watched from the bed. Once we were done, Que turned on his stereo, and Renee stood and moved to the center of the room. She started to dance, swinging her hips back and forth in a rhythm only a stripper would know. She teased, slowly lifting her shirt and unbuttoning her pants to flash different parts of her body until she was fully undressed. And when she touched herself, she moaned. I had never seen her naked before.

Que called her over, and she straddled his legs, humping his crotch. When they started kissing, Raul got off the bed and scooped me into his arms. I felt like a baby against his broad chest and thick neck. Besides Eric and that brief episode with Mark, I hadn't been this close to a man in a while. I studied the side of his face, the golden brown color of his skin, the stubble on his jaw line, and the teardrop tattoo under his eye. He had that masculine smell, musky deodorant and spicy cologne. Those scents used to make me horny, but since I'd been with heroin, nothing turned me on. Smack gave me a feeling no man ever could, a total fulfillment in all my senses. A man could give me an orgasm, but dope gave me a hundred at once.

He carried me into the room across the hall and laid me on the bed. The shades were closed and he didn't turn the light on. His hands took off my pants and shirt, and I was left with only my bra and underwear. I hadn't showered or brushed my teeth in two days. I hadn't shaved in weeks. And I didn't give a fuck.

But before heroin, I had cared. When I'd dated Cody in college, I always dressed in cute outfits and underneath, a sexy pair of panties and matching bra. I'd shower, shave, and lather my body with fruity scented lotion before I'd go to his apartment. I'd brush my teeth as soon as I got up in the morning so I wouldn't scare him off with my breath. Even when I'd kissed Casey, I had gum in my mouth to hide the cigarette smell.

Raul's lips grazed my body. His tongue ran down to my thighs and climbed back. His fingers rubbed my crotch, and I could feel him inhale my smell. And all I thought about was how good I felt.

The scent of the condom and his candy-flavored breath were oddly delicious. His mouth tasted tart like Starbursts. The shot was making me crave sugar again, and if I wasn't going to reach an orgasm, at least I got to taste his candy.

Raul didn't kick me out in the morning. He told me I could stay as long as I wanted, and when his friends came over, he left me alone in his room. He kept checking up on me, bringing me food and movies to watch, and refilling my syringe. I didn't know why he was being so nice. It wasn't like I was special or prettier than the other girls I'd seen hanging out here.

When we moved out of Abdul's hotel, we left behind most of our clothes, and we'd been wearing the same outfit for three days. Que gave us money to buy some new clothes so we went shopping. We each got a couple shirts and a pair of jeans and then we stopped at a bakery for chocolate cupcakes.

On our way home, we passed a library. There was a sign by the door that said: Computer classes, 2-4 p.m. daily, free to the public.

My cell phone showed it was only noon.

I pointed at the library. "I need to go in there for a sec."

"For what?" Renee asked. "You gonna check out a book?"

"I want to use their computer."

She said she'd wait for me outside, but I had to be quick. Her stomach was upset and she needed to shoot up again. We'd shot up just a few hours ago. It seemed like her stomach was upset more than not.

I found the computers along the far wall of the library and got online. I typed in Eric's full name, but only football articles came up from when he played in high school. There wasn't an obituary or any articles about his death. I guess his parents couldn't have an obituary printed or plan the funeral until the autopsy was completed and his body was shipped up to Bangor.

I walked through the middle of the library this time, but stopped when I saw all the kids. Groups of three were sitting on the floor and one kid from each group was reading out loud. Their teacher was sitting at a table close by, watching each group and taking notes.

"Switch," the teacher said. The kids, who were reading out loud, passed their book to a different kid in their group. They were young, kindergarten or first grade, and reading from lesson books.

A little boy, in the group closest to me, got stuck on a word and raised his hand. I started to walk over to the boy, but the teacher stood and went to his side, so I didn't. She helped him sound out the word and then the boy asked what it meant.

"Class, can any of you tell me what the word *believe* means?"

A bunch of kids raised their hands, and the teacher called on a little girl.

"Believe means to know something is true," the little girl said.

"Very good, Mona," the teacher said. "I'll give you a star if you can put believe in a sentence."

"I believe my cat has fleas," Mona said. She scratched her arm and all the kids laughed.

"Nicole," Renee yelled. She was standing on the opposite side of the reading group, close to the front door.

The kids and their teacher turned towards Renee and then to me.

"What the hell is taking you so long?" Renee said, too loud. "I told you I wasn't feeling good."

The teacher's lips were pointed in a frown. "Never mind them, class," she said.

Some of the kids looked away and the rest kept their eyes on me. The ones who stayed had scared expressions.

They thought I was scary?

But in my head, I was wearing the long patchwork dress, standing in the front of the group, holding a notebook full of assignments, and they were calling me "Miss Brown." I had taken them on a field trip to the library, helping them with vocabulary and overseeing their reading lesson.

"Let's go. Now," Renee shouted.

But I wasn't their teacher. I'd been wearing the same clothes for three days, my hair was greasy, and track marks covered my bare arms.

I believed heroin was pumping through my veins. I believed Renee was sick because she needed another shot. I believed I'd be sick too if I didn't do one soon.

"I'm coming," I said and followed Renee through the door.

Renee said we should ride out Que and Raul's offer to stay at their house for as long as we could. She didn't want to go back to sleeping in the park. She said she needed to be close to a bathroom since she was still getting sick a lot. I thought I could give Raul what he wanted for a while. He was keeping me well fed.

What he wanted was sex—all the time. It was like he couldn't get enough of me and, in return, I couldn't slam enough of his dope. Right before he was about to come, he'd whisper strange shit in my ear like how he wanted me to be his boo and how I was all he could think about. He said he'd wanted me since the first time we met, but whenever I came to his house, I was always with Eric. Raul said I looked happy with Eric, so he never pursued me. I didn't correct him either. I was happy when I was with Eric, but that was in the past.

Being someone's girlfriend sounded like a lot of work, and besides, dope made me lazy and emptied all my emotions. But at the same time, I liked being with Raul. He was tender when I needed him to be and gentle when my crotch was sore. He listened when I bitched about my parents, which was every few hours because that's how much they were calling. Michael was calling too.

News of Eric's death had finally gotten out in Bangor, and my parents were crazy over it. They were acting like the cops with all their questions. I told them Eric and I had drifted apart. He'd been hanging around his co-workers who were a bad crowd, and they'd gotten him into drugs. I never said the word heroin when I was on the phone with them. It was sacred like when people said gosh instead of God.

By the end of each phone call, I had them believing my lies. But within a few hours, they'd call back with more questions. They wanted to know why we were staying in a hotel at the time of Eric's death, and I said our apartment was being treated for bugs. They'd bring up the rape and how much I had changed since it happened. They tried to use my weight loss and acne, and my weird behavior at brunch, as signs I was on drugs. I repeated the same excuses: I was running every day and working too much, and was still getting over the flu when they'd last seen me. I told them I'd never even smoked pot, let alone stick a needle in my arm. They didn't call me a liar, but I could hear concern in their voices.

To get them off the phone, I'd tell them I was at work. Raul would have a shot waiting for me, and before I hung up it was already in my arm.

Tim called a week later. He said Eric's funeral was in two days. I asked if I could crash on his couch and if he'd pick me up from the bus station, and he said yes to both. When we got off the phone, I went into Que's room to tell Renee.

"Can I go?" she asked. "I need a break from this place."

I didn't know if she was talking about Que's house or Boston. And why did she need a break? She hadn't gone back to work, and she was getting all the smack and food she wanted for free. I thought we had a pretty good thing going on, and I wasn't sure if I even wanted to leave.

"Can you cover your bus ticket?" I asked.

"I'll get the money."

"What about dope? We'll be gone for a couple days."

"I'll take care of it… for both of us."

I went back into Raul's room where he was waiting for me naked in bed.

"I'm taking a trip," I said and climbed in next to him.

His lips moved over my chest and down my stomach, and then his head disappeared under the blanket.

"Mmm… Where we going?" he asked.

My needle was lying on the nightstand, full and ready to be shot. I reached for it, but I was too late. Raul's head surfaced and he moved on top of me.

"I have to go home for a few days."

He moved in and out of me. But there was something different about it. His dick was warm and there wasn't any chaffing.

"You're not going anywhere," he said and devoured my mouth with his.

It was the condom. He wasn't wearing one. And I wasn't on the pill.

Fuck.

Fuck it. It was too late, he was already inside me. And since I'd been slamming so much dope, a baby wouldn't have a chance of surviving in my body.

"Can you lean up a little?" I asked.

I slapped my arm and fisted air since I couldn't get off the bed to grab my belt. He didn't stop, but he gave me enough room so I could stick my vein.

"You're mine," he said.

My eyes closed, but I could still feel him and hear his breath coming out in moans.

Was I his? As long as he kept feeding me, I guess I was.

CHAPTER NINE

Renee came through as promised. She got the money for the bus ticket and enough dope to keep us high while we were in Maine. Raul gave us a ride to North Station and bought me a one-way ticket. Before we boarded, he lifted me up in his arms and kissed me goodbye. He told me he'd miss me and would purchase my return ticket as soon as I was ready to come home. If he bought me a round trip ticket, I'd return to Boston, but that didn't mean I'd return to his house. That was his way of controlling when I came back to him.

I wasn't sure if I'd miss him the way he was going to miss me. He didn't give me that tingly feeling in my stomach. Raul did have free reign of my body, but he didn't have my heart. His drugs did.

It had been two years since I'd left Bangor, and when the bus pulled onto Main Street, so many memories hit me at once. We drove by the Bangor Auditorium where my high school graduation was held, and the Bounty, where we went clubbing because it was the only place in town that didn't card at the door. We passed the *Bangor Daily News*, where my dad worked. He used to bring me there as a kid to do his filing and photocopying.

We got off the bus with our backpacks and climbed straight into Tim's car. He drove through town and everything looked exactly the same. The ground had a light dusting of snow, and the sky was overcast, which gave the buildings and houses a grayish tint.

My favorite store, The Grasshopper Shop, and our Friday night hangout place, the Wig & Courier, were both still there. There was a line out the door at The Coffee Pot, which made the best sandwiches in town, and I saw Jeffrey, my old hairdresser through the window of The Cut Hut.

We passed Eastern Maine Medical Center. That was where my old roommate, Katy, had taken me the morning after the rape and where the doctor had told me what those bastards had done to me. The rape—that was why I'd left Bangor in the first place. Why did I come back here and re-open all these memories? Eric was dead and his funeral was in the morning. Shit. I needed to get high.

Tim lived in a small one-bedroom on the top floor of a converted house. When we got inside, he asked if we wanted to smoke a bowl, and I said we would after we cleaned ourselves up. Renee and I went into the bathroom and ran the faucet so he couldn't hear us. We did a small shot to get straight again, but not too high. I didn't want Tim to know I was using heroin. In high school, we'd smoked hash and opium together, but smack was different. It was the drug that wasn't talked about to people who didn't use.

Tim smoked us up after we mainlined, and it wasn't long before people started showing up to his place. He had said some of the regulars were going to stop by, but I didn't expect a party. The old gang from high school was all here.

Time must have stopped in Bangor. Everyone looked just the same, and Tim told me they were all still dating their high school sweethearts, still working at the mall, and living at home with their parents. Anyone could see I wasn't like them anymore.

Didn't they want better? Bangor was a sad place. There was fun to be had out in the world, and it didn't involve hanging out at Tim's and sleeping in the bedroom you grew up in.

There were at least fifteen people there already, and I heard someone say more were on their way. No one greeted me with hugs when they came in. They said hello and then completely ignored me. I caught stares and snide looks like they didn't know what I was doing here. Maybe they were just surprised by how thin I'd gotten, but that wasn't a reason to blow me off.

Tim had bought a case of beer, and Renee was helping herself, pounding one after another. I'd never seen her drink before, but tonight she was sucking them down. And it wasn't just beer, she was hitting every joint that was passed to her. The strongest drug in this apartment was weed, so I was hitting the joints too. Tim didn't hang out with pill-heads or the kids who did blow. I wished he did. Renee said a speedball—mixing blow and dope—was a crazy rush.

We were all huddled in the living room, and Emily, Eric's ex-girlfriend from junior year, handed me a water bong. I took a hit, and just as I was passing it to Renee, Emily asked me about Eric. The room turned silent and all eyes pointed at me.

"What do you want to know?"

"Did he really die from a heroin overdose?" she asked. She wrinkled her nose when she said heroin, like the word grossed her out.

"That's what I heard," I said.

"You should know, you were living with him," Tony said. "So you had to have seen it happen."

What did they want from me? A confession? They needed someone to blame for his death and because I was here, that person was me.

"I have a job," I said. "So no, I wasn't there when it happened."

"Were you?" Emily asked Renee.

"Nope, I was at work too," Renee said.

Wouldn't they love to know Renee saw the whole thing and to keep herself out of jail, she waited to call 9-1-1. But I'd never tell them that, just like I didn't tell the cops Renee was lying when she gave her statement.

"Eric was addicted to heroin and neither of you knew?" Tony asked.

Both Renee and me shook our heads. I didn't need to convince them I was innocent. These people didn't mean shit to me, and what fucking difference did it make? He was dead. Couldn't they just leave it alone?

"They're lying," Emily said. "You can't live with someone and not know they're shooting up drugs."

"Look how thin she's gotten," Frank said and pointed at me.

"You were doing heroin with him, weren't you?" Ryan asked.

I couldn't take this anymore. I needed to get out and find a quiet place where I could shoot up.

I told Tim we were going to get something to eat and we'd be back later. He said this wasn't Boston, and everything closed at ten.

We left anyway. We walked down Broadway and stopped when we got to the park. Broadway Park was the one place in Bangor where I didn't have to hide. There was something about the trees, and flowers, and benches that made me feel like I was back in Boston. Maybe it was because it looked so much like our park, Boston Commons.

Screw this place. And screw Eric too. I never should have come back here, and if it wasn't for that asshole dying, I never would have set foot in Bangor ever again. I was better than all those people at Tim's apartment. In fact, they wanted to be like me, living in the big city and away from my parents. And what was waiting for me in Renee's backpack was fucking perfect.

In the middle of the jungle gym, between the slide and wobbly bridge, was a cubbyhole, and we climbed inside. With our legs crossed, we both fit comfortably and used the light from the full moon to guide the needles into our arms. During the nod that was usually filled with warmth and beautiful pictures, I had a flashback of my last night in college.

Katy and I had arrived at Washburn Apartments for the yearly rager the complex threw to celebrate the beginning of spring. Of course, in Maine it sometimes snowed until May, and this year was no different. The ground was covered in fresh powder, and the temperature was dipping well below thirty degrees. We'd spent hours getting ready to look our cutest for Cody and Katy's boyfriend, Brandon, but the night wasn't kicking off like I had planned. My jacket hid the shirt I'd bought just that morning and my new boots were pinching the crap out of my toes.

Cars were parked on both sides of the road and on the snow-filled lawn, and the three parking lots were full. There had to be over five hundred people there already, and somewhere among them were our friends we were meeting. The boyfriends had all gone to Portland to watch the Sea Dogs game and weren't due back until midnight, so we had a few hours to catch a buzz.

Katy and I found the nearest keg and stood in line to buy a cup.

"Having fun yet?" a voice said in my ear.

I turned around and my friend Ben from biology class was standing behind me with three full cups in his hands. He handed one to both Katy and me.

"Thanks, Ben, how'd you score these?" I asked.

"My goal is to get all the pretty girls drunk tonight."

"Well you got any bud," Katy said. "You might as well get us high too."

Ben was never without weed, and sometimes we'd buy from him when our regular connection was dry.

"Come with me," he said with a big smile.

We followed him towards a row of townhouses and stopped when we reached the front steps of his apartment. He pulled out a blunt from his pocket and passed it to me after it was lit.

"Where's your boy?" he asked.

I told him the guys had gone to the baseball game and were coming to the party after.

"He still let you come with all the vultures around here?"

Katy and I laughed.

When the blunt was down to a nub, Ben left us to get more beer.

"What do you think, should we find the crew?" Katy asked.

Blunts got me extra high. Every time I smoked one I felt like I was floating. We'd smoked a bowl in the car on the way to the party, and now I was pretty much locked up.

Standing on the steps, I looked out to the crowd and felt like I was a blade in a field of grass. There was no way we were ever going to find our friends.

"Call Mathy's cell and see where she's at," I said.

"I did," she said. "She didn't answer."

I didn't want to move. Couldn't the girls find us?

"Stop being lazy, come on," she said and pulled my hand, leading me through the mosh pit.

I stopped drinking after my second beer. It was too damn cold outside to put anything icy down my throat, plus my stomach was a little upset. I felt it gurgling, though it wasn't from being hungry because I'd eaten before we came.

A pair of arms slid around my waist, and warm lips kissed the skin between my collar and scarf. I didn't have to look to know it was Cody. I could smell the woodsy scent of his cologne.

"Did you miss me?" he whispered.

From just the sound of his voice, tingly sparks shot into my belly. We'd only been dating for four months, but it felt much longer than that. We had this sexual attraction that I'd never had with anyone else before, and when I was in his arms, I was so turned on.

"More than you know," I said.

I didn't want to just feel his lips on my neck, I wanted to taste them too. He took my hand and twirled me around. On my tiptoes, I hugged his neck and kissed his mouth. His skin was hot, and the minty flavor of his toothpaste stung my tongue.

"How was the game?" I asked.

"It was fun, wait till you hear this," he said and pointed at Barry. "Barry, tell the girls what happened on the way home."

I'd forgotten anyone else was around us. Katy had her arms tucked inside Brandon's jacket, and Barry was holding Mathy. Everyone laughed but me as Barry told the story. I couldn't concentrate, everything around me was starting to spin.

Cody noticed something was wrong and put his hands on my face. "Baby, you okay?"

My stomach was more than gurgling now, it was churning. And my mouth was watering like I was going to be sick.

"Just cold," I said. "I need something to drink, want me to get you a beer?"

"I'll come with you."

"No, stay, I'll be right back," I said and jogged away, heading for the side parking lot by the dumpsters.

I didn't want Cody to see me puke. We weren't at a point where we were showing each other our bodily fluids. I knew I'd be fine once I got out whatever was hurting my stomach and then I'd rejoin the group. Maybe I'd even tell him I wasn't feeling good and I'd go back to my dorm room to sleep.

Halfway to the dumpster, the food rose to the back of my throat and I took off running with my hand over my mouth. Behind the dumpster, I lost it all. The dinner we ate and the two beers, it all came out.

My stomach was still churning, my head was foggy, and the rest of my body was sweating. I sat on the ground, the snow soaking into the butt of my jeans. The spins were getting worse, so I put my head between my knees, trying to make it stop. Behind my lids were circles of blackness like I had rubbed my eyes too hard, but I hadn't touched them.

"Give her another minute," I heard someone say.

"Cody?"

I heard laughing. Two different voices and they were deep.

"Cody, is that you?"

And then all I saw was blackness.

When I woke up, my body was stiff and my muscles ached like I had the flu. I was freezing and reached for the blanket, but my hand grabbed only a fistful of air. Where was my comforter?

Even with my lids closed, I could still feel the brightness around me. Had Katy forgotten to shut the blinds?

I sat up to look for my blanket and opened my eyes slowly so they'd adjust to the light. The sun almost blinded me.

Where was our dorm room? Why the hell was I outside, surrounded by woods and sitting on a mound of snow? My pants were next to me in a clump, my jacket was unzipped, and my shirt was torn at the bottom.

Panic ran through every part of me. I didn't know where I was. And I didn't know why I was half naked.

Scrambling to my feet as fast as I could, I yanked my jeans over my boots and took off running. The button on my jeans was missing and the zipper was broken, so while I staggered through the snow, I held the waist to keep them on.

There were footprints in the snow. I thought if I followed them, they'd lead me to somewhere I recognized.

The heel of my boot broke off from stumbling over twigs. My nose was running. The wind was making my eyes water, and it was hard to see where I was going.

There was a swishing noise up ahead and the trees started to clear. Cars? Cars swished, right? Something was swishing.

A branch hit my face. I tasted blood on my lips.

A road. A main road with more than one lane.

I tripped over a big rock. Both my body and pants fell at the same time. I needed to haul myself back up. I was almost at the road. But so tired.

At the clearing, I saw the street, and across the way was the University of Maine sign. I was fifteen minutes away from our dorm.

I crossed the four lanes of traffic without looking both ways. Cars honked. My pants slid down my waist and every step pounded my muscles like I was lying on a bed of nails.

My other heel broke off at the beginning of Long Road. Cumberland Hall was at the bottom of the hill.

I wheezed from the cold and strain. My toes cramped from the pointy-toed boots.

Someone was leaving Cumberland Hall. "Wait," I shouted.

They held the door and I pushed my way through. Our shoulders hit, and the person yelled, "Ouch, watch it."

I bolted up the two flights of stairs and down the hall to our room. Our door wasn't locked and I threw myself into the room.

"Where the hell have you been?" Katy asked. She closed her textbook and put it on the bed.

She was tucked under the covers. The TV was on. The shades were closed and my eyes still hurt.

"I... I don't know," I said and rubbed my forehead with both hands. Without holding the waist, my pants dropped to my ankles.

She gasped. "Nicole, your jeans, and, and your legs, they're covered in blood."

She was right. I wasn't wearing any underwear, and my thighs were caked with dried blood.

"I woke up in the woods," I said and lifted my head to meet her eyes.

She shook her head. "We looked for you all night."

"I got sick by the dumpsters and then..." I tried to remember what happened after I sat down on the snow. "I don't, I don't know, Katy, I don't remember anything."

She jumped out of her bed and pulled on her boots and jacket. "We're going to the hospital."

I closed my eyes when we got in her car, and when I opened them again we were at Eastern Maine Medical Center.

The doctor was trying to be gentle, but every time she touched my crotch, it burned. Her head rose from between my legs, and said she'd be back with the test results.

Katy hadn't left my side. She'd held my hand through the exam and blood test, and when the police officer asked me questions. Now she sat behind me on the gurney, rubbing my head and pulling out twigs and leaves that had nested into my hair.

The doc opened the blue curtain that separated my gurney from the others and closed it once she entered. She was reading from a clipboard.

"Your blood tested positive for Rohypnol," the doc said.

Rohypnol, like the date rape drug?

She set her clipboard on the table and sat on the stool she used for the exam, but wheeled it next to me. "Two different types of sperm were found during the internal exam," she said and paused like there was more. "And we found traces of lighter fluid on your skin."

Katy wrapped her arms around my chest. I went to move and the IV stopped me, tugging at my arm. I ripped it out. Blood dripped from where the needle was. "What, what does all that mean?"

The doc took a deep breath. "You were drugged and raped last night by two different men, and they burned your chin with a lighter."

My eyes shot open. Renee was sitting in front of me, nodding out. It took me a minute before I realized we were still in the park, crammed into the cubbyhole. And the park wasn't in Boston. I was in Bangor because Eric's funeral was tomorrow morning.

I'd had flashbacks and nightmares about that night before, but not like this and never so detailed. That was the real deal, like it had just happened seconds before and not two years ago. I couldn't wait to get the hell out of Maine.

When we got back to Tim's, everyone was gone, and his bedroom door was shut. We shot up again and drifted in and out while the sun rose in the eggplant and aqua sky.

Tim woke us up only a few hours later and handed us mugs of coffee. Renee and I dressed in the nicest clothes we owned—jeans and button down shirts—and got high after we put our makeup on.

The ground was still too frozen for a burial, so the service was held at a funeral home. Rows of chairs faced the open casket. From the back row, I could see only a small portion of Eric's profile. But next to him was a poster-sized picture from high school graduation propped on an easel. I kept my eyes on the floor. I'd seen enough.

When the holy collared guy started reciting prayers, I fell asleep. I could have stayed awake, but I didn't want to hear all that shit about our heavenly father.

Tim nudged me. Renee was sleeping too and I tapped her on the leg. Eric's mom was standing in front of the casket, saying how much Eric was loved and how it wasn't his time to be with Jesus. Oh, he'd seen Jesus all right. Jesus had sold us the batch of dope that Eric OD'd on.

She talked about Eric's goals of being a pilot—that was news to me—and how he was so talented and surrounded by such inspiring people. Her teary eyes scanned the crowd, and not once did they land on me. I counted how many times she wiped her nose. So far it was eight.

After the ceremony, everyone got up and moved to the other room where drinks and food were being served.

"Let's go see Eric and get the fuck out of here," Renee said. "This place is creeping me out."

I agreed. Our backpacks were in Tim's car, so if he wasn't ready to leave yet, we'd walk to the bus station.

Renee and I stood in line. I didn't look at him until I was right in front of him. The funeral people had done a good job making him look alive. His skin was a light peach, and his lips were red.

What can I say, I thought to myself. Sorry this happened to you? Sorry you took too much? Neither of those seemed right. Eric wouldn't want to hear me apologize, he'd want to know how I was doing.

I've been staying at Que's, I told him. Raul has the hots for me, but I'm not sure if I want to be his girl. He takes good care of me though. Like you would have. My parents have been all over me since you died, and they think I'm doing the same shit you did. We'll keep that between us, okay? It'll be our little secret like the time you saw me naked in our apartment in Chinatown. I hope you're liking the other side and everyone over there is treating you good. Rest in peace, my friend.

I went to the back of the room to wait for Renee and when I got by the door, my parents walked in.

"Were you going to call us?" Mom asked.

Fuck. Renee needed to hurry the hell up.

"I just got in this morning," I said. "I was going to call after the funeral."

My parents looked at each other. My dad's expression caught me first, raised eyebrows and lips pointed down in a scowl.

"I don't believe you," he said. "You haven't answered your phone in three days."

"What's not to believe? My luggage is still in Tim's car."

"Tim?" Mom asked. "Why are you avoiding us? Is there something you're trying to hide?"

"He offered to give me a ride—"

"You need help, Nicole," Dad said.

I couldn't remember the last time he'd called me by my real name.

"We're taking you to Acadia Hospital right now," Mom said.

I wasn't going to that hell hole of a rehab center and sit in therapy with all the dropouts and addicts I went to high school with.

Renee was walking towards us. She gave me a look like she'd meet me outside. I mouthed "Tim" to her and she understood.

"Mom," I said and looked at her. "And Dad, I don't need to go to rehab. I'm fine, I promise."

"Stop lying to us," they both said at the same time.

My parents' voices were so loud people were starting to stare.

Renee had found Tim, and they were standing by the front door, waiting for me.

"I hope you're proud of yourselves," I said. "Causing a scene."

I dashed to the front door. I could hear my parents following behind me, and then I heard Eric's mom call my name. I didn't turn around. I joined Tim and Renee, and we fled down the stairs to Tim's car. When I was in the passenger seat, I saw my parents and Eric's mom running down the steps after me.

"Go, go, now," I said, and Tim floored the gas.

I asked him to drop us off at the bus station, and I called Raul to tell him I was ready to come home. Raul said he'd call the bus company and pay for my return ticket, and he'd pick us up at North Station.

The bus wasn't leaving for thirty minutes, but we boarded anyway and scrunched down in our seats so we couldn't be seen through the window.

I decided not to go into the bathroom and shoot up until we were on our way to Boston. I would have done it in the seat, but the driver was watching us through his rearview mirror

"I've got to tell you something," Renee said.

The bus had started moving, and I was getting ready to go into the bathroom.

"What is it?"

She was chewing her fingernail and her eyes were glued to the floor. "I'm... Fuck," she said and paused. "I'm fucking pregnant."

"What?"

"Yeah, at least two months along."

This couldn't really be happening. Could it? She was using as much dope as I was, so wouldn't that have killed the baby? Two damn months? That would explain her throwing up. But wait. Who was the father? Que?

"Is that why Que and Raul have been so nice to us?" I asked.

"I don't know about Raul, but yeah, Que thinks it's his."

She didn't sound convinced. Who else could be the father?

"Is it his?" I asked.

"There's only been one other dude besides Que."

Renee didn't talk about the men she had sex with. Until we started staying at Que's house, I didn't even know they'd been sleeping together.

"Mark," she said.

"Mark who?"

"Our old boss, Mark. He could be the father too."

Now it made sense. All those dirty looks she'd given me when Mark had paid for BC's tip and when I told her he'd stuck his tongue down my throat. She'd been sleeping with him the whole time? And Que? Damn.

"Does Mark know you're prego?" I asked.

"Why, do you think I should tell him?"

"Shit, Renee. I don't know, we've got a good thing at Que's."

"But I'm pretty sure Mark's the dad."

What the hell were we going to do? Renee might have Mark's baby inside her, and if Que found out, our asses would be on the street. Who would we buy from then?

CHAPTER TEN

Renee's belly was starting to get round, and Que would rub it, calling it his bump of love. The whole thing grossed me out. Not just her pregnancy, but also the way they acted. They pretended to talk to the baby and put headphones on her stomach, so it could listen to rap music. She hadn't gone to the doctor yet, and she wasn't taking those pregnancy vitamins. For all she knew, the baby had three arms sprouting from its chest.

I didn't know what made her want to keep the baby in the first place. Mark would have sprung for an abortion, I thought. But she still hadn't even told him she was pregnant. What was she going to do if the baby came out light skinned and didn't have any of Que's Puerto Rican complexion?

Raul was obsessed with the whole baby thing too. He thought it'd be fun if he and Que had kids close in age, and he was trying to get me pregnant. Fun? That would be about as much fun as checking into rehab. I told him one morning I was going to visit Michael, but really I went to the free clinic. The doctor did an internal exam and I had to pee in a cup to make sure I wasn't pregnant before he gave me birth control pills. He told me I'd have to come back once a month to get another prescription, and the receptionist would call to remind me of my appointment.

Raul got all upset when I got my period and said we needed to try harder. We were having sex at least twice a day, how much harder could we try? I told him it took some women up to a year to get pregnant. He said I was young and in a month or so I'd be carrying his baby. Whatever I did, I couldn't forget to go to the clinic or he'd be rubbing my bump of love too.

Renee said sunlight was good for the baby and asked me to go on a walk with her every afternoon. A baby wasn't like a plant, and

if she really cared what was good for it, she'd stop shooting dope.
Near the end of our walk, we'd buy two pints of ice cream and eat
them before going back home. In between bites, she'd tell me the
baby names they'd picked out and how different their lives were
going to be after it was born. Que was going to give up dealing and
open an auto body shop, and they'd rent a house in the suburbs for
their little family of three. Her plans never included Raul and me.

Raul said Que would never stop dealing because they made too
much money. And moving to the 'burbs wasn't going to happen
either. All their friends lived in the city. What I thought he meant
was their gang lived in the city and they weren't allowed to leave
them, but their gang was something he wouldn't discuss.

Renee and I were walking home one day after finishing our ice
cream, and a parade of police cars passed us, blue lights flashing.
When we saw the cops again, they were double parked in front of
our house. Swarms of officers stood on the lawn, and the front door
of the house was open. We stopped a block away and didn't move
any closer. We knew if we tried to go inside the house, we'd get
dragged into the mess too.

Two officers with canines came out of the house. There was a
yellow lab and a German shepherd, followed by five cops, two
carrying Que's wooden drug cabinet and the others with trash bags
in their hands. The cops had found everything except Renee and me.

Que and Raul were hauled out next. They were handcuffed and
placed in separate police cars.

"How'd they know?" Renee whispered.

"Someone snitched."

She looked at me from the corner of her eyes and her top lip was
curled. "Was it you?"

"Fuck you, Renee, seriously."

"Sorry, it's my hormones, they make me think crazy thoughts."

The same hormones that led her to believe Que would give up
dealing for the baby? Stupid bitch. I couldn't believe she'd accuse
me of tipping off the cops.

"What do we do now?" she asked.

I needed my clothes from inside the house, but we couldn't
stand here all day and wait for the police to clear out. If we did stay,

they might think we were connected and try to question us. I had the important stuff like my purse and cell phone. Renee would have to steal me some clothes from Goodwill.

"Let's go to the park," I said.

We sat on a bench and people watched. Renee was really quiet. I asked her how much time the guys would serve and if we should call their friends to tell them the news. She didn't answer. She only shrugged her shoulders, staring at the trees that surrounded us.

By dark, I was feening and I knew Renee had to be hungry. We didn't have any dope, and I'd spent the money Raul had given me on ice cream that morning. "You have any money left?"

"I've got Que's ATM card."

"You stole it?"

"He gave me one."

He must have really trusted her.

"Let's go to McDonald's," she said. "Then we'll hit up Roxbury for some H."

"Roxbury first."

"The baby needs to eat," she said.

I was already sick of this baby and it wasn't even born yet. The old Renee would've wanted smack first and food later. This was bullshit.

I walked with her to the ATM and while she searched her bag for the card, she complained about how hungry she was. She said she didn't want to wait in line for the food, so she told me to go order and she'd be there in a minute to pay.

McDonald's was only a block down from the bank. I ordered two value meals and stood to the side of the counter, waiting for Renee. After five minutes, I called her cell phone. She didn't answer. Ten minutes later, she still hadn't shown up. The McDonald's guy had set our food on a tray and placed it on the counter. The smell of the burgers was making my stomach growl and my mouth was watering for the orange soda.

"Is your friend coming or not?" the guy asked.

The clock on my phone showed twenty minutes had passed since I'd left her at the ATM. I tried her cell again and it went straight to voicemail.

I stole a couple fries. "I guess not," I said and walked out.

I went to the ATM, but she wasn't there. She wasn't in the park either. That bitch had taken off, leaving me without any dope or money. She'd been really quiet since we saw the cops, so she was probably scheming up a plan to ditch me. I had this feeling I'd never see her again.

I sat on the same bench we'd shared earlier that night and thought about what to do. I needed a loan. Who could I ask? There wasn't anyone in the city I knew besides Michael. But wait. I had money in my savings account that I still hadn't touched. Actually, I'd forgotten I even had the account. I used to get bank statements at the Chinatown apartment, but since Eric and I had gotten kicked out, I never forwarded my mail. There was enough to buy me a week at a hotel and a couple bundles of smack.

I took the cash limit out of the ATM and got on the train to Roxbury. I hadn't been to this part of the city before, but I'd heard things. Bad things like girls getting raped and murdered by gangs and dealers who they owed money to. I wished Raul was with me, but if he were, I wouldn't have to go to Roxbury. I was hoping I wouldn't have to walk too far from the train and could stay close to where there were a lot of people.

A block away from the station, I saw what I was looking for—groups of guys hanging out on both sides of the street. They dressed in baggy jeans with hooded sweatshirts and jackets despite the warm weather. When Raul did drug runs, he wore a jacket too and stashed the packages in the inside pockets. He said if a cop ever approached him, he'd ditch the coat, so they couldn't charge him for possession.

I stopped at the first group of guys. "Montega?" I asked, which was Spanish slang for dope.

They shook their heads and pointed down the street to the entrance of a pawnshop.

In front of the pawnshop were two guys. Thick gold chains with diamond pendants hung around their necks, and jackets were wrapped loosely over their shoulders. One of them had the same tattoo as Raul, a teardrop under his eye.

"Montega?"

"How much?" The tattooed guy asked.

"Bundle," I said.

We exchanged the money and dope by shaking hands and they whistled at me as I walked back to the train.

I rented a hotel room at the border of Roxbury and Boston. I figured I'd stay on this side of town. The rooms were cheaper than what Abdul charged, and they were bigger too, with a king-sized bed and cable TV. Everything I needed, a spoon, rig, and cotton ball were tucked inside my purse.

Renee called in the morning. I didn't know why I answered when I saw her name on the caller ID or why I listened to her talk. I was high, but that wasn't the reason. Somewhere inside me, I cared about her even though she ditched me. She told me she stayed with Mark last night and was going to live with him permanently even after the baby was born. As she put it, he was the father and the right thing to do was to see if they could make their relationship work. What relationship? Mark had been trying to get with me while he was screwing her, and at the same time, she was also banging Que. She didn't ask about what I'd done after she left me stranded in McDonald's or where I'd spent the night. She said she'd call once the baby was born so I could come visit them in the hospital. I didn't want her to call. She didn't give a shit about me, so why would I want to see her? Hell, I didn't really think her pregnancy would last the whole nine months, not with all the dope she shot.

I wasn't lonely when I sat in my hotel room by myself. Smack was my dream maker. And it was the only thing that stayed constant when everything around me was changing. Raul had called my cell and told me they were being charged with possession, distribution, trafficking, laundering and a bunch of other shit I couldn't remember. They were looking at a minimum of fifteen years. Eric was dead, and Renee was off with her baby's daddy. Everyone in my life had split, and I was in the middle, standing still.

A week later, I was on my way back from Roxbury and saw a middle-aged woman working the corner a few blocks from my hotel. She was decked out in hooker garb, a short jean skirt, backless tank top, teased hair, and makeup painted on like a drag queen. I was out of cigarettes and asked her if I could bum one.

When I met someone for the first time, usually the introduction was awkward and there were moments in the conversation where I had to think of something to say. It wasn't like that with Sunshine and me. We clicked instantly. And we both kept interrupting each other because there was so much to talk about.

From the scars on her arms, I knew she was a junkie too and invited her back to my room to get high. Just then, a car pulled up and the guy asked how much she charged for a full service. She told him eighty, and he hired her. I swapped cell phone numbers with her and told her to call when she was done.

She phoned a couple hours later and came over. I split up the dope, taking some from both our bags. Her smack looked more pure than mine. The heroin I got from Roxbury was cut with things like vitamin B-12 and dextrose, which made it less potent. When mixing hers with mine, the hit was strong like the heroin I got from Que.

After our nods, she told me she'd been working the streets for about thirty years and had two kids in their late twenties who grew up in foster care. I told her about my two plus years in Boston, and she asked how I was paying for dope since the guys had been arrested. I said my savings account was almost dry. She said she remembered living on the streets at my age and how no one had helped her out.

"You want to stay with me?" she asked. There was a menthol 100 dangling between her lips, and the ash was on the verge of falling. "I ain't got much, but it'll get you out of here," she said, using her cig to point around my room.

My room wasn't that bad, minus the cobwebs in the corners. But I said yes. If she wanted to help me out, I had nothing to lose. She said I'd have to pay for my own dope, but if I wanted, we could team up and turn tricks together. I had enough junk to get me through tomorrow and a few bucks left to buy a burger. Raul had told me I was good at sucking dick, and Sunshine said if I could get the guys off fast and land some regulars, I'd make a lot of money.

I moved into Sunshine's place the next day. Her pad was a hotel on Massachusetts Avenue, only a few blocks down from the

Roxbury hotel. She'd been living there rent-free for over five years because she banged Frankie, the owner, a few times a week. The only thing I brought was my purse, but that was good because Sunshine was a collector—of everything. In the last five years, I didn't think she threw anything away, including the trash.

We ate scraps from her fridge, eggs and pickles, and listened to old school music, the Beatles and Jimmy Buffet. She said the tunes got her pumped up for work. Before she left for the streets, she told me stories about her clients and the sick fetishes they were into like bondage and blow-up dolls. She even had one guy ask her to bark and lap water out of a bowl. I couldn't help but laugh. I'd met a lot of hookers when I'd lived at Abdul's, but none of them had enjoyed sex as much as Sunshine.

She hit the corner around nine, and I stayed in the room and watched a show on teen pregnancy. The girls they interviewed looked like Cabbage Patch dolls with their baby faces and braces, and their boyfriends were scrawny without facial hair. The parents' of the teens cried when they talked about their daughters and how bad they felt for them, being pregnant at sixteen. Sunshine had told me when we first met that I looked sixteen too. And every time I bought butts at the store, I got carded. I had an idea.

The next morning I got up early and dressed in Sunshine's clothes, a pair of jean shorts and a tank top. Under the tank, I wore a tube top and stuffed the stomach area with a mound of toilet paper. I made a cardboard sign that said "Six Months Pregnant, Please Help" and sat on the corner of a busy street. The people walking by were dressed in work clothes, carrying briefcases and talking on their cell phones. When they read my sign and looked at my bump, they stopped and donated money. The rich had sympathy for teens with baby bumps the same way they did for homeless people with dogs. One woman even handed me her business card after giving me five bucks. She said she was a doctor and would give me exams for free if I came to her office.

By ten that morning, I'd made eighty-two dollars and got a pretty good suntan too. And after a nice nod at Sunshine's, I earned another seventy-eight from the evening rush.

That night was also the first time I met Richard, Sunshine's dealer. He lived in Dorchester, a fifteen-minute train ride from the hotel. I'd gotten used to the way Que ran things, call before you come over, ring the doorbell before entering, and wait for Que to bring you upstairs. Richard was just the opposite. Sunshine didn't have to call, the door to his house was unlocked, and she walked inside without knocking. There weren't any lights on, and the windows were covered with cardboard. Richard's place was even grimier than the frat houses at UMaine. Roaches climbed the walls, cabinets hung from their hinges, there were holes between the wooden planks on the floor, and in the cracks were broken glass, burnt foil, and needle caps. The smell was similar to the sumo guy I'd found dead at Abdul's hotel.

Sunshine had told me during the train ride that Richard had squatters living with him and sometimes they'd give her a hard time, hustling her for money. I knew squatters lived mostly in abandoned homes and warehouses around the city, but I'd never heard of them taking over someone's house. She said a lot of them ran drugs for Richard or slept with him for dope and that he liked to have them around because he thought they kept him safe. How they'd be able to protect him, I didn't know. The squatters were so fucked up they never even looked at us when we came inside. There were two half-clothed, bug-eyed men cuddled on the uncushioned couch. They stared at the black stained walls and scratched their arms so hard they were covered in blood. There was also a young girl sitting on the kitchen floor next to a mound of trash. Her face was spotted with blemishes like mine; her shirt was ripped open, she was snorting lines off a slice of a mirror.

I followed Sunshine to the back of the house, and we stopped outside a closed door. She knocked twice and opened it. Richard was sitting on the floor in the middle of the room, wearing only boxer shorts, and injecting between his big and second toe. He was long, thin, and pale like a Q-tip with ringlets of black hair on his chest and legs, and his face was covered in pockmarks.

Sunshine took a seat on the air mattress, and I stayed in the doorway, watching him do a second shot in his other foot.

He licked his fingers and wiped the blood from the needle hole. "You brought me a present?" he asked Sunshine.

"She ain't no present," she said. "Nicole's a new customer."

She patted the spot next to her for me to sit down. Richard's eyes followed me, and when I sat, he stared at my chest. "You a hussy too?" he asked.

"Not really," I said.

"You got any money?" he asked Sunshine.

Sunshine took out her cash along with the money I'd given her.

"Damn it," he said and his eyes came back to me. "Your lips would have looked nice around my cock."

Not that I'd want my lips anywhere near his cock, but at least I knew that was an option if I ever ran out of money.

He stood and walked over to the closet. Inside on the floor was a black safe with a number pad. The safe looked out of place. I thought he would have kept his stash in a pillowcase or in a Ziploc under his bed.

He handed three bundles to Sunshine, and her and I moved to the door.

"Come back soon," he said to me.

She closed his bedroom door and once again the squatters avoided us, looking at the walls while we left his house.

"Don't pay him any attention," she said as we got on the train. "He's full of himself, but he's got a tiny pecker."

I'd been living with Sunshine for a couple weeks, and we had a routine down. After my morning shift of panhandling, we'd go to Richard's house together and while I hit up the evening rush, she'd go to the needle exchange. And when she came back from work around two, we'd do a shot. For a few nights in a row, she'd been complaining that she hadn't been doing very well on the streets. Johns were only looking for blowjobs instead of the full service, and she made less money. She said younger girls were crowding her usual corner and getting picked up more than her. She wanted to switch up the clientele, so she decided to go to Ted's, a biker bar and asked me to come too. I'd already earned around a hundred and fifty that day, panhandling with my fake baby bump. But some extra cash meant I could take tomorrow off, and letting some guy fuck me for ten or fifteen minutes was easier than sitting out in the hot sun all morning.

She dressed me up in a short black skirt, shiny tank top and black heels, and lathered my face with makeup. When she finished primping and teasing, I looked like I was entering one of those beauty pageants. My face and hair hadn't even been this done up for prom.

We planted ourselves in the back of the bar and leaned against the wall, looking at all the prospects. In the front of the bar was a younger crowd, probably still in college and broke. The women flocked in the middle by the tables, wearing clothes like I was wearing, but they were around Sunshine's age. The bikers with their leather jackets, tight jeans, and steel-toed boots were in our corner of the room playing pool.

It only took a few minutes before two men approached us. They had thick beards, wads of chew in their lips, and they kept spitting into a cup.

"What you looking for, sugar?" Sunshine asked.

"Full rounds, Mama," the guy standing in front of me said. His eyes were almost black, and when he smiled there was dip stuck between his teeth.

"Hundred," Sunshine said. "Apiece."

"Meet us out behind the bar in twenty," the guy said.

Sunshine and I went to the bathroom and into separate stalls. I sat on the toilet, using my lap as a table and dumping three bags onto the spoon. I usually only did two bags, but I didn't want to feel the burn when he shoved his dick inside me. Sunshine had said the men didn't usually do any licking to get you wet first, and I didn't have any lube. She had told me she pretended all the guys looked like Patrick Swayze and that got her all worked up. It was going to take a lot more than fantasizing about some movie star to make me horny on smack.

When the rush hit me, my mouth went dry. I needed to get a drink or my lips were going to stick to the condom when I gave him head. Sunshine was still in her stall, so I told her I'd meet her at the bar and asked the bartender for some tap water. My legs were wobbly, and I sat on a stool, sucking on the end of the straw.

Damn. The nod came fast. And I couldn't help but follow it. I was so warm, and the leather seat was like silk on the back of my legs.

I felt someone lift me up, and I bounced in their arms as they walked. I didn't open my eyes to see who it was. The dream was so beautiful, I was in a boat and the water was calm and sparkly.

I heard a noise, and the sound was so loud it vibrated through my body and wind swished across my face. Then I heard my name. The voice was familiar, and my eyes opened. I was sitting on a bench near the platform of the train. There were a set of legs underneath mine and arms wrapped around my stomach. I turned to my left and saw Michael.

Michael?

And there was a girl sitting to my right.

"What the hell—"

"I found you," Michael said. His face was only inches away. "You were sleeping on a stool in the bar."

"What were you doing at Ted's?" I asked.

"What are you doing dressed like this?"

"Who are you?" I asked the girl.

"I'm Whitney," she said. She was so pretty. Her long chocolate hair was curled around her face and her lips were plump like sausage links. There were tiny freckles under her eyes and her skin glowed like it was covered in glitter.

"Are you his girlfriend?" I asked.

She looked at Michael. From the corner of my eye, his face looked so serious and a little red, and he shook his head no.

"Do you remember seeing me in the bathroom?" she asked. "You bumped into me after you washed the blood off your wrist."

Michael grabbed my wrist and flipped it over, so my track marks were staring right at him. "I can't believe it," he said. He pulled at my other arm, which looked the same. "We had our suspicions but... Cole, let me get you some help."

"They're not what you think."

"Eric died from this shit, I'm not going to lose you too."

"I'm not Eric."

"That's right, you're still alive," he said. "You're coming home with me." The approaching train overpowered his voice, so I couldn't hear what else he said.

I didn't want to stop using smack. There wasn't a reason for me to stop. I wasn't sick and I wasn't dying. People took painkillers and antidepressants, and instead I did heroin. If I wanted to take a day off from dope, I could. I didn't need help to do that.

"You're going to check yourself into rehab," he yelled.

Rehab? First my parents had turned against me and now him too? Michael had always taken my side when I was younger, and now he wanted to put me in one of those places like I was some messed up, helpless kid?

"Why are you trying to punish me?" I shouted.

His arms loosened from around my stomach and fell to his sides.

"I haven't done anything wrong," I said. "If you think you're helping, you're not, you're only pushing me further away."

His eyes turned red and watery. "But you're—"

"I hate you," I screamed. "You're fucking dead to me."

His chin dropped to his chest, and his body went limp, leaning back against the bench.

This was my chance. I bolted from his lap and ran down the platform.

"Nicole! Nicole! Please stop!" Michael shouted.

When the train door started to close, I slid inside and it shut behind me. I turned my back so I wouldn't see him on the bench and sat in an empty seat.

The next train stop was about a five-minute walk to Ted's. I hoped Sunshine would wait for me before doing both guys by herself. I wanted to feel a man's arms around me and hear them tell me how good I was.

I didn't need rehab. I needed money and heroin.

CHAPTER ELEVEN

A fter I left Michael in the train station, I called Sunshine's cell. I'd woken her out of a nod, and she was still in the bathroom at Ted's. While we talked on the phone, she went outside and found the guys waiting behind the bar. I told her to keep them entertained and I'd be there soon.

When I got there, the three of them were trying to decide where we should get it on. The men had ridden their motorcycles to Ted's, so we didn't have a car to use and they didn't want to pay for a hotel room. Sunshine said the alley was as good as a car, and the guys were fine with that.

We moved in the alleyway, in between Ted's and a nail salon, and separated into couples. I stood still, waiting for him to tell me what he wanted, and he bent his head and kissed me. He hadn't spit out his wad of chew, and I tasted bits of tobacco when I licked my lips. I tried to keep my lips in a tight lock, but he opened them with his tongue, moving around in my mouth like he was brushing my teeth.

He dropped his pants, and his fingers pushed down on the top of my head. I opened the condom Sunshine had given me and slid it on. As I gave him a blowjob, I smelled the stench from his pubes. Sweat and dirt, mixed with something sour like stale milk. The condom tasted like antibacterial gel. My mouth was dry from the latex, my jaw was sore, and my lips were sticking, not sliding.

He grabbed both sides of my face and pulled me in for some deep throat action. I choked on him. That was when he pulled me by the hair and slammed me against the wall of the building. He told me he wanted it from behind. I hiked my skirt to my waist and spread my legs. I wasn't wet and I'd sucked all the lubricant off the condom, so I licked my fingers, trying to drench myself with saliva. But I still felt the burn when he rammed into me.

His thrusts were rough and every time he buried his dick, my nose hit the wall. I protected my face with my hands and counted the strokes to keep my mind off the pain.

Eight. Nine. Ten strokes.

Sunshine was about a foot away, and I stared at the side of her face, the wrinkles around her eyes and the gray roots that needed to be bleached. She'd been doing this for thirty years? That seemed like a long time and this was only my first day.

Sunshine moaned and said, "Deeper, baby."

I hadn't said a word, not even a groan. She looked over at me and winked. Her guy was much louder than mine and sounded like he was really into it.

"Give it to me harder," I said and Sunshine smiled.

He gave it to me harder and moaned.

"Faster," I said.

He moved faster.

Sixteen strokes. Seventeen. Eighteen.

I matched his grunts and shouted, "I'm gonna come."

Twenty-four. Twenty-five.

He let out a long moan and leaned into the side of my face. "You've got a nice, tight pussy," he said.

As I pulled my skirt down, he slid off the condom and threw it on the ground.

Sunshine's guy had finished too, and after they zipped their pants, they gave us a hundred bucks apiece.

"See, it ain't so bad," Sunshine said on the way to the train station. "The moaning gets them to bust quicker and that's the secret to turning tricks real fast."

I took a seat next to her on the train and it hurt a little when I sat. If I did this again, I'd have to buy some lube. But Sunshine was right. It wasn't so bad, and I'd made more money in ten minutes than I had panhandling all morning.

I met our next door neighbor, Claire, a few months later. I'd just gotten back from panhandling, and she walked in behind me, carrying all these bags of groceries. The bags looked too heavy for an old woman to be lugging up the stairs, and I offered to carry them for her. She thanked me and gave me all the bags from one of her hands. I followed her to the fourth floor, and she stopped at the room next to mine. I was surprised I'd never seen her before.

"Did you just move in?" I asked, setting the bags by her kitchen sink. "I live next door and haven't seen you around."

"Oh no, honey. I've been here for years," she said.

"I'm Nicole," I said. "Sunshine's roommate."

She shook my hand so gently I barely felt it. "She's such a nice gal, that Sunshine," she said. "I was just going to fix some supper, do you want to join me?"

Considering we'd just met seconds ago, I thought her invitation was odd. But I accepted. Hell, was there such a thing as odd anymore?

What struck me the most about Claire was how motherly she was. She made me a cup of tea and a plate of cheese and crackers before she started cooking, and told me to make myself comfortable. I sat on the couch, drinking my lemon tea and flipping through the photo album on her coffee table. Most of the pictures were cracked and faded. The photographs showed her as a young woman and with her were a little boy and a man I assumed was her husband because the kid looked just like him. But as the boy grew older, his father disappeared from the photos.

"That's my son, Henry," she said, standing next to the couch. She used her wooden spoon to point to the pictures.

Over dinner, I learned she was seventy-eight and widowed, and Henry was in prison, but she didn't say what for. After her husband died of cancer, she got her first job as a baker in a café, and when she retired ten years ago, she moved into the hotel.

Claire washed the dishes, and for dessert, she served homemade cookies with milk. I was so full. I hadn't eaten this much food since Jimmy's Fourth of July party in Cape Cod, but the cookies smelled so good and they were right out of the oven. The chocolate chips were melted and the dough was gooey. I devoured three cookies and as I reached for my fourth, Claire asked where I was from. I told her my story—minus the cause of Eric's death and what Que and Raul had gotten arrested for, and that I used heroin, because I wanted to be invited for dinner again.

Claire had a collection of movies and asked if I wanted to watch one. I didn't have anything going on. I had my period so that ruined my plans for tricking. I told her I needed to make a phone call and I'd be back in a little while.

I shot up and after the nod, I went back to her room. Claire was sitting on the couch and there was a bowl of popcorn on the coffee table. She patted the cushion beside her, and I sat down.

"I hope you don't mind, but I picked out a movie."

I didn't care what we watched, I just didn't want to make any decisions.

"*Gentlemen Prefer Blondes*," she said. "Have you seen it? It's a classic."

I shook my head, and she hit play on the remote.

If classic meant old, then she had definitely picked one. The actresses' clothes and hair were from another time, like my mom in her graduation picture. There was an obvious age gap between Claire and me. My classics were *Pretty Woman* and *Dirty Dancing*.

I fell asleep not too long into the movie. When I woke up, I was lying across the couch, covered with a blanket with a pillow under my head. Claire was sitting on the end of her bed with her legs crossed and her hands folded on her lap. Her lips were spread in a grin, one like Eric had when he was stoned on pot.

"You woke up just in time, my dear. That's Marilyn," she said and pointed to the screen. And then she cupped her hands over her heart and mouthed the words that were being sung.

Marilyn was walking down a set of stairs, wearing a pink dress and matching gloves. She was surrounded by men in suits, singing, "Diamonds are a girl's best friend." Marilyn shimmied her shoulders and Claire shimmied too.

I never thought I'd like hanging out with someone as old as Claire, especially since she didn't do drugs. She hardly drank either. But the more time I spent with her, the less I wanted to be away from her. Our friendship was easy. There wasn't any drama or jealousy like I had with Renee. The only thing she wanted from me was my company, and she'd always say how much she appreciated having me around. I got this feeling that if it weren't for me, she'd be alone.

Claire reminded me a lot of my mom. They hugged the same, squeezing for an extra couple of seconds when you tried to pull away and always making sure I never had an empty stomach. But Claire didn't ask questions like my mom did. That was probably because Claire didn't know I used heroin.

Mom had been leaving voicemails. Dad and Michael too. I didn't listen to their messages and since my mailbox was full, they couldn't leave any more. I already knew what the voicemails said— they loved me and wanted me to go to rehab, and blah-blah-blah. If I had extra money, I'd get a new cell phone number. But my phone was linked to my parents account, and they paid the bill.

Even though it was fall and the weather outside was cool, I always wore tank tops or t-shirts when I was in the hotel. Smack made me sweat. If Claire saw the track marks on my arms and wrists, she never said anything. When I needed to use, I'd make up an excuse to leave, and I'd go back to her room after the nod.

One morning, while Sunshine was at the needle exchange, I curled up in her bed and did a shot. I heard the door open and slam closed and figured it was Sunshine coming home. But I didn't open my eyes to look. The nod was too pretty.

Someone sat next to me and then I felt arms wrap around me. That was when I knew it wasn't Sunshine—she and I didn't hug. My nose filled with Claire's smell, flowered shampoo and baby powder. Her arms shook, and she was crying.

Did she think I was dead?

I opened my eyes. The needle was still in my arm. The spoon, bags, and lighter were lying in front of me on the bed.

"Claire, I'm okay, don't worry."

She didn't let go of me.

"Why didn't you tell me you were addicted to heroin?" she asked.

How did she know it was heroin?

"I didn't think you'd still be my friend," I said.

"Oh honey," she said and kissed the top of my head.

Most people would have freaked out if they found me in a nod with the needle still in my arm. But Claire didn't. I was expecting a lecture. At the least, I thought she'd use the death card, trying to scare me into being sober. She didn't do either. She continued to hug me and then asked if I wanted some spaghetti.

While we ate the pasta, I told her the truth about Eric's death, and the reason Que and Raul had been arrested. I even told her about Renee and her pregnancy, and how she left me stranded at McDonald's. Claire listened and didn't say anything. And when I finished talking, she told me she was going to make a big Thanksgiving dinner for Sunshine and me. I didn't know if she was upset I'd lied or she just liked to talk about food. Either way, she was an excellent cook.

A few days later, Claire came over and invited me to go out and spend the day with her. I'd just gotten home from my morning shift of panhandling and hadn't made shit. It was Friday and those were usually my best days. She wouldn't tell me where we were going but said it would mean a lot to her if I came. I told her I'd go, as long as we could leave in a couple hours and be back before five. I needed enough time to get dressed for my evening panhandling. She said yes to both. When she left our room, I asked Sunshine if she wanted to come too. She said no and we did a shot together.

Claire took me on the same route I used to get to Richard's, but we got off the train a few stops before his and then got on the bus. I couldn't imagine where we were going and what was so important we had to travel so far.

She stopped walking in front of a massive brick building. It took up an entire block and was at least ten stories high. There were bars over the windows and when I squinted, I saw people standing in front of them.

"Where are we?" I asked, trying to look for a sign on the building.

"Henry lives here."

We were at the county jail?

"I want you to meet my son," she said. She looked so happy that I'd come with her.

"I can't go in there, Claire."

"Of course you can, honey."

"No, I really can't. I've got stuff in my purse..." I looked around to see if anyone was listening.

"Hide it over there," she said and pointed to an alleyway.

I could do this, right? I could walk inside a jail and look the officers in the eyes, pretending not to be high. This was the first time Claire had asked for something. And I'd gotten this far. But damn, jail? Really?

I left her on the corner and went into the alley. I stuffed the Ziploc between a dumpster and the wall.

As the steel door of the prison shut behind us, I pushed down the sleeves of my hoodie.

Claire checked in at registration. The man behind the glass wall asked for my ID, and I placed it in the chute at the bottom of the glass. He slid my ID through a machine next to his keyboard and then his eyes moved to my face.

"Nicole Brown," he said, looking at my ID again.

My license picture was taken when I was sixteen.

"Yes," I said.

"Fill out this registration form," he said, dropping a clipboard into the chute. "When you're finished, bring it up to the security line."

Claire led me into the visiting room and chose a table in the back corner. I sat down and exhaled the air I'd been holding in. This was crazy, I was on dope and in jail, but I wasn't behind bars.

A buzzer went off, and the front door opened. The prisoners came inside, and Claire stood on her tiptoes, scanning each face. They were hard to tell apart, all dressed in bright orange jumpsuits with buzzed haircuts.

Claire waved, and a man who looked about my dad's age came over to the table. He had amber eyes, the same color as Claire's. But he looked so different from the pictures I'd seen. His hair was gray, his nose crooked, his shoulders slouched, and he walked with a limp.

After they hugged, she introduced us. Henry stuck out his hand, and his fingers were like ice against my sweaty palm.

Claire said how nice it was I was finally getting to meet her Henry. And Henry said he'd heard a lot about me, and besides Claire, I was the only other person who had visited. None of his childhood friends had stopped in? If I were in jail, I'd want visitors all the time. But besides Sunshine and Claire, who would visit me?

"How you feeling?" Henry asked me.

"Fine, why?"

"You're more than fine," he said. "You're riding pretty high right now."

There were officers standing by both the front and back door, but they were far away and couldn't hear what he said.

When Claire had told him about me, I guess she didn't leave anything out.

"Your pupils are a dead giveaway," he said. "I was a junkie too, you know."

Claire reached inside her purse and took out a tissue, dabbing her eyes and under her nose.

Wait. Was this the reason she asked me to come here? So Henry could lecture me about consequences like he was some straightedge? But I thought my visit meant a lot to her because she wanted me to meet her son?

"Heroin brought me to prison," he said.

He told me about the night he'd been arrested. He'd been on smack and needed money to pay off the dealers he owed, so he held up a store at gunpoint. The owner of the store had pulled out a gun, trying to protect himself, and Henry got scared and fired. The man died instantly. Henry took the cash from the register and got four blocks down the street before the cops picked him up. He was sentenced to life without parole.

"How old were you?" I asked.

"He was twenty-four," Claire said.

"I started slamming junk when I was eighteen, I was living with Mom and stole all her valuables for drug money," he said and reached his hand over to Claire. She held his hand between hers. "And I put her through hell."

For the first time since I'd met her, I saw pain in Claire's eyes. They filled with tears, and as she blinked, the drops rolled down her cheeks. That was why she didn't freak when she'd caught me nodding out. But why didn't she tell me Henry was a junkie too?

"You've seen what dope did to your buddy Eric," he said. "When it comes to heroin, it's either death or jail, there ain't nothing in between."

He was so wrong. I didn't owe anyone money. I didn't own a gun and I'd never commit armed robbery or pull the trigger to get my fix. Eric had OD'd because he wasn't good at using needles and hadn't known how much dope to shoot. Renee got pregnant, but it wasn't from doing heroin.

If they thought they could turn me sober by bringing me here, they were wasting their time.

The buzzer went off, and visiting hours were over. Henry and Claire hugged, and he shook my hand again. His skin was clammy, and my hand slipped out of his grip from the sweat.

"I thought it would mean more," he said, "seeing me in orange and listening to it in here."

That didn't change how I felt. Jail was for people who were stupid enough to get caught or for people who got ratted on like Que and Raul. I was a junkie, not a dealer. And I wasn't stupid.

When we got outside, I went straight into the alley and over to the dumpster. I reached my hand behind it, searching for the Ziploc. My hand grabbed nothing but air.

The bag was gone?

"Claire, I can't find it, will you look?"

She bent to her knees and ran her hand along the crack. "I don't see it, honey."

Where else could it be?

I looked all over, by all three sides of the dumpster, and under the piles of trash on the ground that hadn't made it into the bin. If it wasn't on the concrete, it had to be inside the dumpster. I opened the lid and climbed up the side. I ripped open all the trash bags, rummaging through the food and papers. The Ziploc wasn't in there either.

I jumped to the ground and took off my hoodie, ringing out the soaked sleeves. There was a banana peel stuck to my sneaker, and my hands were brown and sticky.

Someone had stolen everything I had, my needles, spoons, and a whole day's worth of smack. Who would do that to me? And how did they find my bag?

I had three dollars in my wallet. And five hours to make enough money to replace it all or I was going to be dope sick.

CHAPTER TWELVE

We didn't get back to the hotel until five, which didn't give me much time to dress and stuff my baby bump. I packed my stomach as fast as I could with Sunshine's socks and plopped down on a new corner, at Huntington Avenue and some cross street. Usually I chose a spot closer to the Prudential Building, but if I wasted anymore time walking, I wouldn't make any money.

Huntington was busy, but the people were barely looking at me when they walked by, and they seemed much younger than the usual business crowd. Some even laughed at my cardboard sign. They didn't understand how badly I needed their money and how sick I was going to be if I didn't earn enough.

I started calling out, "Can you spare some change," to everyone who passed. That didn't help either. It was like I was invisible.

One guy dropped a couple pennies in my hand. "Use a condom," he said.

Wasn't it too late for a condom?

"I did, it broke," I yelled, but he was already walking away.

He must have heard me because he turned around. "People like you shouldn't be having sex," he said.

What did he mean by people like me? Because my sign said I was sixteen? My sleeves were rolled to my elbows, so maybe he saw my track marks. That didn't matter though, just because I used heroin didn't mean I shouldn't have sex.

A group of teenagers were coming down the sidewalk and all of them were wearing Northeastern hoodies. I'd forgotten that Northeastern University was on Huntington Avenue and only a few blocks from where I was sitting. Damn, that was the reason I wasn't making any money. College students didn't have spare cash like business people. I'd picked the worst place to panhandle, but it was too late to move spots. It was already six o'clock and the evening rush was over.

I went back to the hotel and counted the cash I'd made during both shifts. I had eight bucks and that was only enough for one bag. I used three bags for each shot and needed at least three more shots to get me through until morning. I was thirty-seven dollars short.

I searched the room, looking in all the spots where Sunshine might hide an extra stash. But I knew there wasn't smack in the room. Junkies didn't plan for times like this. And there wasn't anything of Sunshine's I could pawn. The TV was too heavy for me to carry, and pawnshops didn't buy clothes or makeup.

I called Sunshine's cell to ask if we could meet up, but she didn't answer. I phoned a second and third time and still, she didn't answer. Where the hell was she? She needed to change and paint her face before hitting the streets, and it was already dark.

I didn't want to work the corner without her. Pimps forced new girls into their cars and beat them until they agreed to be one of their whores. Sunshine knew all the pimps, so when I was with her, they left me alone. But she wasn't answering, so turning tricks wasn't an option.

I knocked on Claire's door, and she invited me in. The fish she was cooking made me queasy. It had been eight hours since my last shot. A couple more hours without dope, and I was going to be really sick.

I asked her for money, and she gave me the two dollars she had in her wallet.

"That's all you've got?" I asked. "Will you go to the ATM?"

"My check hasn't come in yet, so I don't have any more to give you."

I thought of the Ziploc and how she had told me to hide it in the alley.

"Did you steal my bag of heroin?"

She was standing at the kitchen counter, mixing something with a big spoon. "Why would I do that?"

"For the same reason you wanted me to meet Henry," I said.

She walked over to me and put her hands on my shoulders. "I wanted the two most important people in my life to meet, that's all."

"Then why did he lecture me?"

"You and Henry share the same past," she said. "Who better to hear it from?"

"The only thing I share with Henry is love for the needle. He murdered someone for—" I said and stopped.

Her eyes welled up, and her hands dropped from my shoulders.

"I'm sorry," I said. "I shouldn't have said that."

Still, it was too much of a coincidence that I'd gotten lectured and had my dope stolen on the same day.

"Just tell me, did you take it?" I asked.

"I don't steal people's things," she said. "Plus, I was with you the whole time."

She was right. She'd never left my side while we were inside the prison.

I told her I'd see her tomorrow and walked out the door. I paced the hallway, trying to come up with a plan. I could suck Richard's dick for a bag or two, but I needed more dope than that. I'd have to give him head all night, and I'd be too sick in the morning to panhandle.

I had to call Michael. He'd start in about what I had said to him at the train station, and I'd have to listen to all that rehab shit again. But I didn't have anyone else to ask.

He picked up after the first ring. "Are you okay?" he asked.

I needed to come up with something good.

"I've been calling you nonstop," he said. "Why is your phone always shut off?"

What would make him want to give me money?

"I've been looking for you too on the streets," he said, "since I don't know where you live and..."

The streets? I had the perfect lie.

"Cole?"

"Yeah, I'm here," I said.

"Will you go to rehab? For me? Please?"

"I'm in trouble."

His voice was even more panicked than before. "What's wrong? What happened?"

"I'm pregnant and I need money for an abortion."

"You're what?"

"I can't have the baby, you know, like this," I said.

"Have you been to the doctor?"

"The abortion costs five hundred and I've scheduled it for tomorrow morning."

"Come over, I've got the money," he said, and I hung up.

I didn't have a lot of time. I needed to get the cash and go straight to Richard's so I could catch Sunshine before she left for work. She usually kept a few clean rigs in her purse.

When Michael opened the door, his face looked like I had kicked him in the gut. My stomach wasn't any better. I was starting to feel dope sick, and pretty soon I'd be throwing up.

He moved to the side of the door. "Let's talk," he said.

I stood in the living room, and he took a seat on the couch. He asked me to sit next to him.

"I don't have much time," I said. "So say what you have to say."

He shook his head and put his hands on his cheeks. "What happened to you?"

What happened to me? Women got pregnant all the time and chose to have an abortion. Since I was slamming dope, wasn't that the more responsible decision?

"You had everything going for you," he said. "And now look at you."

I crossed my arms over my stomach, trying to hold the food down. "Are you going to give it to me or not?"

"Is it because you didn't get help after the rape?"

"That doesn't even make sense," I said.

"Then why are you pregnant and addicted to heroin?"

"I don't know."

I liked the way smack made me feel. I liked watching the needle glide into my vein and feeling the chamber empty into my body. I liked how it took me away into a dream, where I didn't have to think about my past or future or make any decisions. Everything inside me and around me was beautiful when I was high.

Why wouldn't everyone just leave me alone? I had to listen to Claire and Henry this afternoon, and now Michael too? How was I hurting them? This was the first time I'd asked anyone for money.

"I just don't want to be pregnant anymore," I said.

"Are you selling your body?"

"It doesn't matter."

"It does to me," he said.

"I'm selling it to anyone who will buy it. Now give me the money, so I can go."

His face cringed like I was the most disgusting thing he'd ever seen.

This was another reason why I used heroin. The look Michael had just given me and the questions he asked wouldn't have sunk in if I were on dope. But because I was sober, I felt his look all the way down to my toes.

"Do you want to die?" he asked.

I wanted to get out of here. And to make that happen, I needed to try a different approach.

I sat on the chair across from the couch and looked him in the eyes. "Michael please, I just want to get rid of this baby," I said. "I'll come back to your apartment after the abortion and do whatever you want me to."

"You promise me? You swear on my life?"

"I swear."

He stood from the couch and disappeared into his bedroom.

I wasn't going to die, at least not from heroin. I was good at injecting. I knew how much dope to shoot so I wouldn't OD and how to get all the air bubbles out of the rig. Panhandling wasn't going to kill me, and Richard was harmless. Michael was just trying to scare me.

There was an envelope from CVS on his coffee table, and to keep my mind off puking, I opened it up. The pictures were all of Michael and some guy posing in front of Boston Harbor and Fenway Park. I didn't recognize the dude. He wasn't one of his college friends. He must have been a buddy from work.

I flipped to a photo and it showed—no. Michael had his arm wrapped around the guy's neck. And. And they were kissing. The next few pictures showed different stages of their kiss, from a peck to full-blown tongue shots.

Michael was gay? But he always had a girlfriend. In high school and college, the girls were all about him, and all my friends had a crush on him when we were growing up.

I put the pictures back in the envelope and placed it on the table. All except for one, the photo where their eyes were open and Michael's tongue was in the guy's mouth. That picture went in my purse.

"His name is Jesse," he said from the doorway of the living room. He walked over to me, put the cash on the coffee table, and kneeled on the floor with his hands on my knees. "And we've been dating for over a year."

"A year?"

He nodded his head. "I'm in love with him."

A year ago, I'd found heroin. How funny, we'd both fallen in love at the same time.

Why didn't he tell me he was gay? We used to talk about everything, our relationships, dirt on our friends, and even stupid things like TV shows. And then I started using, and our friendship changed. When we spoke on the phone, I was high and did all the talking. I couldn't remember the last time he'd shared something personal with me.

"Do mom and dad know?" I asked.

"Not yet, they've been too worried about you, but…"

My mouth started to water.

"They won't have to worry anymore," he said. "You're going to rehab tomorrow, right?"

"Michael, I'm—"

"You promised me," he said.

"Yeah, yeah."

"Why don't you stay the night, and I'll take you to the doctor tomorrow?"

My stomach cramped, and a hot flash sent drips of sweat down my back.

"I don't feel good," I said. "I think I'm going to be sick."

He put his hand on my forehead. "You're burning hot."

"Will you get me some water?" I asked. "Water and Tylenol?"

"Why don't you lie down on the couch."

I knew if I moved, I'd throw up. That wasn't such a bad thing, I thought. At least if I hurled, it would get him out of the living room for a second.

He helped me out of the chair, and after my second step, I leaned forward. My stomach churned and puke poured from my mouth. My sneakers were covered with chunks, and it splattered on my shirt.

"Don't move, let me get you a towel and a clean shirt," he said and sped off towards the bathroom.

When I heard him open the closet door, I grabbed the cash and ran out of his apartment. I bolted into the stairwell and shut the door behind me. Hopefully, he'd check the elevator first, which would buy me some time.

I made it out the back door of his building, and there was still no sign of him. I took side streets, and by the time I got on the train, I knew I'd lost him.

When I got inside Richard's bedroom, I gave him the five hundred dollars. What he handed me was the fattest sack of dope I'd ever seen. There was enough smack to last me about a week if I rationed it like Eric had.

I sat in the back of the train on the way home. The jerking and stopping made me throw up all over the floor again. A little taste would take all my sickness away, but I didn't have a rig and I couldn't snort a line in front of all these people. After each heave, more people stared or got up from their seats to move further away.

I held my stomach and ran to the hotel. There was a note taped to the outside of our door. It was from Claire and it said to meet her at Boston Medical.

Why was she in the hospital? And if she was sick, how did she have enough time to leave a note?

Before I went anywhere, I needed to get straight first. Sunshine wasn't home, and there weren't any rigs lying around, so I snorted the powder. It took a few lines for the hot flashes to stop and for my stomach to feel good enough to walk to the hospital.

Claire was sitting in the waiting room of the ER. When she saw me come in, she stood and pulled me into her arms. "What's going on?" I asked.

"It's Sunshine."

"What's wrong with her?"

Claire told me she'd heard Sunshine crying in our room and rushed over to see if she was all right. She found Sunshine on the floor, and there was foam coming out of her mouth. But that wasn't all of it. Her face was swollen and bruised. She'd been beaten up and there was blood on her legs.

Had someone raped her?

The last time I'd been in a hospital, dried blood had been all over my legs too.

"Did she tell you who did this to her?" I asked.

Claire shook her head.

"Is she going to be okay?"

She said she didn't know.

We sat by the reception area, waiting for the doctor. Claire cried and held my hand. She'd let go to blow her nose and then squeeze my fingers again.

If Sunshine was going to be in the hospital for a while, I needed to find a way to get needles. Maybe I could steal them from the hospital. There had to be a storage room with boxes of rigs, or I could snatch some from those carts the nurses pushed around.

What about the hotel? If Sunshine couldn't fuck Frankie, would he let me stay for free or would I have to bang him too?

Damn, Sunshine. Why did you have to let yourself get beat up?

Someone was always screwing things up for me. Eric had died, leaving Renee and me with one less income. Que and Raul had gotten arrested and that left us with no place to live and no more free dope. And then Renee took off and I was alone. Now Sunshine, too?

At least I had a fat sack of dope. Yes. I didn't have to panhandle with a whole week supply of heroin. And if I could get some needles, life would be really good.

CHAPTER THIRTEEN

Finally, around two in the morning the doctor came into the waiting room and gave us the news on Sunshine's condition. He said when she came in, she was under cardiac arrest from overdosing on heroin. He injected her with Narcan, which reversed all the symptoms. Once she was stable, he took her into surgery and repaired her collapsed lung. Her kidneys were bruised, and her lip and forehead were stitched closed. He didn't say anything about the blood on her legs. But he said once she healed, she should have a full recovery. He told us she'd be in the hospital for about a week, and if we'd like to go see her, he'd give us a couple minutes.

In the elevator, Claire warned me how bad she would look. Claire was right. I didn't recognize Sunshine. Most of her face was wrapped like a mummy, but her eyes were black and swollen. Her hair was a tangled mess, and her bangs were pink from the blood. There were tubes in her nose and an IV in her hand.

Claire sat on the bed and rubbed Sunshine's leg. She was still asleep, but that didn't stop Claire from telling her how much we loved her and how we'd been praying. Maybe Claire had prayed, but I was still thinking about needles and how I was going to steal them from the hospital.

"It's time for us to go," Claire said.

I was standing at the foot of the bed. In the corner of the room by the chair was a plastic bag and printed on the front were the words: Patient Property, Boston Medical.

"I'll meet you in the lobby," I said.

When Claire left the room, I opened the bag and inside were her clothes and purse. I found her container of clean rigs and tucked it under my jacket. Just then, I heard someone coming down the hall and rushed back over to the bed.

"She needs her sleep," the nurse said from the doorway.

I said goodbye to Sunshine, and Claire and I went back to the hotel.

Sunshine was awake when we visited her the next afternoon. Her eyes looked more swollen than they had the night before, and her face was still wrapped in gauze. But she talked just fine and wanted to know if I'd scored any dope. I told her I'd gone to Richard's.

"What happened to you last night?" Claire asked.

Sunshine didn't answer right away. And when she finally responded, her words came out slow like she had to think first. She told us she was walking home from the store when some guy pulled her into an alley, put a gun to her head, and asked for all her money. She told him she only had a couple dollars, and he punched her in the face and knocked her to the ground. He beat her and kicked her in the stomach before leaving her there to die.

"What did he look like?" I asked.

"He had a mask on," Sunshine said.

"Did the police question you?" Claire asked.

Sunshine nodded. "I didn't have nothing to tell them."

"Someone must have seen—"

"It was dark and I didn't see nobody around," Sunshine said.

Claire turned in her chair to face me. "You need to be careful at night," she said. "Those streets aren't safe."

Sunshine getting beat up wasn't going to keep me off the streets. If I didn't hook, I wouldn't have enough money for dope.

I remembered then we were out of toilet paper and went into Sunshine's bathroom. I unraveled half the roll and stuffed the wad into my purse. When I came out, Claire was sliding our chairs away from the bed to the far wall.

"Our conversation must have tuckered her out," Claire whispered.

The side of Sunshine's face was resting on the pillow and she was snoring. We left the hospital so she could get her sleep.

Frankie came knocking on my door the next morning. He told me if I wanted to stay for the week, it was seventy-five bucks. I needed to either pay up or fuck him. Claire must have told him how long Sunshine was going to be in the hospital. The choice was easy to make. I didn't have any money to give him.

When I first started tricking, I hated doing older men. Their skin was wrinkly and hairy, and they had bad breath. But I'd grown to really prefer them—even more than younger guys—because the sex didn't last very long. And if I were on top, that position made them bust real quick.

I rode Frankie on the couch and he came within a minute. Before he left, he said he'd be back in a week to collect again.

We visited Sunshine every afternoon and on the sixth day, the doctor let her go home. Claire got her settled in bed, and once she left to make dinner, Sunshine asked if I had any dope.

"I'll spot you, but you owe me," I said.

I had enough smack for two more days. But if I had to feed her too, I'd be dry by morning.

I dumped three bags on a spoon and heated it with a lighter.

"Hurry up," she said and searched her arms and legs for a vein. "The morph's wearing off."

She said the morphine IV they gave her in the hospital didn't get her high, but it kept her from being dope sick.

"I've been dreaming about this shot," she said. "The shit's been haunting me at night."

The only time I'd dreamt of heroin was during one of my nods, but I'd never gone more than eight hours without a shot. I also hadn't been doing smack for as long as she had.

I filled the syringe and walked over to the bed. "You owe me," I said again. Sunshine's memory wasn't too good.

She found a vein on the back of her thigh and stuck it, but she hit muscle. "Will you stick me?" she asked, wiping the blood off the needle hole.

I injected the vein, and she fell back against the pillow with her eyes closed. The purple bruises on her face were fading, and the swelling on her cheeks were going down. The stitches were still noticeable, but they were starting to dissolve too.

She kicked off the blanket and I saw bruises on her inner thighs. I wondered if those were from the rape. She still hadn't said a word about it. Claire and I hadn't asked her either. When she was ready, she'd tell us.

Since Sunshine's face and body were still bruised, we agreed not to trick until she was healed. To make money, we panhandled together. My jacket was too tight for a baby bump, so I changed my sign to read: Homeless and Hungry. We couldn't sit on the sidewalks or benches, since they were covered in snow. We used a milk crate to sit on, but it didn't fit us both so we took turns sitting down. I thought we'd make a lot of money panhandling in the winter, but people didn't seem to feel bad for us.

We started tricking about a week after she got out of the hospital. The bruises on her face had turned yellow, but at night they were hard to see. We'd be lucky if we got one or two Johns the whole night, and usually they only wanted head. We charged twenty bucks for a blowjob, but we really made nineteen after the cost of the condom. Sunshine said the winter was the worst season for hooking. But come spring, we'd be making good money. Spring was five months away.

If we were low on cash, we'd steal. We'd try all the door handles on the cars parked on the sides of the street. When we found one unlocked, we'd take everything—CD's, Walkmans, radar detectors—and bring it to the pawnshop. Sometimes we'd get a big score like a diamond ring or gold necklace, and those finds would buy us a whole day's worth of junk.

One night, I was walking back to the corner after finishing a trick and saw a minivan parked in front of an apartment building. The guy was unloading a trunk full of boxes and electronics and kept the truck open while he brought the stuff inside. I wasn't too far from the hotel. If I could snatch something and bring it right home, I could sell it at the pawnshop in the morning. But I had to hustle. The guy only spent a few seconds in the lobby and came right back out to the van. I waited for him to take in his third load and then darted over to the van. There was a DVD player sitting on top of a box, and I grabbed it. When I got to the corner, I looked over my shoulder and he was chasing me.

"You're dead!" he yelled.

I booked it as fast as I could, trying not to trip over the mounds of snow. Up ahead, a woman was coming out the back door of a building and I slid inside before the door shut. I hid behind the set of mailboxes and peeked over the top. The guy was only a few feet from the door. His back was facing me, and he kept turning to the right and left like he was looking for me.

"I know you can hear me," he shouted. "If you come out now, I won't hurt you."

How could he hurt me? He didn't know where I was hiding, and the door to the building was locked.

He turned towards me, but I ducked just in time. "That's my six-year-old son's DVD player."

A part of me felt bad for taking something from a six-year-old. But I could get thirty bucks for it.

"Keep it, you piece of shit," he shouted. "I hope you rot in hell."

He walked back in the direction he came. I stayed hidden behind the mailboxes for at least an hour. I wanted to make sure he was really gone and not waiting for me in a doorway or behind a dumpster.

I sold the DVD player for twenty-five bucks. I would have gotten thirty if I'd stolen the remote too. I took the money and went to Richard's to re-up. I was doing all our dope buying since Sunshine had gotten out of the hospital. With both of us going to Richard's, we were wasting too much money on train tokens. So we bought an extra bag with the six bucks we saved in train fare, and while I was out buying, she went to the needle exchange.

It was just after New Years when I met Heather at Richard's house. She had rotted teeth and red spidery veins on her face, and she was only nineteen. I'd sit and talk with her while I waited for Richard to finish banging one of his squatters. She was a tweaker who smoked and mainlined crystal meth. Her pupils were always dilated, and she'd pick the skin off her arms and legs, killing the bugs, she said, who were eating her skin. Most of the time, she talked about the police and how they were setting up a raid on Richard's house. She said she could hear the cops talking outside his windows. I never saw any cops when I came in or left. Heather was just paranoid, but that's what meth did to people. That crystal was some crazy shit.

I told Heather about the DVD player I'd stolen and how the guy almost caught me.

"Boost from stores," she said. "That's what I do."

"But stores have cameras."

"If you have a receipt, it's harder for them to bust you."

She'd find receipts in trash bins, grab the items off the shelves, and return them for cash.

So on my way back from Richard's, I decided to try it. I collected all the receipts I could find in the trash and sorted through them, looking for items I recognized like shampoo or soap. There was a receipt from CVS for vitamins and razor blades. I stashed the receipt in my pocket and went into the store. I took the vitamins and razor blades off the shelf and brought them to the checkout line. The clerk gave me cash, twenty-three dollars and change.

I left CVS and went to Walgreens, returning baby formula and cough syrup. This was so much easier than stealing from cars. I could do it during the day when it wasn't so cold, and I didn't have to bargain with pawnshop owners for more money.

But even after adding store boosting to my daily lineup of panhandling and tricking, Sunshine and I were still short on money. Between the two of us, we shot two hundred and fifty dollars worth of heroin a day, plus the two packs of cigarettes we smoked. If it weren't for Claire feeding us dinner, we'd never eat. I made pads out of wads of toilet paper instead of buying tampons. I washed my hair with the little bars of soap Frankie put in the rooms. I used the same soap to do laundry too and washed my clothes in the kitchen sink. We stole markers from Frankie and used them as eye shadow and liner and borrowed Claire's tweezers to pluck the hairs from our legs and armpits.

Just when I thought the winter was behind us and tricking season was finally here, Boston was hit with a blizzard. When I woke up and looked out the window, there was at least three feet of snow. The streets weren't plowed, and the sidewalks weren't shoveled, and the snow was still falling. I turned on the news and it said all trains and taxis were shut down until further notice.

"You ain't deaf, turn that shit down," Sunshine said from her bed.

I turned the volume up. "You need to see this."

She threw her pillow on the floor and sat up. "What's so damn important?" Her face froze when she saw the TV screen. "The trains are working, right?"

"No, and the taxi companies are closed too."

She walked over to the window and held onto the ledge, pressing her nose against the glass. "Guess you'll be walking to Richard's."

"He lives a couple miles from here," I said.

"Then you better start walking."

"You know I can't go. It's too cold out there, and the sidewalks aren't cleared."

She sat on the edge of the bed and put her hands on her forehead. "How much dope you got?"

"Three bags."

She emptied her purse on the floor, and only two bags fell out.

"It's supposed to snow like this until Friday night," I said.

It was only Wednesday.

When it came to snow storms, Boston wasn't like Bangor. Bangor had plows and places to dump the snow like fields and parking lots. Boston was all city. Even when it snowed only a few inches, the trains ran slow. It would take days for the city to move all this snow. I didn't have days. I only had a couple hours before I'd be dope sick.

I cooked up Sunshine's dope and split it between two rigs. The shot didn't get me high. I didn't even feel a rush. A few hours later, we shot our last three bags and I didn't get high from that either. We usually shot three bags each, just to get straight. If we wanted to get really high, we'd shoot four.

Sunshine stretched out on the bed, and I curled up on the couch with my eyes glued to the TV. I hadn't prayed when she was in the hospital, but I was praying now. But the forecast was only getting worse. Overnight, the snow was supposed to change to hail.

When I was a senior in high school, some asshole had run a red light and smashed into the passenger side of my car. Seconds before he hit me, the accident played out in my head. I knew the crash was going to total my car and possibly even hurt me. Panic ran through me. My hands shook and I gripped the wheel so my face wouldn't slam into it.

Withdrawal was like my car accident. Dope sickness was driving towards me. I could feel it, and I could see it coming when my hands started to shake. And because Sunshine had told me what to expect, I played out the next two days in my head. Cramps, vomiting, diarrhea, and it was all going to hurt. Really bad.

Three hours after my last shot, the stomach cramps hit, like a combination of food poisoning and PMS. I tried to sleep it off, but when I closed my eyes, my head would spin. Sweat dripped down my forehead and soaked the pillow. The wet stain felt cool against my burning skin. Then I'd shake from the chills. The heroin gods were moving the thermostat from right to left every few minutes. I couldn't get warm enough and I couldn't cool down.

Dope seeped out of my pours. I could smell the sweetness in my sweat and when I peed.

The food I'd eaten the night before came up, and I ran to the bathroom to puke. My stomach gurgled, and diarrhea poured from my ass. I didn't know which end to put on the toilet. So when I had to do both at the same time, I leaned off the toilet and puked in the shower.

From the bathroom, I heard Sunshine moaning and throwing up, spitting and then moaning again.

"I need the toilet," she yelled.

There was no way I could get off the pot. She was throwing up in our only bucket, and that wouldn't cover both my ends.

"I'm not done yet," I said.

"But I'm gonna shit in the bed."

Frankie would give us a change of sheets. But if I got sick on the couch, I didn't think he'd give us a new one.

She came into the bathroom, stripped off her clothes, and squatted in the shower over my pile of puke.

"What are you—"

She added diarrhea to my puke pile. The sight and smell was too much for my stomach. I heaved into the shower and it splattered all over her feet. She barfed after I did and then cursed me out for making her throw up too.

She ran the water in the shower to wash off her legs and feet, and then she left the bathroom. The water went down the drain, but nothing else would. I covered the clump of vomit and shit with toilet paper and then realized we only had half a roll left.

I crawled out of the bathroom and into the bed. I was only on it for a second before she kicked my legs and pushed me to the ground.

"What was that for?" I asked from the floor.

"I ain't sharing the bed," she said. "I'm too sick."

I looked over the edge of the bed. She was wrapped in a cocoon, and her head was buried in a mound of pillows. I didn't want to share a bed with her either, but the couch was wool, and my skin itched like the chicken pox.

My upper body hurt worse than my lower half so I kneeled in front of the bed, resting my head and arms on the mattress. Her foot kicked my shoulder so hard I landed on the floor again.

"Get the hell away," she said. "Your smell is making me sick."

"You don't smell any better."

If I had more energy, I would have picked her up and thrown her on the ground. But I couldn't even crawl back to the couch, so I stayed on the floor and watched TV. Sunshine flipped through the stations. She'd settle on a movie and during the commercials, she switched to the news. I closed one eye, trying to ease some of the pressure building behind my lids. But then I saw two TV screens, and that made me dizzy.

From the floor, the bathroom looked miles away. My bladder was full, but I didn't have the strength to crawl there. I peed right where I was. There was so much of it, and it was so warm, like I was taking a bath.

When Claire came in, she helped me to the couch. She took off my wet shorts and put me in a pair of sweatpants. She fed me juice and tea and I puked them both up. After she rinsed out the bucket, she washed my face. The washcloth felt like needles scraping over my skin.

"Don't. It hurts," I said.

"Poor thing," she said. "I'll just sit with you, okay?" She reached for my hand and massaged my fingers. That didn't feel good either.

The weather was punishing me, but I didn't know what for. I was a good person and didn't deserve to detox like this. In rehab, they had medicine to help with all these symptoms—that was what Sunshine had told me anyway. We didn't even have Tylenol and neither did Claire. Why hadn't Eric picked Florida or California instead of Boston?

It was like both my legs had been cut off, and I was left without a wheelchair. I had money too. I'd made sixty bucks the night before the storm, and I couldn't even use it to buy heroin. Richard didn't deliver bags of dope, only pounds, and there was no way for him to get to us anyway.

I took a sip of orange juice, and as soon as I swallowed, I gagged. The juice came out of my mouth and nose at the same time. I made it in the bucket, but it still got all over me. Claire helped me change again and put my hair in a ponytail. She buried her nose under her shirt and sat by my feet. The smell was getting to be too much for me too.

"Bucket, bucket," Sunshine yelled and Claire brought it over to her.

The sound of her puking made my stomach churn, and I barfed all over the floor.

Specks of morning light came through our blinds. I remembered when Eric and I had gone to Que's and tried heroin for the first time. The light from Que's blinds had sparkled when I was high. That first hit from his pipe had tasted so good.

I just wanted a taste. I crawled off the couch to the middle of the room, sweeping my hand over all the trash. I found an empty bag, opened it, and licked the inside. I searched for more and ripped the tops off, wiping the packets over my tongue like they were postage stamps. I licked spoons and bottle caps caked with resin, biting off the clumps of tar like it was taffy. But none of it got me high. All it did was change the taste on my tongue from orange juice and bile.

Night came, and the snow continued to fall. Sunshine said we'd be dope sick for around seventy-two hours. Thirty had passed. We weren't even halfway through it.

Claire brought us food and more juice. We ate and drank, and barfed it all up. She updated us on the blizzard. It wasn't going to stop snowing until tomorrow night. By then, I'd still be detoxing and probably too sick to go to Richard's.

When I closed my eyes, I saw heroin. Mounds of brownish powder, buckets full of wax paper packets, piles of clean rigs. I wasn't sleeping. It was more like a daydream where my brain was teasing me. I couldn't sleep. Every bone ached, every muscle cramped, and when I moved, I puked.

Sunshine cried. She said how much she hated heroin and then listed all the reasons why. It made her sick when she didn't have any, it took away her children, it got her beat up, raped, and put her in the hospital.

How did dope get her beaten and raped? She was held up at gunpoint, but that wasn't the smack's fault.

"So he raped you too, huh?" I asked.

She didn't answer.

"I know how it feels," I said. But I didn't say any more. The words just weren't there, and my throat burned when I spoke.

"I ain't got it in me no more, I'm quitting junk," she said. "I'm too old for this shit. I'm getting a real job and moving away from here."

I didn't want to feel like this ever again. I wanted to go back to having fun. Fun like when Eric and I had gone to the Cape for Jimmy's bash and when we tripped on shrooms at the club. And like the fun I'd had before moving to Boston. In high school and college, I'd hang out with my friends and go to parties and have the best time.

But besides Claire and Sunshine, and Heather, Richard's squatter, I didn't have any other friends. All I cared about was money and dope. I stole and whored out my body just to buy smack, and then I'd shoot up and have to whore it out again. There was nothing fun about being a junkie.

If I went to rehab tomorrow night after the storm, I wouldn't have to detox and could start right in with the meetings. But did I really need rehab and meetings? Rehab was for people like Sunshine who'd used for years and couldn't stop. I could stop as soon as all this dope was out of me. And I was going to stop. When the roads cleared, I wasn't going to Richard's. I was going to apply for jobs around town and save enough money for an apartment. Maybe I'd have Claire move in with me. And I'd smoke pot. Yes, I'd go back to only smoking pot.

I heard the trucks outside. I could hear them over the TV, their metal plows scraping against the pavement. Sunshine shouted one swear after another. I didn't know if they were happy shouts or shouts of pain. I didn't bother to ask. I buried my head under a pillow and tried to fall asleep.

"It stopped snowing," Claire said.

Her words woke me. Claire's voice was like my mom's on Christmas morning when she came into my room and said, "Santa came."

The gnawing in my stomach, the aching in my bones, the pounding in my head were all still there. But I had energy. Enough energy to get to Richard's.

"Where are you going?" Sunshine asked from the bed.

"Richard's," I said, sliding on my jeans and sneakers.

Claire didn't say anything. She didn't have to, the disappointment was on her face. I had told her that morning I was going to stop using, get a job, and find an apartment to rent. I had asked her if she'd move in with me, and she said yes, as long as I was sober.

Tomorrow. Tomorrow I'd stop. One little shot wasn't going to change my plans. I was already somewhat detoxed and a couple bags of dope wouldn't set me back.

"I'm coming with you," Sunshine said.

We finished getting dressed and moved to the door. Claire was leaning on it, holding the knob like she wasn't going to let me through.

I stood in front of her and put my hands on her shoulders. "It will be my last time," I said. "One final goodbye."

I meant it. I'd get closure and I'd stop after this shot.

"You can't go," Claire said.

"Why not?"

"Because this won't be your last time. Can't you see how addicted you are?"

"Claire, I promise. Now please move," I said.

"No."

"If you don't let go of the door, I'm going to hurt you, and I don't want to do that."

"Then hurt me," she said.

My hands dropped from her shoulders and clenched into fists. I punched the door on both sides of her face, and pressed my nose against hers. "Get the fuck out of my way."

"Look what it's done to you," she shouted back.

I felt the skin on my knuckles burst open and blood seep down my wrists.

"You're just like my Henry," she said.

I took her hand and yanked it off the knob, pushing her away from the door. She stumbled back and tripped over a pile of Sunshine's clothes. When she landed on the floor, she let out a cry. I wanted to help her up, but I wanted heroin more.

I walked through the door, and Sunshine followed me. We took the train to Richard's, and outside the station she puked. She was leaning against a wall, taking deep breaths and still retching. I told her to wait for me at the corner, and I went in and bought eight bags for us to share.

I rushed back to meet her. "Can you make it to McDonald's?" I asked.

She nodded and held her stomach as we walked to McDonald's and locked ourselves in the handicapped stall. I dumped four bags on each spoon and cooked it all up. The metal needle sparkled under the florescent light. The skin on my arm looked purple from all the track marks.

The rush wasn't like when I had first smoked dope with Eric and Que. It was better. My back slid down the wall of the stall. My feet and hands went numb. My eyes closed, and before me was a magical land made of nothing but heroin and paraphernalia. The grass was needles, the plants were poppies, and the waterfall was cooked-up H. Willy Wonka was giving Sunshine and me a tour of his factory. And as we walked around, he let us sample the goods.

I'd only gone two days without smack. Sunshine had said after you detox, the high was always stronger than when you shot up every day. Damn. She was so right.

CHAPTER FOURTEEN

Sunshine and I left the McDonald's bathroom, turned some tricks, and I went back to Richard's to re-up again. The next day wasn't any different, more tricks and more heroin. I'd broken the promise I'd made to Claire, and I went to her room to apologize—not for lying, but for pushing her away from the door. She told me she'd seen the devil in my eyes, and she never wanted to see that side of me again. I gave her my word. But if she ever stood in my way, I didn't know if I could keep that promise. Heroin was stronger than me.

I had convinced myself I could stop using, like dope was something simple like chocolate. But heroin was my air. It had a hold of me like we were chained together. And those shackles weren't just around my wrists, they were tied around my brain too. Once that powder was injected, I forgot about the puking, diarrhea, sweats, chills, and all the fun I used to have before dope, like none of it had ever happened. At the end of the high, all I could think about was getting my next fix.

The rush and the nod weren't the only things I was addicted to. It was scoring the dope and riding home on the train, knowing those bags were in my purse. It was dumping the powder onto the spoon and watching it turn to liquid. It was taking the orange cap off the rig and filling it. It was seeing the flash—my blood creeping into the chamber—and emptying the chamber into my vein. I'd fallen in love with the steady rhythm of working, buying, and shooting.

But shooting dope wasn't as easy as it used to be. The veins in my left arm were tapped out because I'd stuck them too many times. I had switched to my right and those were toasted too. Finding a vein was like a game of hide-and-go-seek. I'd poke anything that looked green or popped up when I used a tourniquet. My body was scarred with needle marks, and when I missed the vein, my muscles ached.

I lost track of time. My days all started and ended the same. Weeks blended together, and I didn't know if it was June or July. I shot up first thing in the morning, before I peed or brushed my teeth. I went to Richard's to score and split the dope with Sunshine. I panhandled and shot up. I boosted and then shot up. I shot up and hit the streets. I sucked dick and screwed, and shot up in between Johns. I shot up and went to bed.

When I had my period, I couldn't hook and was short on cash. I'd wake up sick and hug the toilet, and make all these promises to myself. Tomorrow would be the day when I'd change my life, I thought, in between heaving and shaking. I'd get a job and an apartment with Claire, and I'd stop using. Tomorrow came, but my plans didn't.

As time passed, though, there were slight changes. The weather got warmer and then cooled off when the leaves turned from green to bright oranges and reds. Three bags wouldn't get me straight, so I had to shoot four. And five if I wanted to get high. I stopped looking my tricks in the eyes. I used to like seeing all the different shades of blue and hazel. But I'd seen so many eyes, the colors started to repeat.

By the middle of the winter, my body began to change. I stopped getting my period. Sunshine hadn't gotten her period in years and said it was a combination of junk and being too thin. I was the skinniest I'd ever been, and everything I ate, I threw up. Food wasn't staying down, even when I was high. I put condoms on all my Johns and my stomach was flat, so I knew I wasn't pregnant. Actually, my stomach caved inward, and my ribs stuck out. Just as I was getting ready to buy a pregnancy test, I felt blood in my underwear. My period was light and lasted only two days.

And then my molar got infected. The gums around my tooth swelled and turned dark red. I used Claire's floss and mouthwash, but it didn't help. I called a dentist and the secretary told me the minimum charge to come in was eighty-five dollars. Without insurance, tooth extractions or cavity fillings would set me back a couple hundred at least.

I couldn't eat on that side of my mouth, and when I slept, even the pillow hurt my cheek. I went downstairs to Frankie's office and asked for a pair of pliers.

"What do you need them for?" he asked. He didn't even look up from his computer.

"My tooth, I have to get it out."

He stood from his chair and told me to sit, and open my mouth.

"Yup, that sucker needs to pulled all right," he said. "You don't got the strength to yank out a big molar like that, let me do it."

He opened his desk drawer and took out a pair of pliers and a bottle of gin. He cleaned the pliers with the flame of his lighter and told me to drink.

"This isn't gonna feel good, you ready?"

My head was already leaned back against the chair and my mouth was open. He splashed more gin over the tooth and then gripped the pliers around it. I held onto the armrest and closed my eyes. The metal tasted awful and the pressure was shooting pain into my head.

"One," he said. "Two," and then he pulled.

Tears filled my eyes and my nose ran. But the pain was gone once the tooth was out.

He told me to keep my mouth clean and rinse it real good or the hole wouldn't heal. I bought a bottle of mouthwash and after each blowjob, I gargled and spit.

One morning, I woke up to Claire singing "Happy Birthday."

She had opened all our windows. The sun was bright, and the birds sitting on our window ledge were chirping and tapping the glass with their beaks. For months, we had quiet mornings, and now those damn flying pests were back from their winter vacation.

Mid-song, I ran to the bathroom and threw up.

"Do you want some Rolaids?" Claire asked from the bathroom doorway. "They might help settle your tummy."

I shook my head and heaved up another mouthful.

"Come by my room when you feel better," she said and closed the bathroom door.

I stuck my head under the faucet and let the water run into my mouth. I lifted my head to spit and froze when I saw my reflection in the mirror.

I grabbed some toilet paper and scrubbed the mirror, but it didn't help.

If it weren't for my blue eyes, the scar under my chin, and my nose, I wouldn't have recognized myself. My skin had turned gray, and there were brown smudges under my eyes from yesterday's markers. Boils, scabs, whiteheads, and blackheads covered my face. My teeth were yellow, and my gums were caked with plaque. Sections of my hair were dreaded. My lips were dry and cracked. I was twenty-four today. Damn, I looked worse than the morning after I was raped.

"I need the can," Sunshine said, knocking on the bathroom door. She didn't wait for me to answer. She walked in and sat on the toilet. Since the storm last year, we'd given up on privacy.

Was the mirror lying? I couldn't really look this bad.

I touched my face, running my fingers over my cheeks and across my forehead.

"It's the junk," Sunshine said. "It ruins your skin."

I turned towards her. Her front teeth were missing, and her cheeks were scarred with pockmarks.

She wiped herself and flushed the toilet. "Slam some dope, you'll feel pretty again."

I sat on the couch, cooked up five bags, and couldn't find a vein. I poked my ankles and thighs, and eventually found one on my left boob. The rush was warm and tingly.

The room wasn't as messy as usual. The trash on the floor was organized into piles, and all the wax-paper packets of heroin were scattered on top like sprinkles on a sundae. Sunshine was on the bed. Her eyes were so deep and rich, they looked like blueberries bursting with juice. I traced the track marks on my arm with the back of my finger, drawing hearts and diamonds, and squares. I spotted a pattern on my other arm. It was the Big Dipper, and I found the little one too.

Claire cooked my favorite for dinner, lasagna with meat sauce. After we ate, she surprised me with a homemade cake, chocolate on chocolate, decorated with purple flowers. She also made me a card. She wrote how much she loved me and thought of me as a daughter. At the bottom of the card, she wrote, "God willing, my final breath will be taken before yours."

The card dropped from my hands and swished in the air before it hit the floor.

Claire got up from her chair, kneeled in front of me, and wiped the tears from my eyes. "I didn't mean to upset you," she said and pulled me into her arms.

I buried my face in her neck. "I don't ever want to lose you."

"Honey, I'm seventy-nine years old."

Both sets of my grandparents had died in their early seventies. But she seemed healthy, and I'd never seen her sick or take any medicine.

During one of my nods, I had dreamt that Claire and my mom were in the delivery room and I was giving birth to a baby girl. Would Claire live to see that happen? If I kept using, probably not.

Sunshine and I hit the streets once it turned dark. At midnight, I told her I needed to use the bathroom and left her on the corner. I went into an alley and sat on the ground next to a box of rotten bananas. I opened my cell phone and placed it on my lap. I knew the screen would show two new voicemails. And it did.

When I lived at home, mom would make my birthday an all-day celebration. She'd decorate my room with balloons and serve me breakfast in bed. For lunch, she'd take me out of school, and we'd eat burgers and sundaes at Friendly's. And after dinner, more cake and ice cream, the whole family played Monopoly until they carried me up to bed.

The phone felt heavy in my hand and hot against my ear. I heard a beep, and the message began to play.

"Happy Birthday, baby girl," Mom said. "I love and miss you so much." She started to cry. "I decorated your room this morning with purple balloons."

"It's been two years since we've seen you, and we think of you every day," Dad said.

I could picture them, mom at the kitchen table, twirling the phone cord between her fingers. Dad on his recliner in the family room with the cordless phone. When one finished talking, they'd nod and the other would take over.

"Cole," Dad said. His voice turned shaky. "You're killing us."

"Steve, don't, it's her birthday," Mom said.

"All right, fine. Happy birthday, pumpkin," Dad said.

Mom sniffled. "Please come back to us," she said, and they hung up.

I thought of Claire and how I would feel if I lost her. She was my best friend and took care of me. But I was their daughter. Was that how they felt when they thought about losing me?

There was one more message, which I assumed was from Michael. I didn't listen to it. I hit the delete button and emptied my mailbox.

All I had to do was call my parents and tell them I wanted help, and I'd be in rehab before breakfast. I could see the whole thing play out in my head. Claire would walk me to my parents' car, telling me how proud she was I'd decided to get sober. Michael would carry my bags inside. My parents would hug me and visit during family weekend.

And then Claire wouldn't have to check on me anymore. My parents would stop crying. Michael would forgive me for taking his money.

Maybe tomorrow, I thought.

I dumped my purse onto the ground and cooked up. The hit was strong, and I threw up all over the fruit. Claire's dinner had tasted so good. But it didn't look as pretty splattered over the bananas.

I stuffed everything back in my purse and stood up. I straightened my skirt and tightened my ponytail, walking down the alley. As I got closer to the street, I heard a guy's voice. And then a second guy spoke, and a third. They were talking in ghetto slang, as Raul had called it.

I peeked around the side of the alley where a group of men were standing close by with their backs against the building. They were all dressed in red—a gang color. Hats dipped over their faces, and gold teeth shined in their mouths.

I put my hood over my head and walked in the opposite direction.

Sunshine was on the corner of the next block. Her pink fur coat looked like a big cone of cotton candy.

A car was driving towards me, its headlights were so bright I had to squint. The car began to slow down and veered to my side of the road. It had to be a John looking to hire, I thought. I moved across the sidewalk and onto the street. I took off my hood, unzipped my jacket, and hiked up my skirt.

The guys in the gang stopped talking and from the corner of my eye, I saw them step onto the curb.

As the car got closer, the backseat window rolled down. Then the driver's window.

I heard what sounded like an explosion, followed by bang after bang.

Sunshine screamed.

I felt a sharp pain in my chest like I'd been stabbed with the tip of a crowbar, and I reached under my tank top. I felt something wet. And when I pulled my hand out, my fingers were covered in blood.

The sidewalk seemed to move under my feet. Maybe my feet were moving. But I was definitely falling.

My back hit the ground first. My head was next, pounding onto the pavement. The pain made everything look white for a moment. And then all I saw was black.

CHAPTER FIFTEEN

I sat on our couch with my feet on the coffee table. With Sunshine at the needle exchange, I finally had some time to myself. I'd been out of the hospital for two days, and the doctor's words were still echoing in my head: "The bullet was a few inches from puncturing your heart, and still we were able to save your fetus."

I didn't know what he meant by fetus. Was that some organ I hadn't learned in biology class?

"You're eleven weeks pregnant," he said.

A nurse had come in after the doctor left and lubed my stomach with jelly. She moved a wand over my belly and told me to look at the screen. "There's your baby," she said. She printed a picture of the bean-shaped blob and gave it to me.

I was eleven, almost twelve weeks pregnant. I had to get this thing out of me.

I didn't tell Claire or Sunshine about the baby. Since they were both mothers, I figured they'd be upset if I told them I was getting an abortion, and I didn't want them to try and talk me out of my decision. I mean, how could I have a baby? I didn't even know who the father was. He could be any one of my tricks, one with a big enough dick to break the condom. Fucker.

The clinic charged four hundred dollars. I already had an appointment set up for tomorrow morning, I just didn't have the money yet. I'd made two hundred and forty last night, and all of that was going to Richard. Claire didn't have any money and neither did Sunshine.

I thought I'd start with Frankie and see how much I could get out of him.

He was sitting behind the front desk, eating what smelled like fish. I wanted to hurl.

"Four hundred," he said. "That's how much they cost these days?"

I assumed Sunshine hadn't been the only hooker he'd slept with over the years. He'd probably paid for several abortions, so what was one more?

"I'll pay you back," I said.

He took a bite and chewed with his mouth open. "With what? After the abortion, she's going to be out of commission for a bit," he said and pointed to my crotch.

I hadn't thought of that.

But hopefully I wouldn't be sore for too long. Blowjobs weren't going to pay for my dope.

"Look kid, I'll give you a hundred bucks, but it's only cause I feel bad for you."

He took a hundred dollar bill out of the drawer and handed it to me.

"Get lost and don't ask for anymore," he said

I went back to my room. Sunshine would be home soon from the needle exchange, and she'd want her dope. I grabbed my purse and headed for the train station.

Walking down Massachusetts Avenue, I decided to stop at Michael's first since his apartment wasn't too far out of my way. We hadn't spoken in a year and a half, since I'd stolen his money. But he still left me voicemails and once in a while, I saw him driving down the street where Sunshine and I worked. I'd hide my face in my jacket or run into an alley so he wouldn't see me. One time, he had even asked Sunshine if she'd seen me, but she told him she didn't know anyone who fit my description.

I asked the doorman to let Michael know I was here. He made me wait on the sidewalk while he called from the desk phone and after he hung up, he let me inside. He escorted me through the lobby and to the elevator, and didn't take his eyes off me until the door slid closed.

Michael was waiting for me in the hallway. As I walked towards him, he said, "What are you doing here?"

"It's been a while, huh?"

I moved past him and went into the kitchen, leaning against the fridge.

"Too long. I've miss—" he said and stopped.

My foot tapped on his floor. I didn't have time for all the I-miss-you crap. "I'm pregnant."

He shook his head. "I don't believe you."

"No, I am, the doctor put that wand thingy on my stomach and I saw the baby, and everything."

"And you came here because you want money for an abortion?"

"Michael—"

"I'm not giving you a penny," he said and crossed his arms.

I remembered just then the picture I'd stolen of Michael and Jesse kissing. It was still in my purse. "Have you told mom and dad you're gay?" I asked.

I took his silence as a no.

He still hadn't told our parents? He wasn't as strong as I thought he was.

"You want me to get clean, but you won't come clean too?" I asked.

He grabbed my hand and pulled me through the kitchen and into the bathroom. He stood me in front of the sink and held my face towards the mirror.

"Look at yourself, Cole. Do you see who you've become?"

I knew exactly what I looked like.

"You used to be my best friend, someone I trusted, and a loving daughter who made our parents proud," he said. "What happened to you?"

I knew what smack had done to me, I didn't need him to remind me.

"Give me the fucking abortion money," I yelled.

"And if I don't?"

"I'll show mom and dad the picture I stole of you and Jesse kissing."

His hands dropped from the sides of my face like my skin had burned his fingertips.

I turned around and looked into his eyes.

"I'm not ashamed of who I am, so show them the picture," he said. "And unless you're ready to go to rehab, don't ever come here again."

I walked out of the bathroom and let his front door slam behind me.

I walked through Richard's front door and went straight to his bedroom without stopping to talk to Heather. Richard was on the floor, injecting into his stomach. I stood in front of him, between his legs.

When he pulled the needle out, he looked up at me.

"I need a favor," I said.

I told him I was pregnant and wanted to borrow three hundred bucks for an abortion. I told him I'd pay him back a little each week with interest.

"I'll give you the money," he said. He put his hand on my thigh and his long, dirty fingers crawled like ants until they reached the zipper on my jeans. "But I want you in return."

Three hundred was more than I made in a night. And if I closed my eyes, Richard would just be another one of my tricks.

"You're going to have to wait a little while, I'm going to be sore and—"

"I've waited this long, haven't I?" he asked.

I told him we had a deal, and he gave me the money along with the two bundles I paid for.

At the clinic, the secretary handed me a clipboard and asked me to fill out all the sheets. The waiting room was full, but I found an empty seat and wrote my name and address.

There was a woman sitting next to me with a big pregnant belly and her teenage daughter was on the other side of her. The daughter was reading a pamphlet on birth control.

Some of the girls in the room had flat stomachs. And some had little baby bumps, sitting next to their men or their moms. The clinic performed abortions up to eighteen weeks and gave doctor referrals to girls who decided not to abort. Maybe they were all here to get rid of their babies too, or they were here to take the clinic's prenatal class.

Toys were scattered around the floor—puzzles, trucks, and a playhouse. Michael and I used to play house in our playhouse. I'd pretend to home school our imaginary kids, and I'd read to them from my picture books. Michael would pretend to mow the lawn and fix things that were broken. We never pretended I'd be a pregnant junkie when I grew up.

I pictured myself in three months, coming here with Claire with a big belly and swollen ankles to take the baby class. She'd come to the hospital too when I was ready to give birth, and she'd wipe cold washcloths over my face. She'd cut the umbilical cord.

"Ms. Brown, the doctor is ready for you," a nurse said.

I handed the clipboard to the nurse and she led me into a room where she took my height and weight. I was five-five and the scale said ninety-six pounds. She wrote the numbers in my chart and brought me into another room at the end of the hall.

"Change into this," she said, giving me a paper gown. "The doctor will be in shortly."

There was a chair in the corner of the room, but I sat on the table instead and put my feet in the stirrups. The paper on the table crackled as I got comfortable.

I heard a knock at the door, and then the doctor walked in. She introduced herself as Dr. Nina Allen and sat on the stool in front of me. She had a little teddy bear clipped to her stethoscope and a gold band around her ring finger. She was probably someone's mom too.

"Are you ready?" she asked.

I lay back on the table, and she moved around the room, getting the tools she needed.

There were posters all over the walls, but the two by the bed stood out the most. One showed a woman getting the wand and jelly exam. Her belly was huge, and she was looking at the screen with a smile on her face. Her husband wasn't with her. Maybe she didn't have one and her mom would help her through labor.

"This is going to feel a little cold," the doctor said.

The second poster showed a mom at a park, sitting on a bench and her daughter was playing in a sandbox. The park looked like the one I had always gone to with Renee and Eric. The mom was reading a magazine, but kept it low on her lap so she could watch her daughter at the same time.

This was my chance, I thought. A chance to change my life and live like a normal twenty-four-year old girl. A chance to get heroin out of my life.

But could I do it—raise a child, be a mother, and be responsible for something other than myself?

The voice in my head kept saying, "You're not alone." I had Claire and my parents, and Michael. I had people who loved me and would help me raise my baby. I could do this. And I could stop using. Not for me, but for my baby.

"Stop," I shouted.

I sat up on the table and pulled my feet out of the stirrups. "I've changed my mind."

The doctor showed her square teeth. "Are you sure?"

I was sure—I wasn't going to kill for heroin. Everything else, I'd figure out.

"I'm sorry I wasted your time," I said and got off the table to get dressed.

"This is very common, you know," she said. "A lot of women have a change of heart right before the abortion."

I hated that word.

"And they turn into wonderful mothers," she said.

I put my shirt on and thanked her. I paid the seventy-five dollar doctor fee at the desk and took the train home.

I sat on our couch again with my feet on the coffee table. Sunshine still wasn't home yet. My stomach gurgled, shooting gas into my chest. That was the baby, I thought. Kicking the heroin out of its little body like I was going to.

I'd never had a reason to quit dope before. And now the reason was in my belly. That little bean-shaped blob was going to grow into something special. A good student, maybe even a journalist or a doctor. And when my baby got old enough, I'd share my story and how I got clean when I found out I was pregnant.

"Mommy quit heroin because of you," I'd say. "I loved you so much and didn't want to hurt you."

I rubbed my palm across my stomach.

"Where are we going to live now?" I asked my belly. "Should we move home to grandma and grandpa's house?"

I didn't want to live in Maine, but living with Sunshine wouldn't be good for the baby or me. I needed to eat healthy and drink lots of water. At least that was what the printouts said, the ones the secretary at the clinic gave me.

I could move in with Claire. She ate three meals a day. And maybe I could get a part-time job to help her with groceries and rent. I had twenty-five weeks to plan until the baby was born.

The dope I'd bought that morning was on the coffee table by my feet, staring at me. I'd shot five bags before going to the clinic, and I had five left. That was enough for a good nod. My last nod. And then I was going to be a mother. There was a new feeling inside me that I'd never felt before. A feeling that was stronger than the love I had for heroin.

The five wax-paper packets with their stamped emblems—a skull and crossbones—were lined up on the table. I opened each one slowly and dumped the powder onto a spoon. The spoon was caked with resin, all black and dirty. I took the orange cap off the rig and filled the syringe. My foot was bruised and the tattooed fireworks were spotted with needle marks. In the middle of the inked Boston skyline, there was an open hole and a bump under my skin. The rig stabbed one of the buildings. I drew blood into the chamber and emptied it into my vein.

In my nod, I was sitting in the park with my daughter on my lap. She had blue eyes like me, and her brown curly hair was in pigtails. She had pink pouting lips and tiny ears with pierced lobes. She was talking and laughing, and bouncing. I understood what she was saying even though she had a hard time pronouncing her r's and th's.

She touched my face with her little hand. "Nose," she said, touching my nose. "Lips," she said and moved her fingers down to my mouth. "Tummy," she said and patted my stomach.

"Yes, baby," I said. "You came from mommy's tummy."

"Wet mama, diaper full."

I felt her butt and it was wet. She must have leaked through her diaper. My pants were wet too. Not wet, but soaked and it didn't look like pee. It was thick and bloody.

I stood her up and turned her around. Her butt was covered in blood, and my hands and shirt were too.

My eyes shot open from the nod, and I looked down. I didn't see anything on the front of my jeans, but my underwear felt wet. I went into the bathroom and pulled down my pants. My underwear was covered in blood, and when I sat on the toilet, something came out of me, something tissue-like with clots of blood.

I reached for my cell phone and called the clinic. I told the secretary what was happening and she told me to go the ER.

"This is normal, right? My last period or something?" I asked.

"No, Ms. Brown, I'm afraid it's not normal. It sounds like you had a miscarriage."

That wasn't possible. In my heroin dream, I saw my baby. She was there in my arms and she called me "Mama." I was going to be a mother.

"I was wrong, there's not that much blood and..."

But there was a lot of blood. The toilet bowl was stained red.

"The doctor will check you out and perform a D&C if need be."

"What's that?" I asked.

I heard her say words—cervix and uterus and vacuuming—and I hung up the phone.

I got in the shower to clean myself off. Blood ran down my legs and into the tub and swirled around the drain and turned pink as it mixed with the water. Pink for my little girl.

There was three hundred and twenty-five dollars in my wallet. I'd stop at Richard's before going to the hospital and spend it all on heroin. I'd get high and forget this ever happened. And if Richard asked about the abortion, I'd tell him I had it this morning.

It wasn't a lie. My baby was dead. But I'd killed her. I'd given myself an abortion.

CHAPTER SIXTEEN

O ver the years, most of my heroin dreams had been action-filled. I'd dreamt about being in planes and helicopters, flying like a bird, swimming in the ocean, and running through fields of flowers. In all of them, I'd always been alone. That was except for a few, like the one where Sunshine and I had been at Willy Wonka's factory, or when I had been with my baby girl, and the one I was having now. I was sitting in the back of a raft, floating down a river. And in front of me sat several people, men and women, even a child, but I didn't recognize them.

Woods surrounded both sides of the river, and the sun was shining above. It was my favorite time of year. The air was crisp, and the leaves were different shades of reds, oranges, and yellows.

Water splashed into my mouth, tasting sweet like candy.

Waves rocked the boat. The raft weaved from side to side to avoid hitting the boulders that stuck out of the water.

My bangs flew into my face, and my lifejacket fit snugly around my stomach.

We came to a pool of water with mountains of rock on three sides. The raft pulled up to a wooden dock. The child stepped onto the dock first, and the women followed, and then the men. I was last. I reached for the handle bar on the dock, and one of the women slapped my hand. She pushed the raft and I drifted away from them.

The boat came to a dead stop in the middle of the pool. The water was calm. There weren't any oars.

"Help," I yelled to the people on the dock. "Throw me a rope."

Claire appeared on the dock. Somehow, she was alone and everyone else was gone. Then my parents and Michael showed up and stood behind her. By Claire's side were Sunshine, Richard, Eric,

Renee, Que and Raul. Tim's dreadlocks poked Eric's face, and Frankie's pot belly squeezed in between Sunshine and Claire.

"Claire," I shouted. "Come get me."

They all put their hands in the air and waved. And then they disappeared.

I put my hands over my head, getting ready to dive and swim to the dock. Just then, the waves returned, and the current moved the boat. The wall of rock opened into a tunnel, and the raft floated through.

At the end of the tunnel, I saw it. The peak of an enormous waterfall. The boat stopped at the tip of the drop and teetered along its edge. Would the raft make the drop? Would I?

I wanted to jump off the edge, glide through the air and feel the water spray over my face.

I moved to the front of the boat, bent my knees, and took a deep breath. My throat was tight. And suddenly, it was hard to breathe.

From somewhere up above, I heard my name.

"Nicole, Nicole," a woman said. Her voice was familiar. "Open your eyes."

A fish jumped out of the water and stared at me. It was yellow and blue, and its fin was pointy like a shark.

I heard her voice again.

"Nicole, baby, we love you," she said.

Something hard was in my mouth. I looked down and didn't see anything except water. But I could feel it when I touched my lips. It was a long tube.

I tugged on it, and the tube loosened and moved.

"Nicole, no," the woman said. "Michael, call a nurse."

I yanked on the tube again.

The raft rocked back and forth over the ledge.

Hands touched mine and they tried to pry my fingers off the tube.

I gagged as the tube came up and out of my mouth.

The raft and river disappeared, and all I saw was darkness. Was the dream over?

Were my eyes open? I touched my lids and they were closed, so I opened them.

The light was blinding.

A needle was in my wrist, attached to another tube that ran along my arm and into a machine. A blanket was pulled up to my stomach. And from my stomach to my chest was a white and blue, dotted—shirt?

Four sets of eyes looked down at me. Mom and Dad. Michael and Claire.

My throat was so dry. "Where am I?" I asked and coughed.

"Mass General," Mom said.

"Is that a town?" I asked.

"No, honey," Mom said. "Mass General is a hospital in Boston."

A hospital? Had I been hit by the train? Motorcycle? Car? Did I still have my legs? I reached down and touched my thighs. Legs were still there and both arms too.

"You overdosed, Nicole," Claire said.

I overdosed? But that was impossible. I knew how much to shoot and how much my body could handle, and Richard didn't sell junk that was laced or cut. Though I'd been shooting a lot more since the abortion—that was what I called it anyway. Six bags, six or seven or eight times a day for the last six months. I used more than Sunshine, and she was a vet.

"Cole, you almost died," Michael said.

What happened to the raft? I wanted to be back on the raft, teetering along the edge of the waterfall. Anything would be better than the looks on their faces.

I closed my eyes.

When I woke up, there was a tray in front of me with apple juice, water, broth, pudding, and Jell-O.

Mom took a spoon off the tray. She scooped up a cube of Jell-O and held the spoon up to my mouth.

I wasn't hungry.

"It'll give you strength," she said.

My eyes shut, I couldn't keep them open.

A man in a white jacket was standing next to me. He was reading the machines behind my bed and writing on a chart.

"You're awake," he said.

I wasn't sure what I was.

He asked if I wanted to talk in private and I said yes. He turned around and said something to Michael and my parents and waited for them to leave before he spoke.

"You're a medical miracle, Nicole," he said. "With all the damage you've done to your body, I don't know how you're alive right now."

He said on Tuesday evening I'd been admitted to the hospital and had gone into cardiac and respiratory arrest from the heroin I'd injected.

"What's today?" I asked.

"Saturday."

I'd been asleep for four days? I didn't even feel dope sick, which was strange. I thought.

He said I had grand mal seizures throughout the first night, and my organs began to shut down, so I was put on a ventilator.

"Your body is weak, but it'll repair itself as long as you stop using heroin," he said. "If you don't, I'm afraid the damage will be progressive and eventually fatal."

He had gray hair and wore glasses, and had probably been a doctor for longer than I'd been alive. It wasn't that I didn't believe what he said. I saw the damage when I looked in the mirror. I just didn't care.

"In addition, you're malnourished, dehydrated, and your teeth are decaying from regurgitating the acid in your stomach," he said.

I touched the back of my mouth with my tongue and felt the hole where my molar used to be.

"Do you vomit regularly, unintentionally or self-induced?"

"I'm not bulimic," I said.

He wrote something down in the chart. "A side effect of long-term heroin use is vomiting."

The queasiness and lightheaded feeling had stopped after the abortion, but the puking hadn't.

He asked if I had any other questions, and I asked when I could go home. He said in a couple of days.

"You were given another chance," he said.

I moved my hand to my chest, a couple inches from my heart. The bullet hole had healed, but it had left a scar.

He walked to the door and turned around. His hand went in the air and his finger pointed at me. "I don't want to ever see you in my ER again," he said and left the room.

Claire came in a few minutes later. I was glad to see her and not my parents. She sat on the bed and put my hand on her leg, covering it with hers. "I thought I'd lost you forever," she said.

"I'm still here."

But not for much longer. Tomorrow morning, I was going to leave the hospital regardless of what the doctor said. I wanted a shot with a new rig and seven bags in the chamber.

"If I hadn't gone to your room to check on you, you wouldn't be here," she said.

Was I supposed to thank her for saving my life? Did I want to be saved? I was tired, I knew that much. Tired of panhandling, tired of boosting, tired of turning tricks, tired of being short on cash, and tired of going to Richard's.

I was tired of thinking about how I'd murdered my baby.

Was I tired of using? I was tired of chasing that first high—the one in Que's bedroom and the one in the McDonald's bathroom. No matter how many bags I shot, I was never going to catch it.

"How would you feel if you came into my room and found me on the floor, convulsing, with foam coming out of my mouth?" she asked.

She touched my forehead, brushing the hair off my face. Her fingers glided down to my cheeks, and I thought of all the boils and whiteheads her fingertips were caressing.

She cupped my chin in her palm. "I really want you to think about that and consider how I felt when I found you," she said. "You wouldn't do that to me again, would you?"

And then she left my room.

Outside the door, I heard my mom say, "Did you tell her how you found her on the floor, foaming at the mouth?"

There was silence.

"Do you think it scared her into going to rehab?" Dad asked.

More silence.

"Thanks for everything you've done, Claire," Mom said. "You saved our daughter's life."

My parents and Michael came into my room, and I pretended to be asleep. Their breathing was loud, and their feet squeaked when they walked towards me.

Mom pulled the blanket up to my chin. Her touch had always been so soft and tender, and it still was.

I didn't have to pretend to be asleep for long. I was so tired. Whatever the nurses had put in my IV was some good shit.

When I woke up, my parents were sitting by my bed, and Michael was leaning against the wall. Sun was pouring in through the blinds, and I smelled coffee.

Had they slept in my room last night? Mom was wearing a shirt with faces painted on it. Had she been wearing that yesterday? I couldn't remember.

Michael moved to my other side and my parents stood, all of them surrounding me. They looked like they were staring at an open casket, saying their last respects.

Who was going to speak first? It wasn't going to be me.

Mom sat on the mattress by my waist and ran her fingers along my arm. She looked so clean and smelled like fabric softener and vanilla. Her eye shadow was sparkly and medium brown. I bet she didn't use markers like I did.

There was nothing about me that was clean anymore. I didn't deserve to be clean, not for everything I'd done. The nurses should have left me in my dirty clothes instead of dressing me in a clean gown.

"We don't want our baby to die," Mom said.

I felt the same way, but mine had.

"And that's going to happen, Cole, if you keep this up," Dad said.

Dad looked clean too. I could smell his aftershave, citrus with a hint of musk.

"Will you go to rehab and get sober?" Michael asked.

Michael's hair was gelled, each strand placed just so perfectly. His shoes were the same color as the brown stripes in his shirt. But

Michael had a secret, and I doubted if my parents knew what it was. He wasn't the cleanest, but he was cleaner than me.

Would I go to rehab—sit in meetings, listen to other addicts tell their stories, work the Twelve Steps, talk to counselors, and promise to never do junk again? And stay clean?

What would life be like, looking through clean eyes?

I wanted the needle.

But I was tired too.

CHAPTER SEVENTEEN

For two days, I lay in my hospital bed and listened to my parents and Michael talk about rehab. They said the same things they'd probably said in all their voicemails—they loved me and missed me, they didn't want me to die like Eric—and so I agreed to go. The rehab center was in a 'burb outside Boston, but they didn't have a bed for me and wouldn't for a couple days. In the meantime, we'd all stay at Michael's.

My decision was more for them and the baby than for me. My parents looked tired and older since the last time I'd seen them. For them and for the child I'd killed, the least I could do was get clean. I also didn't want to hurt Claire anymore. She had told me that before she died, she wanted to see me sober. And like she said, she was seventy-nine.

I left the hospital wearing the clothes I'd come in with, with my purse and cell phone. Those were the only things I owned, everything at Sunshine's was hers. In the car to Michael's, I looked in my purse and it was empty except for my cigarettes, lighter, wallet, and the picture of Michael and Jesse kissing. The bags, spoons, and rigs were gone. Claire must have cleaned out my purse before she brought it to the hospital.

"I have a surprise for you," Mom said as we walked into Michael's apartment. She took my hand and pulled me into the guest room.

Her suitcase was on the floor under the window, and her cosmetics were on the dresser.

"Look in the closet," she said.

I opened the closet door and there was a rack full of clothes. Did she want me to see her wardrobe or her new Nikes still in the box?

"I didn't know your size," she said from the doorway. "But hopefully everything will fit."

"This is all for me?"

"Honey, you don't have any clothes to wear in rehab, so of course it's all yours."

She said rehab like it was my first day of school.

The shirts were all a size small and the jeans a size two. I couldn't remember the last time mom had bought me clothes, and pants that were a single-digit size. I hadn't looked at the tags on Sunshine's clothes. I just put them on and they fit.

"Thanks, Mom."

She walked over and gave me a hug. "We're just happy you're in our lives again."

I was too, but that didn't mean I'd stopped thinking about heroin. Actually, it was the only thing on my mind.

Before I'd left the hospital, the doctor had given me a prescription for six pills of Xanax. I had asked for Klonopin or methadone. He said Klonopin shouldn't be taken in short-term doses and methadone had worse withdrawal symptoms than heroin.

"Take two pills a day," the doctor had said. "They should help take the edge off a little."

The Xanax was about as strong as rubbing coke on my gums. If there was an edge, I was way fucking past it. My stomach was jittery and my hands were shaky. My brain was swimming laps, and heroin was at one end and rehab was at the other. If my parents weren't shadowing me around the apartment, I'd be looking for alcohol or glue, or computer duster, anything that would get me high.

I wanted a minute alone, so I got off the living room couch and locked myself in the bathroom. I ran the faucet and the shower and sat on the toilet taking deep breaths.

"Unlock the door," Mom said from the hallway.

"I'll be out in a sec," I said.

My chest was tight, but the steam was clearing my lungs.

I heard a drill, and the screws on the door handle fell to the ground. Then the whole handle crashed to the floor, and the door swung open.

"You're not going to shut us out," Dad said.

He handed the drill to Michael. Michael took off all the handles from every door in the apartment.

Dad wasn't kidding. There was literally no way to shut them out.

"We're going to get through this together," he said.

I went to bed after dinner. Mom changed into her pajamas too and got into bed beside me. She opened a book and read. She dragged her nail over the corner of the page and flicked it a few times before turning it. Sometimes, she'd lick her finger, flip, and hold the corner of the page between her pointer and middle finger.

Heroin. Heroin. Heroin.

"Do you want to talk?" she asked.

I was on my back, counting the popcorn bumps on the ceiling. There were eighty-nine in the spot above my head, but I could have miscounted.

"About what?" I asked.

"The last four and a half years you've spent in Boston, rehab, Claire, anything?"

Except for rehab, everything on her list was personal. If I told her all the things I'd done, it would only upset her more.

"How about rehab," I said.

She put her book on the nightstand and rolled on her side, facing me. "We believe in you, Cole, and we know it'll work if you just give it a chance."

If the rehab counselor ever asked me why I did heroin, what was I going to say? I didn't wake up one morning and decide to be a junkie. Dope helped me forget about the rape, but that wasn't the reason I used. I came from a good family and my parents loved me. I wasn't picked on in school and dated lots of boys.

"How do you know it'll work?" I asked.

"You're a fighter, baby and you always have been. And when you want something bad enough, you don't stop until it's yours."

I couldn't think of a single thing I'd fought for. I gave the cops my statement, and when there weren't any leads, I didn't fight to find the guys who raped me. I dropped out of college because I couldn't take the looks and stares from the other students. I didn't fight for my relationship with Cody. I pushed him away because I couldn't stand to be touched anymore. I couldn't fight off the urge to use and caused the miscarriage. The one time I fought for what I wanted was when I pushed Claire away from the door. And Claire didn't deserve that.

My mom didn't know me at all anymore.

I told her I was tired, and she switched off the light. I listened to her breathe. And eventually, dad shut off the TV in the living room, and I heard Michael go into his bedroom.

I watched the minutes change on the clock. I counted the seconds in my head. It was two-thirty and mom was still awake. I felt her eyes on me, her hand rubbing my head, her fingers tickling my arm every time I moved. Heroin. Heroin. Heroin was on my brain and it wouldn't go away.

I got up from the bed and went into the bathroom, turning on the faucet just enough so the water trickled. Hopefully mom would think I was peeing. I had to hurry.

I moved into the hallway and stood in front of the closet where Michael kept his jackets and skis. If I opened the closet door, she'd hear me. I'd just have to go to Richard's in my shorts and bare feet.

I tiptoed into the family room, and dad wasn't on the couch. He was asleep on an air mattress by the front door. There was no way out of this apartment.

Michael should have something that would get me high. I searched through the kitchen cupboards and hidden behind a box of cereal was a half bottle of vodka.

"What are you doing?" Mom asked from behind me.

I held the vodka to my chest and turned around. My hands were shaking so bad the vodka looked like waves.

"You're trembling," she said.

"Please," I said. "Please don't take this away from me." I was hugging the bottle like it was Blinkie, the glow worm I lugged around as a child.

Her eyes had been staring at the bottle, but they weren't hard like they had been seconds ago. They were soft and watery.

She reached her hand towards me, and I took a step back.

"I'm not going to take it away from you," she said. She reached forward again, and her arm went around my shoulder. I held the bottle against my heart.

She walked with me to the living room, and when she turned to go to the guest room, I led her to Michael's office. As soon as we got inside, I wiggled out from her arm and crawled under the desk. I crouched into a ball and drank until my throat burned.

She climbed in and sat next to me. I couldn't look at her. I looked at the wall and swallowed.

She pulled a piece of hair off my sticky lip.

I took another swig.

Her hand touched my back, and she gently pushed forward, so she could squeeze in behind me. "Relax, baby, it's going to be okay," she said. Her legs went straight, sticking out from under the desk and they pressed against mine.

She rested her chin on my head. Her fingers circled around my shoulders and down my arms. "Summertime, and the livin' is easy," she sang softly.

When Michael and I were growing up, mom had always sung that song whenever one of us was hurt. And by the time she'd dabbed our cut with peroxide and wrapped it with a Band-Aid, the song would be over.

I didn't taste the next gulp or the one after, the same way I hadn't tasted the beer I drank in college, or the blood that had dripped down my throat when I blew coke, or the bitterness that had covered my tongue when I shot heroin.

"Your daddy's rich, and your mamma's good lookin', so hush little baby," she sang.

The bottle was empty. And even though I was buzzed, vodka wasn't heroin. Booze didn't give me that warm feeling throughout my body and it didn't let me nod into a beautiful dream.

"One of these mornings you're going to rise up singing, then you'll spread your wings and you'll take to the sky," she sang.

I leaned back with my head on her chest.

Her arms crossed over mine. "But till that morning there's a'nothing can harm you with daddy and mamma standing by."

My shoulders relaxed, my chest loosened, and my eyes closed.

Mom's heart was beating so loud it woke me up. Or maybe it was the cramp in my neck or the awful odor I smelled. Still, I was comfortable with my head on her chest, and I wasn't ready to get up.

"What the hell—"

"Shh," Mom said. "She's sleeping."

But I wasn't anymore. Dad and Michael were kneeling in front of the desk and their hands were covering their noses.

"Can you grab me a bucket and rag?" Mom asked.

The smell was coming from the pile of puke next to mom and me. I didn't remember getting sick.

"You slept in her vomit all night?" Dad asked.

"I didn't want to wake her, it's been a rough night for her."

Dad looked into my eyes. "You drank the whole bottle?" he asked, holding the empty fifth in his hand.

I shook my head. "Only half."

Michael lifted me out from under the desk and carried me to his bathroom. He set me down on the toilet and ran the bath water.

I leaned forward, holding my stomach, and he bent down so we were eye level.

"It's that bad, huh?" he asked.

I nodded.

"The rehab center called. They can get you in tomorrow morning," he said.

They'd give me drugs to take away all this fluttering and the cravings, and meds to help me sleep. One more day. I could do this, for him, my parents, and the baby.

He stood, and I grabbed his arm. "I was pregnant, you know."

He looked down at me with a crease between his brows.

"The second time, not the first," I said. "I was eleven weeks and decided to keep the baby, but I lost it…"

"I didn't know, I couldn't believe—"

"I know. And I'm sorry for what I said."

He put his hand on my shoulder and squeezed before he left me in the bathroom.

The bubble bath turned cold, but I didn't get out. Mom brought me a plate of toast and some coffee. She turned on Michael's radio, and some weird music started playing. Birds chirping and waterfalls with this opera-like voice that sang in the background. The last time I'd taken a bath was in my parents' tub, a few weeks after the rape. Mom had played the same kind of music and tried to make me eat. That was before—heroin, heroin, heroin. I needed to shut my brain off.

I'd have to change my whole life if I wanted to stay sober after rehab. I wouldn't be able to talk to Sunshine anymore or visit Claire, knowing Sunshine lived next door. I'd have to move out of Boston because I'd be too tempted to go to Richard's or Roxbury. I'd have to retrain my brain to think bags were to hold sandwiches, spoons were to eat cereal, rigs were tractor-trailers, and John was just a guy's name.

I lay in bed, tossed and turned. It was still bright outside, but I thought a nap would get rid of my hangover. The TV was playing in the living room, and the smell of lasagna was coming out of the kitchen. I paced between the window and door. There was nothing to look at besides the four white walls. White walls, white powder. Brown carpet, brown powder. Black nightstand, black resin. Silver handle, silver spoons. I was surrounded.

Dad asked me to watch a movie with him. He told me the name, but I forgot it after a few minutes. I couldn't concentrate on what the actors said or follow the plot.

I helped mom cook dinner. She asked me to take the bread out of the oven, and the baking dish hit my arm. I screamed when it burnt my skin, and the pan dropped out of my hand. The loaf rolled around on the floor. I'd ruined dinner.

"Put your arm under the faucet," Mom said. She already had the water running, washing vegetables for a salad.

I put my arm under the stream, and it cooled off the burn.

"I'll get you some Neosporin," she said.

My track marks still looked fresh, like I'd shot up just a second ago.

"Don't bother, my arm is full of scars anyway," I said.

She turned my arm so she could see the marks on both sides. And then she bent her head and kissed the skin by the deepest hole. "They'll heal, honey."

No they wouldn't. Like the doctor had said, I was damaged.

I wanted to call Sunshine. I hadn't spoken to her since the morning of my overdose. Claire had told me Sunshine came to see me the second day I was in the hospital, but I was still unconscious. When Sunshine was in the hospital, I visited her every day.

Besides the balcony, there wasn't anywhere in the apartment where I could talk without my parents hearing me. And when I had gone on the balcony to smoke a cigarette, mom came with me and wouldn't let me stand close to the ledge.

I grabbed my pack of cigs and opened the sliding glass door. Mom was right behind me and I turned around. "I want to say goodbye to Claire," I said. "Will you just give me a minute?"

"A minute," she said and sat on the couch closest to the balcony.

It was just after ten o'clock, and the people walking on the sidewalk below looked like shadows under the streetlamps. If I weren't at Michael's, I'd be working the track with Sunshine. Hopefully, I could catch her in between tricks.

I dialed her number from my cell phone.

"Hello?" she said, after the third ring.

I could hear cars swishing by and honking. She was in our usual spot.

"How are you doing?" I asked.

"Ain't been high since you left," she said. "Been going to Roxbury and getting shit that's cut. So weak, it barely gets me straight."

"You miss me? Wait—why aren't you buying from Richard?"

"When you coming back?" she asked.

"Sunshine, I'm going to rehab."

"Just come home and go to Richard's for me, will you?"

"Why won't you go?"

"I can't," she said.

"Did something happen? Did he get busted?"

"No."

Mom was staring at me through the glass. She pointed to her watch, and I held up my half-smoked cig.

"Will you tell me what's going on?" I asked.

"He hurt me, okay? There was no guy who pulled me into the alley and held me at gunpoint. Richard put me in the hospital."

Richard? She'd made up that whole story to protect Richard? But why? Because his drugs were better than anything we could buy on the street? I thought of the blood on her legs.

"He did more than just beat you, didn't he?" I asked.

"He raped me, and then he fucked me with a—" she said and stopped.

I waited for her to keep going, but she didn't.

"I ain't going over there," she said. "So get your ass back here."

Mom opened the sliding glass door. "Come on, Cole, time's up," Mom said.

"I'll talk to you soon," I said to Sunshine and hung up.

I wondered why Richard had snapped. What had she done that had caused him to beat and rape her? But what really mattered was that she had lied to me. I'd gone to Richard's house every morning for years. She knew how evil he could be and never once had she warned me.

Mom packed all my new clothes into one of Michael's suitcases, and we got into the car. I sat in the backseat next to her, and Dad drove. Michael turned on the radio but kept the volume low. We pulled out of the underground garage and drove down Massachusetts Avenue. Ten blocks behind us was the track where Sunshine and I tricked. We passed the Prudential Building, where I had panhandled. We turned onto Commonwealth Avenue, where Que and Raul had lived. The park, where I had hung out with Eric and Renee. The bench, where Renee and I had slept the night Eric had died, the same spot where I'd seen the squirrel eating an acorn and thought my life was perfect.

Twenty minutes later, Dad pulled off the main road and parked by an unmarked brick building. There wasn't a gate around the property or a security guard inside the door. Mom held one of my arms and Dad held the other. Michael rolled my suitcase up to the desk. He gave my name to the receptionist, and she picked up the phone, telling someone I was here.

A man with a red ponytail and thick glasses came out to greet us. He said his name was Walter and shook all our hands. He told me to say goodbye to my family and that I'd see them again in thirty days when my visiting privileges were instated. I gave them all hugs, and they told me they were proud of me.

Walter brought me into his office where he asked me a bunch of questions about my drug use. He searched through my suitcase, and a female nurse patted me down and checked my underwear and bra. He gave me a copy of the rules and daily schedule, and then he brought me into a second office with an exam table and lots of diplomas on the walls.

Dr. Paul examined me. Since I'd already detoxed in the hospital, he wouldn't give me any meds. He told me the facility didn't believe in methadone therapy or anxiety pills, they took a natural approach to rehabilitation with yoga and meditation. He said he'd give me a vitamin to help me sleep.

"Can I at least have a Xanax," I said. "I'm freaking out here."

Dr. Paul pointed a flashlight in my eyes and took my pulse. He unlocked a cabinet and took something out, dropping it in my hand. It was a pill, about the size of a dime.

"Can I have some water?"

"It's chewable," Dr. Paul said.

"What is it?"

"A vitamin with extra B-12."

It tasted like the Flintstone vitamins mom gave me as a kid. If this was a joke, I wasn't laughing.

Walter showed me to my room, which was smaller than the room I'd shared with Sunshine. The comforters on the twin beds had giant Chinese symbols on them, and there was a framed poster of a woman stretching on the beach.

"The girls' bathroom is down the hall," Walter said. "Justina will show you."

He pointed with his head towards the beds. There was a girl standing between them. I hadn't noticed her when I looked around the room.

"Group is in fifteen," Walter said. "I'll see you there."

I wheeled my suitcase into the room. "Which bed is mine?"

She pointed to the one closest to the door. "What are you in for?" she asked.

"Heroin. You?"

She was about my size with hair so blond it was white, and the sides were dyed red. There was a horseshoe shaped-ring through her septum, and she had two different color eyes, a brown and a blue. None of my tricks had had two eye colors. Maybe she'd lost a contact lens.

"Meth," she said and smiled. Her teeth were like Heather's, black and rotted. "I'm here on a court order."

She was like Henry, dumb enough to get caught.

"I tried to kill my mom during a binge," she said. "Tied that bitch up with rope and dumped gasoline on her. But I'd used up all the butane on a hit, so I couldn't set her on fire."

They'd stuck me in a room with a crazy?

Group was held in a room off the cafeteria with couches set up in a circle. I sat next to Justina and watched everyone take their seats. There were about fifteen of us, guys and girls of all different ages. Since I was new, Walter asked everyone to say their name and drug of choice. There were a few alcoholics, oxy-heads, an ecstasy popper, a huffer, and the rest did either coke or H.

One of the guys in group looked familiar. Actually, it was his nose I recognized. It tilted to the side, and there was a chunk of flesh missing on the bridge like a dog had bitten him. I'd seen him at Richard's, he was one of his squatters. He stared at me and gave me that look—I know you from somewhere, but I can't think of how. I mouthed "Richard," and he smiled back.

Walter pointed at me. "It's your turn," he said.

I said my name and hoped he'd move on to the next person. The B-12 hadn't kicked in yet.

"And what's your drug of choice, Nicole?" Walter asked.

"I love to chase the dragon," I said.

The junkies in the group laughed and nodded.

Walter asked how everyone was feeling.

Some guy said he was happy, but horny. A woman said she was constipated. Justina said she was feeling nervous because my suitcase was red and that was an angry color.

The color of my suitcase made her nervous? She'd tied up her mom and tried to set her on fire. Justina was a crazy bitch.

"The sides of your hair are red, does that mean I should be nervous too?" I asked.

"Nicole, group is a place where we can all be honest with our emotions," Walter said. "Justina was just expressing that the color red triggered a feeling inside her. Why don't you share how you're feeling?"

"I'm pissed off," I said.

"And why is that?" Walter asked.

I decided not to say anything about Justina. We shared a room, and when I was sleeping, she could easily tie me up and set me on fire too.

"I asked the doctor for a Xanax and he gave me a Flintstone vitamin. I don't see how Fred is going to help with my heroin cravings."

Walter frowned, but everyone else smiled at me.

After group was cleaning time. We were all assigned a duty, and mine was vacuuming. It didn't take me long, most of the place was tiled, and someone else was responsible for mopping.

When I got back to the room, Justina was there. She'd been given the girls' toilets, and there were only four. She told me it was lunchtime and brought me to the cafeteria. I took a sandwich and a soda, and we sat at an empty table.

Dustin, the nose guy, came in and sat across from me.

"It's nice to see someone familiar," he said.

"How long have you been here?" I asked.

I tried to think of the last time I'd seen him at Richard's, but I couldn't remember.

"Couple weeks. It's hell and these fruitcakes are making me do yoga and shit."

I couldn't picture Dustin doing yoga. I could picture him beating someone up or mainlining, but not yoga.

"Your parents bring you here?" I asked.

He nodded. "You?"

I nodded too. I told him about the overdose.

"Was that your first time in the hospital?" he asked.

"Yeah, for an overdose."

I'd been to the hospital before—the morning after the rape and when I'd got shot in the chest and after my miscarriage, but he didn't need to know all that.

"I've died four times and been to three rehabs," he said. "They're all the same, but this one doesn't believe in meds, which sucks."

I agreed, but he already knew that.

He was good looking in that rough street kind of way. He had scars on his hands and one on his chin like mine. His was from a fight, not a lighter. He had a thick Boston accent—didn't pronounce any r's—and told me he was a Southie. He was twenty-six and had played hockey at UMass until he got injured sophomore year and got hooked on Percs and Vics. He dropped out of school and had been on the streets ever since. Our pasts were somewhat alike.

If I was going to get sober, I had to start thinking like a sober girl, not a hooker who thought of men as dope money. When I looked at Dustin, he was taking a bite of his hot dog and I pictured his lips around my nipple. I hadn't had sober sex since I'd been raped, but that had to change. Dustin had nice lips. And eyes that were icy blue like Cooper, one of my regulars.

After lunch, I went to individual counseling. My therapists were Walter and Sandra, who had been sober for ten years. Walter wasn't an addict, he had just chosen to study addiction in school. They both held a notebook and pen, and took notes while I told them my story.

"Did you speak to anyone after you were raped?" Sandra asked.

I shook my head.

"What makes you want to talk about it now?"

"You asked about my past," I said.

"Do you want to get sober?" Walter asked.

I thought about his question and rubbed my stomach.

"I lost a baby from heroin."

"That's not what I asked," he said.

"My family hurts because of me," I said.

"I didn't ask that either."

"Well, that's the best I've got right now."

Sandra said my first session went well and she'd see me again tomorrow.

The next meeting was held in the same room as group, but the couches were in rows and there was an easel with a big pad of paper in the front of the room. On the paper were the Twelve Steps.

I read Step One: "We admitted we were powerless over our addiction – that our lives had become unmanageable."

I was definitely an addict. Unmanageable? I managed just fine, but I was tired.

The first day dragged on.

Yoga was held in what they called the sunroom, with wood floors and lots of windows. The yoga instructor wore spandex shorts and a sports bra and had a six-pack. She kept telling everyone to breathe, breathe in the air around us and release the negative energy. I was in this position she called downward dog and Dustin was in front of me. He was wearing gym shorts and his butt looked nice under the mesh. He looked at me, upside down from between his arms and rolled his eyes. I laughed. I couldn't help it.

The instructor came over and lifted my butt higher in the air. "Breathe, Nicole," she said. "And deactivate your mind."

Heroin and Dustin's ass were both active in my mind.

I ate dinner with Dustin, and we hung out in the rec room before lights out. He made me laugh—not just about how bad the food was or Walter having the hots for Sandra or Justina's hair—but about Richard and Heather, and the people on the trains, and boosting from old ladies. I laughed so hard, I cried. I couldn't remember the last time I'd really laughed. Nothing had been funny—chasing the high, or tricking, or stealing from cars, or killing my baby. But Dustin was.

On my third night, I was hanging with Dustin again in the smoking lounge, sitting in plastic chairs with a small table separating us. Lights out was in ten minutes, and the last smoker had just gone to bed. Dustin was holding his cigarette, but he wasn't smoking it. I wasn't smoking mine either, I wanted the cig to last the whole ten minutes.

When I was with Johns in an alley or in their cars, I was always grateful for the dark. But here on the porch, I wished for light. I wanted to see Dustin's face, the curve of his neck, and the way his body looked when he shifted in his chair.

Dustin was different than all the men I'd met since I'd moved to Boston. He hadn't asked for anything, and he hadn't pushed himself on me. I was different too, acting like I had when I'd dated Cody in college. When I was with Dustin, I cared how I looked, how my breath smelled, and what words came out of my mouth. He didn't have drugs or money to offer. And for the first time in a long time, I didn't want either. I wanted his attention, and he gave it to me. I wanted to be the reason he smiled, and when I talked to him, he grinned at me.

He moved to the edge of his seat. "I want to tell you something, but you can't laugh at me," he said.

"I won't laugh, I promise," I said, crossing my legs to keep my knees from shaking.

My heart was beating so loud I worried he could hear it.

"I haven't kissed a girl sober in a really long time."

"I haven't either," I said. "A guy, I mean."

What if I wasn't a good sober kisser? Would Dustin still flirt and eat all his meals with me?

"Come here," he said.

I put out my cigarette and slowly got up from my chair to stand in front of him. He tilted his head up. It was too dark to see the blueness of his eyes, but I knew they were looking into mine. He pushed his face into my stomach and I ran my fingers through his hair. I felt his breath through my shirt, and it warmed my belly, sending butterflies to my chest and sparks to my crotch.

He pulled his face out of my shirt and my hands went to his cheeks.

His hands went to my outer thighs, and he gently drew me closer.

I bent my head, inching down to his face, and pressed my lips against his. They were soft and tasted sweet. His tongue poked in my mouth and circled around my tongue.

My body was on fire.

"Lights out," someone yelled from inside.

His hands gave me a final squeeze, and he pecked my lips.

"I don't want to stop," he said.

I smiled. I never wanted the kiss to stop.

Before I stepped through the sliding glass door, I faced him again. "I'll see you in the morning?"

"Do I have to wait that long?" he asked.

"Good night, Dustin," I said and walked through the lobby and up the stairs to my room.

I got into bed without brushing my teeth. I didn't want to wash Dustin's taste out of my mouth.

By the fourth day, I still hadn't graduated from Step One. The addiction part, I admitted to. But I didn't believe my life had become unmanageable. Kara, my Twelve Step counselor said it would take time and that was why rehab was a ninety-day program. I didn't think time would change my mind. I was managing just fine before I'd gone into the hospital. Sometimes I'd been short on cash and had gotten dope sick, but Claire went through the same thing. She had a hard time paying her bills and got a cold in the winter. Kara told me there was a difference between Claire and me. I didn't understand what the difference was. I was a lot of things—a hooker, a thief, and an addict—but I managed all of them.

Walter and Sandra told me Dustin wasn't good for my sobriety. They said we spent too much time secluded from the group.

Romantic relationships were grounds for getting kicked out. I told them Dustin and I were just friends. They said Ed, the night shift aide, had seen us kissing in the smoking lounge. I told them Ed was lying. But we'd been kissing for the last two nights. Sandra said they were giving me one more chance, and if I screwed up again, I was out.

At dinner, I told Dustin what Sandra and Walter had said. My hands shook under the table. What more did they want from me? I'd told them about the rape. I didn't lie during my therapy sessions. I even did their stupid yoga and meditation, and they were threatening to kick me out over a kiss? This was bullshit. The kiss had nothing to do with my sobriety. My counselors were supposed to be helping me, not lecturing me about boys like I was a kid. I was a fucking adult and they needed to treat me like one.

I pushed my tray of food, and the meatballs splattered all over the table.

"They told me the same thing," Dustin said. "Nicole, I like you, and I don't give a fuck what they say."

I liked him too. I wished my tongue were the fork he'd just put in his mouth.

That night, I sat with the group in the rec room. Dustin had gone to his room after dinner and hadn't come back yet.

Molly, a sixteen-year-old who was addicted to huffing paint thinner, asked if I wanted to play charades. She said everyone was going to play. I guess that was what the group did while Dustin and I kissed in the smoking lounge.

I told her I'd be the scorekeeper and sat off to the side while they acted out movie scenes.

Dustin came into the room and slipped something into my pocket. Everyone was so busy either acting or shouting out guesses, I didn't think they even saw him come in.

I reached in my pocket and pulled out the note. It said, "Let's go to Richard's and kiss some more."

I felt my face turn red.

Dustin was standing in the hallway by the stairwell, waiting for me to answer. I smiled and nodded. He held up his hand, showing two fingers and then pointed down. I was supposed to meet him at two, by the stairs. I nodded again.

At lights out, I got into bed wearing everything but my sneakers. I thought about getting high and kissing Dustin and where we would live and how we'd make money. I'd be going back to everything I'd left behind for rehab. But it'd be different because I'd be with him. I'd have someone to share things with, unlike Sunshine who wanted to keep our money and dope separate. And he made me tingle more than I'd ever tingled before.

I got out of bed a few minutes before two. My suitcase was too big to drag around, and since I didn't know if we'd be walking or hitchhiking, I put on three shirts and my jacket. My purse and cell phone were locked in a safe in the main office, but I didn't care.

Dustin was waiting for me at the end of the stairs. He held out his hand, and I grabbed it. We walked down the hall to the front lobby and Libby, the night shift receptionist, asked where we were going.

"We're out of here," Dustin said.

"Let me call Walter and—"

"Call anyone you want," he said. "My girl and I are still leaving."

A block away, there was a taxi waiting for us. We got in the backseat, and Dustin gave the driver Richard's address.

"I don't have any money," I said.

Dustin pulled out a few twenties.

"Where'd you get that?" I asked.

"I'm going to treat you real good, you'll see."

He rested his hand on my thigh as we drove towards the city. It was snowing outside, and the flakes sparkled from the streetlights.

My parents were going to be really upset when they found out I'd left. I'd gone to rehab for them and Claire, and my baby. But tonight, I was going to get high for me.

CHAPTER EIGHTEEN

The taxi pulled up to Richard's house, and Dustin paid the driver. I'd only been gone for two weeks, but it felt much longer. A lot had happened in those two weeks. Meeting Dustin was the most important of them all.

But as I got out of the cab, I remembered the conversation I'd had with Sunshine on Michael's balcony. I was about to see the man who had beaten and raped her. And I owed that same man my body. I needed to come up with a different way to pay Richard back.

Dustin held my hand as I climbed up the front steps and opened the door for me. The squatters on the couch didn't look at me when we walked inside. That was something that hadn't changed.

"I'm back," Dustin yelled, drawing out both words.

The three guys on the couch and the two girls in the kitchen came charging towards us. They all hugged Dustin and wanted to know where he'd been. He said his mom had busted him breaking into her house and trying to steal her credit card.

"Didn't stay too long, did you," the guy with the Mohawk said.

"Nah, wanted to be with my girl," Dustin said, squeezing my hand. "Everyone, meet Nicole, you've probably seen her around here, she's a regular."

They all stared at me and half nodded. They were lying. Besides Heather, none of them had ever looked at me before.

Dustin introduced me and told mini stories about each person so I'd remember their names. It was like group where he said their name and related their story to their drug of choice. Cale was a coke-head and Tommy was a tweaker, so those were easy to remember. Tommy and Dustin had grown up together in Southie. Shank had the Mohawk and wine corks through his lobes and he used special k. The girls, Sierra and Erin, were twins, and I couldn't tell them apart. They both did H and by the way they acted around Dustin—licking their lips, giggling as he spoke, eyeing his body— he'd had a thing with one, if not both of them. A few more squatters appeared, but I stopped listening. Unless one of them was going to give me some dope, I didn't care who they were.

Heather came into the living room, zipping up her pants and straightening her shirt with Richard close behind her. She hugged me. "Where have you been," she said. "I've missed you."

Her pupils were so dilated I couldn't see the brown of her eyes.

Dustin's fingers were hooked to the back pocket of my jeans, and when he pounded fists with Richard, his fingers tightened around my butt.

Richard's eyes followed Dustin's arm, the arm that was behind me. "You with him?" Richard asked me.

"Yeah, she is," Dustin said. His hand left my butt and clung to my shoulder.

"We need to talk," Richard said to Dustin. "Big moves coming up."

Dustin told me he'd be right back and disappeared with Richard.

The squatters drifted back to their rooms and their spots on the couch, and Heather pulled me into the kitchen. She asked again where I'd been, and I told her about my overdose.

"Richard's been edgy since Dustin left," she said. She lifted her shirt and showed me the bruises and bite marks on her boobs. "Shit hurts too, but I know he's just showing me some love. We're sort of together now."

Heather and Richard? Together? I thought of Sunshine and the bruises on her inner thighs. I didn't know if I should tell Heather about what he'd done to her, but I decided now wasn't the right time.

"So you and Dustin, huh?"

"Yeah…"

Heather said Dustin was Richard's main runner and not just in Boston. Dustin ran drugs to New York City, and Burlington, Vermont, and Providence too.

"Dustin's a good guy," she said. "But he's got a bad temper like Richard."

I'd never seen that side of him. But I'd only known him for a week.

"You ready, baby," Dustin said in my ear.

Heather must have seen him coming, because she asked me about rehab.

"Got some dope and clean rigs," he said.

I gave Heather a hug, told her I'd talk to her later about rehab, and Dustin took me into one of the bedrooms. He locked the door behind us.

"That's my bed," he said.

He pointed at the first of three twin mattresses on the floor. Foils and spoons littered the carpet, and there were drawings on the walls made with crayons. Pictures of naked women shooting dope, and hands with bent fingers, creating what looked like gang symbols. Next to Dustin's bed was a drawing of a little boy with big blue eyes and a bright smile holding a hockey stick in his hands.

"Did you draw these?" I asked.

He pulled out a bundle—ten bags—and rigs for both of us. "Sometimes I have a hard time sleeping," he said.

We sat on his bed with our backs against the drawing of the little boy, and he cooked up the dope. He handed me a full rig, and I rolled it back and forth over my palms. I was clean for the first time in years, and if I relapsed, I'd have to detox all over again.

I watched him stick the rig into his ankle and wipe the blood off the needle hole. I knew how good that smack would feel after weeks without it. Should I relapse? I was still a junkie no matter how many days I'd been clean. And I stuck the needle into my ankle too.

"Feel good, baby?" he asked.

I felt more than good. My chin dropped.

He gently pushed me back against the wall.

His lips were on mine. "I can taste the dope on your tongue," he said.

I couldn't taste him, but I could feel his tongue all warm and wet inside my dry mouth.

Curled up next to Dustin on the twin was the best I'd slept since the hospital. And in the early morning, we shot up again. After the rush reached its peak, he took me into the bathroom for a shower. He turned on the water and stripped off his clothes. I'd never seen his body before. His skin was pale and tight around his muscles, and his forearms were scarred like mine. A thin line of hair ran from his belly button to his pubes.

"You like what you see?" he asked, catching my stare.

I felt my face blush.

"My turn," he said and pulled my shirt over my head. He unhooked my bra with one hand and unzipped my jeans with the other. I was naked in less than five seconds.

The bathroom was bright even with the light off, and I felt like my whole body was glowing. His eyes went to my chest and stopped at my crotch before traveling down my legs. It was a good thing I'd shaved the day before we'd left rehab.

"Water's warm, come on," he said.

He opened the plastic shower curtain, and I stepped in.

The tub began to fill because the drain was clogged with hair, and cockroaches floated around my feet.

There wasn't any shampoo, just a bar of green soap covered in a brownish film. Dustin told me not to use it. I wasn't going to anyway.

We kissed under the spray, and he slid his hands up and down the sides of my stomach and around my boobs.

"You're so beautiful," he said and held my face.

My hands were on his stomach, touching the muscles that stuck out of his skin. I moved to his chest and then his arms.

His fingers went between my legs and poked inside me. I was high and not really horny, but his fingers felt smooth, and the water made me wet.

He was hard and I rubbed it, and tugged, and turned around so it pressed against my ass. I bent over, holding the edge of the tub. Black ants crawled near my hands, and I flipped my hair over my shoulder so they wouldn't crawl up to my head.

He gently slid in. I was loud, moaning and saying his name, and he pumped faster. But he never stopped caressing the sensitive skin on my butt, and he reached around to squeeze my nipples.

From his pounding, my hands slipped from the greasy edge, and he caught me before I fell in the bath of cockroaches. He picked me up and turned me around, wrapping my legs around his waist and my arms around his neck, and we kissed. The muscles I'd touched just minutes before were holding all my weight as he stroked at the same time.

His body shook when he came. His arms tightened around me. I didn't come, but being so close to him was as good as coming.

"You want to get out of here?" he asked, brushing his lips over mine again.

The water had turned cold, but I wasn't.

I squeezed his neck so he wouldn't let me go. And he didn't. He stepped out of the shower and set me on the counter, standing in front of me with my legs and arms still around him.

"Baby," he said, "we need to find some place to live."

I knew where I wanted to live and that was by Claire. I missed her and hadn't talked to her since my last day at the hospital. Frankie would probably have a room we could rent, and Dustin had enough money for at least a week's stay.

"There's a hotel on—"

"Wherever you want," he said. "I'll move anywhere with you."

Since Richard didn't have any towels, Dustin dried me off with handfuls of toilet paper and helped me get dressed. He put my clothes on much slower than he'd taken them off. And when his clothes were back on too, we took the train to Massachusetts Avenue.

Frankie was sitting at the desk, and he eyed up Dustin when I asked if he had any rooms. He said he had one on the first floor. Dustin paid for a week, and Frankie held out his hand with the key. I went to grab it, and Frankie's fingers closed around mine.

"You're looking good," he said.

I'd gained a few pounds in rehab since they fed me three meals a day.

Dustin leaned over the countertop and stopped only inches from Frankie's face. "Give her the key. Now."

Frankie turned towards me and let go. "If you ever need Sunshine's discount, you just let me know," he said.

I thanked him and we went to our room.

"Who's Sunshine and what's her discount?" Dustin asked. He was sitting on the bed, flipping through the TV stations.

He didn't know I was a hooker. He'd never asked how I'd made my dope money, but I figured he just assumed.

"Sunshine's my old roommate, she lives on the fourth floor."

"She screw him for free rent?"

"Something like that."

"Have you?"

"No," I lied.

"She's a hooker, right?"

I nodded and asked how he knew. He told me all hookers named themselves Sunshine.

I always thought Sunshine was her real name. Even in the hospital, the nurses had called her Sunshine.

"So you were a hooker too?"

He was still looking at the TV and had settled on a movie. The scene was familiar, but I couldn't think what movie it was.

"I was," I said.

His gaze shifted to me. "That's some nasty shit," he said. "I don't want you ever doing it again, you hear me? I'll take care of you."

He'd probably think carrying some John's baby for eleven weeks and causing my own abortion were nasty too. I guess I could never tell him, which also meant he couldn't find out about the deal I'd made with Richard.

I sat next to him on the bed and rested my head on his shoulder.

"You ever fuck Richard?" he asked.

I pulled back and looked him in the eyes. "No."

"Are you lying to me?"

"No, I swear, he's never touched me."

"Good, because I'm not sharing any more women with him."

I thought of Sierra and Erin, and the way they'd looked at Dustin.

"I don't want you going over to Richard's either. I'll get you plenty of dope, just stay away from his house."

But I needed to go to Richard's one more time. Before Dustin and I had left his house, Richard cornered me in the hallway and told me he hadn't forgotten about our deal. I had to work something out with him, and make him promise to keep quiet.

Dustin left me the next morning to do a run, so I went upstairs to Sunshine's room. She answered the door wearing a long t-shirt.

"Can't say I'm surprised to see you," she said.

I took a seat on the couch and she sat down next to me.

"Did you just get out?" she asked.

I told her about Dustin and how we'd stayed at Richard's the night we left rehab and checked into the hotel yesterday. Her back went straight when I said Richard's name like I'd pinched a nerve. I'd said his name so many times in the past, but maybe I'd just never noticed her reaction before.

There was a reason I'd come to her room before Claire's. Even if she didn't want to talk about it, I still had to ask. "What happened between you two?"

She went over to the bed and fumbled with her purse until she found her dope. "I told you, he beat—"

"No, why did he do it?"

"Shit, I don't work for free," she said. "If he wanted a piece of me, he had to pay up, but he didn't like that answer."

That was what had caused him to snap? She had said no to sex, and he beat and raped her? Damn, Sunshine didn't deserve that. Heather wasn't kidding when she said Richard had a bad temper.

"You watched me go to his house every day," I said. "And never once did you warn me about what he did to you. How dare—"

"I'm a junkie, what do you want from me?"

"Richard could have beat the shit out of me too, and it would have been your fault," I said.

"I'm sorry, but you would have done the same thing."

She was probably right.

Before she stuck in the needle, I told her to stop going to Roxbury. I said if she gave her money to Dustin every morning, he'd get her dope from Richard.

And when she shot up, I left.

I knocked on Claire's door, and she opened it with a blank expression. Then her eyes squinted like she was trying to figure out who I was.

I waited a few seconds and said, "Claire, it's me."

"Why aren't you in rehab?"

She stood in the middle of the doorway and didn't invite me in.

"I met someone and we left together. I want you to meet him, his name is Dustin, and—"

"You left after a week? For a boy?" she asked. "Are you sober?"

She knew the answer, so I didn't know why she asked.

"I was, I—"

"Then I don't have anything to say to you."

She started to close the door, and I stuck my hand in the doorway. "Claire, I've missed you, that's why I came back to the hotel. I'm living downstairs with Dustin and..."

She looked at the floor.

"Claire?"

"You promised me," she said. "Promised and promised that you were going to get sober."

I had promised my parents and Michael too. And the baby.

"I love you, Nicole, like a daughter," she said. "But I can only take so much."

"Claire, wait."

"You've broken my heart for the last time." The door shut in my face.

Maybe I shouldn't have left rehab.

I went to my room and shot five bags. And four hours later, I shot six more.

I remembered Heather telling me that the squatters did most of their runs at night. So when Dustin left the next afternoon to go to Providence, I went to Richard's after dark. When I opened the front door, Shank was on the couch, sitting between Sierra and Erin.

"What's up, Nicole," Shank said.

I'd been spotted. It was too late to back out.

The twins were dressed in bras and panties. They were touching themselves, squeezing their nipples, rubbing their crotches, and moaning. Shank's Mohawk swished from right to left like he was watching a tennis match.

"Have any of you seen Heather?" I asked.

One of the twins stopped pinching her nipple long enough to point to the back of the house, and I slipped into Richard's bedroom. Heather wasn't in there, which was good. I didn't want her to know about our deal either.

Richard was lying on the air mattress and through the white sheet, I could see he was naked. I stared at his lighter-shaped penis and the black bush around it. That was the dick that had raped Sunshine.

His hands moved to his dick and scratched. Those fingers, scarred and filthy, had beaten her.

"Coming to pay back your debt?" he asked. He sat up as if he was getting ready for something.

"Richard, we can't. I'm with Dustin now, and you're with Heather. You know it's not a good idea."

His body didn't move, but his lips were almost pouting.

I told him I'd pay back the three hundred, plus another hundred for interest. I said I needed a couple weeks and then we'd be even, our old deal forgotten and to never be mentioned again, especially to Heather or Dustin.

He didn't say anything.

"Are we good?" I asked.

He nodded his head just as coke-head Cale came bolting into Richard's room. "We have a problem," he said.

Richard shot out of bed and reached for his clothes.

"It's not the cops," Cale said. "It's Heather, you need to see this."

The three of us rushed down the hall to the far bedroom. We pushed through the doorway past Shank, Sierra, and Erin. Heather was sitting on a mattress with a knife in her hand, cutting all the skin off her arm. She was singing, "Bugs, bugs go away, come again another day."

Blood was pouring out of her arm, chunks of skin lying on the bed. She was having a meth psychosis, and if we didn't get her to the hospital, she'd bleed to death.

"Someone call 9-1-1," I said.

Everyone just stared, and Heather continued to cut and sing.

"Richard, do something," I said.

Richard shook his head. "We've got to get her to the street, the cops can't come here," he said.

He started barking orders. Sierra took away the knife, and Erin wrapped Heather's arm in a trash bag. Tiffany called 9-1-1 and reported Heather's location. Once everyone had an assignment, they all began to move. And when Shank and Cale carried Heather out the front door to leave her on the corner, I followed behind them and went to the train station.

When I got home, I buried myself in bed. Even after I shot up, I could see Heather holding that knife, gushing blood, and chopping her skin. She'd lost a lot of blood, and I didn't know if she even made it to the hospital. I called Mass General and asked if she was there. Without her last name, they said they wouldn't give me any information. I called Boston Medical and Brigham and Women's, but they wouldn't tell me anything either. I didn't have Richard's cell phone number, and I couldn't call Dustin and ask him for it.

At least since heroin didn't produce psychoses, it wasn't as scary as meth. But Eric's lips had turned blue, and he'd foamed at the mouth before he died. Sunshine was blue and foaming when Claire had found her, and I'd overdosed too. Maybe dope was just as scary.

I wasn't asleep for more than twenty minutes when I heard Dustin come home. The door slammed, the springs in the mattress squeaked, and then he was on top of me. With my eyes closed, I waited to feel his lips on my neck and his hands on my tits.

My eyes shot open when I felt his hands clamp my neck, his thumb pressing on my windpipe. His lips were pulled back over his teeth, and he was snarling like a pit bull.

I couldn't breathe.

"What the fuck did I tell you," he shouted. "You fucking whore, why didn't you listen to me?"

I should have expected this. But with all the drama that happened at Richard's, I didn't think the squatters would even remember I was there. The twins. Those bitches wanted Dustin and ratted me out.

I reached for his hands and tried to pull them off my neck. "I'm sorry…"

His fist whipped across my face. My eye socket pounded with pain, and I let out a cry.

I tasted blood seeping down my nose and onto my lips.

His arm went back, preparing to swing again.

"I just wanted to say goodbye to Heather," I said. "She's my friend and I knew I wouldn't see her again."

"I would have taken you there. Why didn't you just ask me?"

"I…"

The snarl changed to a look of remorse. "Why did you make me hurt you?"

"I'm sorry, I'm so sorry."

"I want to be with you forever," he said. "But if Richard ever touched you, we'd be done, don't you get that?"

He threw the comforter off me. "I need to know you're mine."

He yanked off his clothes and got between my legs. While he moved on top of me, he held my face. He wiped the blood from my nose and kissed the skin around my eye.

"All I've got is love for you," he said quietly.

He moved in and out, and up and down.

"So much love," he said, his voice deep.

His breathing turned heavy, and then his body went limp on top of mine.

In that moment, two things were decided. Once I gave Richard the money, I'd never lie to Dustin again. He loved me and wanted to protect me. I couldn't be mad at him for that. And I was going to be with him forever too.

Dustin was gone all the time doing runs. Sunshine was never home anymore since she'd met some guy and was at his place when she wasn't tricking. Claire wanted nothing to do with me, so I spent my days in our room with nothing but TV and heroin. And at night, I sat in the hallway outside Claire's room with my back against her door, talking out loud and hoping she was listening. I told her about

Dustin, how much he loved me and took care of me. I talked about Heather and how she was admitted to the psych ward after the doctors repaired her arm. I told her I missed her. She never came out of her room, but I could hear her sniffling on the other side of the door. Just knowing she was there was enough. Sometimes I'd fall asleep there, and Dustin would carry me down to our room. He'd tell me I didn't need Claire, I had him, and I should leave her alone. But I couldn't. I'd never leave Claire.

After two weeks of not leaving the hotel, I went for a walk. The hotel was sucking all the air out of me. I headed down Massachusetts Avenue, to where Sunshine and I had tricked and the place where I'd been shot.

I owed Richard four hundred dollars and didn't know how I was going to get the cash. Dustin gave me money for food, but if I didn't eat, I'd end up in the hospital again. I couldn't trick with Sunshine because I'd promised Dustin I'd never do it again. Boosting was my only option. So while I walked, I searched through every trash bin on the next four blocks and returned the items on the receipts.

I boosted for a couple hours each night and hid the money in the back of our toilet. If Dustin ever found the cash, I'd tell him I was saving for an apartment, a place of our own we could fill with furniture and framed pictures of the two of us. But an apartment that wasn't too far away. I still needed to be close to Claire even if she wouldn't let me in her room or talk to me through her door. And once I paid off Richard, that's what I'd save for. Dustin couldn't be angry with me for that. He'd never told me not to leave the hotel, he just didn't want me at Richard's.

But he did get angry—not because he'd found the cash—because he didn't think I should be sleeping outside Claire's door. He'd been finding me there asleep for weeks, and he snapped one night after carrying me home.

He set me on the bed and stood in front of me with his hands on his hips. "How can she be so important when she won't even let you in her room?"

I wrapped my arms around my knees and rocked.

He kicked the trash bucket and punched a hole in the wall by the fridge.

Had something gone wrong during his run? He couldn't be this mad because I was sleeping outside Claire's door.

"She's my best friend," I said.

"What if Frankie found you there passed out?" he asked. "I'm sure that scumbag would love to put his hands all over you."

Frankie had keys to every room in the hotel. He could stop by anytime when Dustin wasn't home and put his hands on me. But if I said that to Dustin, we'd be moving out tonight.

"Is Claire more important than me?" he asked.

He didn't need to keep bringing Claire into this. I knew what would happen if another guy touched me.

"I won't fall asleep there anymore," I said.

He stopped kicking. There wasn't much left of the trashcan anyway, the plastic bucket was in pieces. He didn't believe me. Dope made me tired, so it was hard not to fall asleep when I was up there talking to her.

"I promise," I said. "When I get tired I'll come back to our room."

He sat on the edge of the bed by my feet. "I wish you'd just leave her alone."

"I'll never leave her and don't ask me to. Claire's old and she needs me—"

"She won't even let you in."

"I'm going to keep going to her room until she does," I said.

I crawled under the covers, burying everything but my eyes. He got under too and our backs faced.

Just as I was about to fall asleep, he cuddled behind me. "I'm sorry," he said.

I wasn't going to apologize. He could set any other rule he wanted, but not one that had to do with Claire.

"I just want you to be careful. There's a lot of shady people in this hotel, and if something ever happened to you..."

I'd won. But he'd made his point very clear. If I ever fell asleep there again, we'd be moving out of the hotel, and Claire would be added to the list along with no tricking and no going to Richard's house.

"You know, someday we're going to get out of here and you're going to have to leave Claire," he said.

I rolled over to look at him. "What do you mean?"

"Don't you want to quit all this shit and start a family?"

The only way we could stop using was if we left Boston. Dustin knew that too, that's why he said we had to get out of here. And that was exactly what I wanted—moving far away from our dope connections, living in a little house on the beach with kids running around. But what about Claire? Maybe Dustin would let me bring her too.

"Of course I do, I want that more than anything," I said.

"I just need some time," he said. "We need a car and a place to live, and we won't be able to work while we detox, so I need to save for all that."

I wasn't going to put all this on him. By tomorrow night, I'd have enough to pay off Richard, and then I'd boost to save money for our move.

I took my clothes off and kissed his soft lips, and he pulled me on top of him.

When we'd had sex in the past, I'd always been so high I couldn't come. And before I'd met Dustin, Casey was the only other person who had gotten me off. None of the guys had known how to make me come, or didn't care enough to, or the heroin wouldn't let me. But tonight I'd slept off my high outside Claire's door.

As I rode him, he rubbed my clit, and I felt a surge of tingles inside my crotch. The build-up was much more intense than when I fingered myself, and I shuddered and collapsed on top of him.

He told me how wet I was and how much that turned him on, and he flipped me onto my back and got on top of me. He bit my lower lip while he moved in and out, and then shuddered like I had. After he came, he held me in his arms and said he'd never felt like this with any of the other girl he'd been with. I felt the same, and it wasn't because Dustin was the first guy to make me come. It was because he was perfect for me.

The next night, I left the hotel earlier than usual to boost so I could spend a few hours at Claire's door before I got sleepy. But boosting took longer than normal. Most of the receipts I found were drenched with slop. And when I finally had one I could use, the cashier wanted to give me a store credit instead of cash. I had to speak to a manager.

I knew I was cutting it close. Dustin said he'd be home by ten, and the clock behind the register said seven minutes before ten. Dustin would check Claire's door, and if I wasn't there, he'd come looking for me. But I needed this money. With the seven dollars I'd get from the return, I'd have the four hundred to pay Richard back.

I left the store and I ran as fast as I could to the hotel. A block away from home, I saw smoke and specks of ash, and smelled fire. People on the street were shouting. Red and blue lights from the ambulances and police cars flickered across the buildings across the street.

I didn't know what building was on fire, but whichever one it was, it was on the same block as the hotel.

I pushed my way through swarms of people, and on the corner, I saw the smoke, and flames shooting through the windows of the third and fourth floors of the hotel.

Claire.

Dustin grabbed me before I got to the front door. "Where have you been?" he shouted. "I almost died looking for you." I could barely hear him over all the screaming.

"Is Claire out here," I said, searching the crowd, scanning each head for her gray hair. "Where's Claire?"

"They're getting everyone out," Dustin said. "They'll get her out too."

Frankie joined us on the sidewalk. His face and hands were covered in soot. "Got the first two floors evacuated," he said.

"What about the fourth floor?" I asked.

"The fire's bad up there," Frankie said.

"Are they looking for Claire?"

Frankie shrugged his shoulders. "I think so," he said.

The firefighters pushed us off the sidewalk to spray with their long hoses. Three firefighters came out the front door with four of the residents. Two I recognized from the third floor.

"Get all the men out," someone yelled.

"Chief, the men are out," a firefighter shouted back.

And not ten seconds later, the top two floors caved inward and crashed onto the second floor. Burning wood flew through the air. People began to scream and run across the street. The firemen hosed off the burning ambers that sparked on the sidewalk.

I stood still, staring at what used to be the fourth floor, Claire's home. And now she was part of the burning rubble.

The last thing Claire had said to me was I had broken her heart.

CHAPTER NINETEEN

Once the fire was out, the crowd cleared. The other residents had mumbled about finding hotels nearby to rent or going to the shelter. Dustin, Sunshine, and I were the only stragglers left. Frankie was around too, talking to the cops and filling out paperwork.

We sat on the sidewalk across the street, looking at what was left of the hotel: the frame, charcoaled pieces of furniture, planks of wood from the first floor.

My elbows rested on my bent knees, my butt ground into the hard pavement. But I couldn't feel my body or the cold air that whipped past me.

Sunshine cried over losing all her clothes. Frankie yelled about the fine the city was going to slap him with because the sprinklers weren't up to code. Dustin wanted to know where I'd been when the fire started.

Did the clothes and the fine, and three hundred and ninety-three dollars I'd stashed behind the toilet really matter?

My best friend was dead.

Claire was a kind high I couldn't get from shooting. She came into my life to show me love and tried to teach me there was more to live for besides a needle and a bag of dope. Even though I was an addict, losing her only made me want to use more. Maybe I should have listened to her.

Sunshine, Dustin, and I checked into a new hotel, a few blocks down from Frankie's. Dustin let Sunshine live with us. She came home every afternoon with clothes she bought at Goodwill and rebuilt her wardrobe. At night, she worked the streets and saved enough for her own room. After a week, she moved down the hall.

She probably made a deal with Lucchi, the hotel owner. I didn't know.

Ten days after the fire, I still hadn't left our room. I hadn't showered either. Dustin complained I was like a dead fish in bed and he had to do all the work. But he never said anything about how bad I smelled.

The fire hadn't slowed Dustin down, he took off every afternoon and came back late at night. Sunshine broke up with her man and started dating a new one, and worked the same schedule as she always had. And then there was me, replaying that whole night in my head, cursing the seven bucks that cost me Claire's life. If I hadn't gone boosting, I would have been home when the fire started. I would have gotten Claire out of the hotel, and she'd still be alive.

Since I couldn't go to Claire's room and rest against her door, I talked out loud like she was sitting next to me. I had full conversations, and in my mind, I heard her answer and saw her face. So when she asked me to visit Henry for her, I did.

Like Claire and I had done two and a half years ago, I sat in the visiting room and watched all the prisoners come in through the double-locked doors. When I saw Henry, I waved. His hair was a little grayer and he walked with care, nursing his limp. His amber eyes were just like Claire's.

He sat down across from me and asked how I'd been doing since the fire. I told him I'd moved into a new hotel. The mattress was just as lumpy as our bed at Frankie's, and the TV had to be kicked because some of the stations had bad reception.

"How are you really doing?" he asked.

"I'm sad."

But he already knew that. He probably also knew about my fight with Claire over leaving rehab.

"She was sad too," Henry said.

"That's my fault," I said. "I let her down."

"That's addiction for you, constant let-downs and never-ending promises. Don't you think I let her down too?"

He had years to apologize for his mistakes. Claire died with a broken heart I'd caused.

There was a woman at the next table placing her newborn baby in the arms of a prisoner. The baby was tiny against his broad chest, and the pink blanket clashed with his orange jumpsuit.

"That's the first time he's held his daughter," Henry said.

Henry was looking at the couple too.

"How do you know?" I asked.

"That's Vic, my celly, doing two years on a drug charge," he said. "He came to prison a few weeks ago, and his girlfriend was nine months pregnant."

I thought of my baby and the pink blood that had swirled around the drain while I showered off my miscarriage. And then the last time Claire had held me in her arms.

"She listened to you, you know, on the other side of her door," he said. "She listened to everything you said."

The buzzer went off, and the other inmates stood, saying goodbye to their visitors.

Henry and I stood too. There was a gold band on his ring finger and he took it off. "I want you to have this," he said and placed it in my hand.

The band looked old and was scratched. I held it up in the air to read the engraving on the inside: a date and the word "love."

"It was my dad's wedding band," he said. "Mom gave it to me when I got sober in prison. I want you to get sober and wear it for Claire."

I put the ring in my pocket and gave Henry a hug.

"Make her proud," he said in my ear and then pulled away. "Before it's too late."

I didn't say anything. I didn't even nod my head. He turned around and walked through the double doors.

On my way home, I stopped by Sunshine's room. The only time I saw her was when she dropped off her money or picked up her dope, and she never stayed long enough to talk.

I knocked on her door and waited a few seconds, but she didn't answer.

Halfway to my room, someone shouted, "Hey you."

I turned around, and a girl was poking her head out from Sunshine's room. The overhead light was flickering so I couldn't see her face.

"Did you knock?" she asked.

The girl's voice was strangely familiar.

"I was looking for Sunshine," I said.

"Come back, I'll wake her."

The girl was standing at the foot of the bed yelling Sunshine's name, and I leaned against the door, staring at her back, and trying to place her voice. New York-ish accent, raspy tone. Her black hair was dreaded.

No, it couldn't be.

She turned and faced me. "Sorry, Sunshine's knocked out—"

Renee looked exactly the same, but her baby bump was gone. It had been years, of course the bump was gone.

"Holy shit, Nicole is that you?"

"What are you doing in Sunshine's room?" I asked.

"I live here."

I pressed my fingers against the door to stop them from shaking. "Since when?"

"I met her on the streets a couple weeks ago, she needed someone to cover half the rent," she said. "How do you know Sunshine?"

"I moved in with her after you left me stranded in McDonald's."

The next time Sunshine dropped off her money, I'd have to warn her about Renee. If Sunshine was looking for a permanent roommate, Renee wasn't that person.

"Sunshine always talks about a Nicole," she said. "But I had no idea it was you, girl."

"Funny, she's never talked about you," I said.

She smiled and then opened her mouth to say something but stopped and walked over to the coffee table. She took a bundle out of a red purse.

"You want some?" she asked. "It's real good."

I walked into the room and handed her the rig from my pocket and took a seat on the couch.

For leaving me at McDonald's with no money or dope, she owed me this shot. And more.

"Who's your dealer?" I asked.

"Jose, Que's cousin."

She told me Que and Raul had each gotten fifteen-year sentences, and since they'd been in jail, Jose had taken over their business.

"Where's your baby?" I asked.

There weren't any toys in the room and none of the clothes on the floor looked small enough to fit a kid.

"With my mom," she said. "But hell, you probably guessed that would happen. I'm no mother."

"No, I thought you'd give the baby to Mark."

She laughed so hard, she almost dropped the spoon. "You should have seen Mark's face in the delivery room when Mason came out, looking just like Que."

Poor kid. I didn't know what was worse, having Renee as your mom or having your dad in prison.

She gave me back the loaded rig and held hers up in the air, clinking it against mine.

"To old times," she said.

And we both shot up.

Spending all my time in my hotel room talking to Claire wasn't helping me get over her death. It was turning me into a crazy. So when Renee stopped by and asked if I wanted to go for a walk, I said yes. And quickly, our walks turned into an everyday thing, like when she'd been pregnant. Mostly, she did all the talking. She'd tell me how Que and Raul were doing in jail and how she was going to marry Que in prison once the warden approved the ceremony. With good behavior, she said he'd be out in eight or nine years. She'd take Mason back from her mom, and they'd be a family.

"Does Que know you hook?" I asked one day while we were sitting in the park. We were on a bench, watching kids slide down what was left of the snow banks.

She'd been working the track with Sunshine every night. And Sunshine said Renee did overnighters with her clients too, staying in their hotel rooms, doing gangbangs, and S&M shit.

"I need to make money," she said. "I don't have a Dustin to take care of me."

Dustin had only met Renee once, but he liked that I had someone to hang out with. Once Renee and I had started going for walks, I showered every day, and in bed, I got on top and rode him like I had before the fire.

She got up from the bench, and we walked through the Back Bay. She turned down a street I'd never been on and climbed up the steps of one of the townhouses.

"What are you doing?" I asked as she knocked on the front door.

"I need to re-up."

"Jose lives here?"

"He couldn't move into Que's old place," she said.

Dominick, a friend of Que and Raul's, answered the door. Renee walked past him, and I stayed on the sidewalk.

He pointed at me. "Look who we have here, Raul's boo," he said. "I was just talking to Jose about you."

I wasn't Raul's anything.

And I really shouldn't be here. If Dustin found out I was at another dealer's house, he'd be pissed.

"Jose, come see who's here," Dominick yelled.

Jose came to the door. His soul patch had grown since the last time I'd seen him and now hung to his chest in a braid. "Damn girl, never thought I'd see you again," he said. "Aren't you gonna come in?"

A woman and her little white dog had been walking towards me on the sidewalk, but she turned around when Jose came out.

I'd stay for a just a couple minutes, and if Renee didn't want to go, I'd leave without her.

I followed Jose inside, and Renee was sitting on one of the couches with Federico, another cousin of Que and Raul's. Federico looked just like Raul with a teardrop tattoo under his eye, but he was much shorter and had a barbell pierced at the end of each eyebrow.

On the coffee table was a mound of little baggies with a pill in each of them. Federico opened five of the bags and chopped up the pills with a razor blade.

I sat on the other couch between Jose and Dominick.

"There's a rave in Worcester tomorrow night," Dominick said to me. "You should come with us."

"Renee's coming, aren't you, girl," Federico said.

"You know I wouldn't miss it," Renee said.

Federico separated the powder into lines and snorted one. Jose and Dominick each did a line too.

Dominick handed me the straw. "Roll with us," he said.

I thought of Dustin.

"I can't, we've got to go, Renee just came for some dope," I said.

"Nicole, we've got time to do some E," Renee said.

The shot I'd done that morning was wearing off. Even if I shot up again, it would only get me straight. But ecstasy would get me high for at least four hours. And an E high was pretty damn good.

I took the straw from Dominick and snorted the line. When I was done, I handed it to Renee.

She shook her head. "Can't, my nose is all fucked up from snorting dope," she said. "Federico, give me one of the pills."

She brought the pill into the kitchen and I heard her run the faucet.

Jose rolled three blunts and we smoked them while we waited for the E to kick in. At first, I felt heaviness in my chest from the weed. Then slowly, I stepped out of my body like I was watching myself from the outside. That was the E coming on. And when I re-entered, my skin craved to be touched. I ran my fingers up and down my neck and around my ears.

Renee turned up the music. The vibration of the base shook my muscles, tickled and rubbed my joints.

Jose blacked out the windows with sheets and shut off the lights. He cracked glow sticks and danced on top of the coffee table, tracing patterns in the air. Pink and green and blue rays, swirling like a kaleidoscope.

Dominick touched my arm. My skin was water and his fingers were fish.

I touched his arm. My fingers wriggled and glided across his silky skin and the roughness of his arm hair. My hands moved to his head and swept across his cornrows. The texture sent sparks through my body.

My feet slipped out of my sneakers. My toes spread and crossed.

My teeth needed to bite, and my tongue wanted to lick. My head bent down to Dominick's hand and I slid one of his fingers into my mouth. His skin was the best thing I'd ever tasted. My teeth grinded his finger, my tongue flicked his nail and circled around his cuticle. He rubbed and tugged my knuckle with his teeth.

The glow sticks darkened to red, navy, and forest green, and the CD was skipping.

I was coming down, swallowed in the corner cushions of the leather couch with my toes in Dominick's mouth and my fingers rubbing my own head.

Jose got off the table, turned off the stereo, and flipped on the light.

My gums were sore from Dominick's nails, and my jaw was tight from chewing his finger, but I wanted to roll again.

In the lit-up room, Dominick released my toes from his mouth, and Federico pulled his hand out of his pants.

The spot on the couch where Renee had been sitting was empty.

"Where's Renee?" I asked through clenched teeth.

"Bathroom," Federico said.

The clock on the cable box showed it was just past four. What felt like only minutes were really several hours. Still, I had plenty of time before Dustin would be home.

"Let's do another pill," I said.

Federico crushed four more pills and set a whole one aside for Renee. He bent his head to snort the line, but stopped when Jose said, "How long has Renee been in the bathroom?"

Federico shrugged his shoulders. "She said she wasn't feeling good."

"I'll go check on her," I said. "Where's the bathroom?"

Jose pointed towards the kitchen. "First door on the left."

My toes were wet from Dominick's spit, and they slid on the wood floors.

I knocked on the bathroom door, and when Renee didn't answer, I jiggled the knob. The door swung open, but she wasn't inside.

I went back to the couch. "She's not in the bathroom."

"When did you see her get up?" Jose asked Federico.

"Don't know, seemed like just a couple minutes ago," Federico said.

The guys all looked at each other, and Federico said something in Spanish. Jose took off up the stairs to the second floor. When he came back, he was out of breath. "She's not in the bedrooms." He walked into the kitchen and opened the back door to check the porch. "The pill's still here," he said. "She never took it."

The rest of us went in the kitchen too. Renee's water glass was in the sink. Full. And the pill was on the counter.

Jose pointed to the closed door next to the bathroom. "She wouldn't go down there," he said. "So where'd she go?"

"What's down there?" I asked.

"If she did go down there, we would have heard the dogs," Dominick said.

"The music was too loud to hear anything," Federico said.

"What dogs?" I asked.

Jose opened the door and raced down the wooden steps. "Motherfucker."

Dominick and Federico flew down the stairs, and I followed and stopped on the bottom step. Three pit bulls sat in the middle of the room, chomping on steak bones. Trash bags were placed in circles around the basement floor, and there were gaps where it looked like some of bags were missing.

Jose counted the bags in each circle. "We're missing two bags," he said, standing by one of the gaps. "Two fucking bags and none of us saw her leave?" Spanish came pouring from his mouth so fast I only caught random words. Heroin. Set up. Kill.

Jose ran to the steps and his hands clamped my throat. "Where the fuck did she go?"

"I don't know." And I didn't.

His shoulder jabbed into my stomach and he lifted me, folding me over his back.

"I don't know anything," I shouted. He carried me up the stairs and threw me on the couch.

Dominick stood behind me, holding my shoulders. Federico sat beside me and cuffed my hands. And Jose stood between my legs, pointing a gun at my chest.

"I'll blow your fucking face off if you don't start talking," Jose said.

"We went for a walk and she brought me here," I said. "She told me she needed to re-up, that's all I know."

"What was in her backpack?" Federico asked.

"I don't know," I said. "She always carries one."

The guys talked more in Spanish.

The steaks were in her backpack, I thought. That bitch had set me up. She had waited for all of us to start rolling, fed the dogs the meat so she could grab the bags, and slipped out the back door without anyone hearing her. She knew the guys would be bagging the pills for the rave tomorrow night.

"Whose idea was it to roll?" I asked.

"Renee's," Federico said. "She asked me before any of you guys even sat down."

"Don't you see, she had the whole thing planned out," I said.

"And what about you?" Jose asked.

"Do you think I'd still be here if I was in on her plan?"

Jose straddled my legs and pressed the gun against my temple. "Tell me everything, where she lives, who she's working for, and I might let you get out of here alive."

When Dustin came home, I was in the bathroom, squeezed between the shower and toilet. My eye was swollen from where Jose had hit me with the gun, and my nose wouldn't stop bleeding.

"Where's my girl," Dustin yelled from the bedroom.

I buried my head between my knees and undid my ponytail so my hair covered the bruises on my neck.

"Are you sick?" He crouched in front of me and lifted my chin with his fingers. "What happened, baby?"

For the past hour, I'd come up with excuses for why my face was so swollen and bloody—I had gotten jumped in the street or Renee had beaten me for drugs. But none of those lies would get me out of the trouble I was in. Jose knew where I lived, and he knew Dustin ran drugs. And he had said if I didn't find Renee and have her return the bags, he was going to kill Dustin and me.

I took a deep breath, and the whole story came out. When I got to the part where Jose bashed the gun across my face, Dustin punched the wall by the shower.

"I'm going to fucking kill him," he yelled. "No one touches you but me."

It was a good thing I'd skipped the part where Dominick and I were sucking each other's fingers.

"I'm so sorry," I said. "I shouldn't have even gone inside their house, this is all my fault."

He paced between the bedroom and bathroom. "Do you remember where they live?"

I nodded.

He grabbed my arm and lifted me up.

"Where are we going?" I asked. He pulled me down the hallway and out the front of the hotel. His fingers were clamped so tightly my skin was bruising.

"You're going to show me their house," he said. "And then I'm going to take you somewhere safe."

The van Dustin used for his runs was at Richard's, so we took a taxi to Jose's neighborhood, and Dustin asked the driver to pull over at the corner of Jose's street. I pointed out the townhouse, and Dustin said to wait in the car while he checked it out. He came back after several minutes and gave the driver an address in Southie.

"Who lives in Southie?" I asked.

He dialed a number on his cell phone. "You home?" he asked the person on the other end. "I'll be there in fifteen."

"Dustin, who lives in Southie?"

"Shut up," he shouted. "I need to think."

Dustin had said he was going to kill Jose, but I hoped he wasn't serious. Jose was a member of the same gang Raul and Que were in.

Jose carried a gun, and his teardrop tattoo meant he'd killed someone.

I tried to warn Dustin, but he wouldn't listen. He said he'd heard of Jose's gang, but his was just as tough and had more people. I didn't know Dustin was a gang member. I also didn't think he carried a gun.

The taxi pulled up to a house, and Dustin told me to get out.

"I'll be right back," he said to the driver.

He clamped my arm again and pulled me up the front steps. The outside light was on, and a guy was standing in front of the screen door. He opened it, and we both went inside.

"This is my girl, don't let anything happen to her while I'm gone," Dustin said to the guy and the woman who was in the kitchen. "I'll be back later to pick her up."

He turned me around so my back faced the couple. "There's enough here so you won't be sick," he whispered, slipping a few bags and a rig into my pocket.

"Where are you going?" I asked.

"I need to take care of this mess."

I told him to be careful and kissed him. He kissed me back, but his lips were stiff and he pulled away too soon.

I watched him run down the steps and get in the backseat of the taxi.

"Can I get you something to drink?" the woman asked as the cab drove away.

My eyes shifted between the guy and the woman, wondering who they were and how long I'd have to stay here. I wished Dustin had taken me with him. If he got killed because of me, I'd never forgive myself.

"Come on," the woman said, putting her arm around my shoulder. "Let's get you a drink."

She brought me into the kitchen, and I sat at the table while she opened cupboards and filled glasses with some light brown liquor.

The heroin had long worn off, and my stomach was queasy from withdrawal and the E I'd taken. The liquor burned my throat as it went down.

"You want some ice for your eye?" she asked.

I shook my head, and she took the seat across from me, tapping her glass with her long red fingernails.

"You must be the reason why my brother left rehab," she said.

She had the same icy blue eyes as Dustin, and her blond hair looked stiff from hairspray.

The guy stood in the kitchen, his bald head leaning on the side of the doorway. Under his wife-beater was a chest full of hair, and his stomach flopped over the waist of his jeans.

"That's Dale, my husband," she said. "And I'm Lexy."

"I'm Nicole."

"Dustin do that to your face?" he asked.

"No," I said.

"You guys in a lot of trouble?" he asked.

"I don't—"

"Your brother can't be getting us involved with his shit," he said to Lexy. "My parole officer will have my ass back in jail if she finds out I'm messing—"

"Relax, Dale. No one's going to tell your parole officer nothing," she said.

He poured himself a drink.

"Ignore him," she said. "He's been a little edgy since he quit drinking."

He downed the full glass and poured a second one.

"So what did my brother do this time?"

Her nails tapped the table, and Dale turned around, his cheeks puffed full of booze until he swallowed.

I asked if I could use her bathroom, and she told me it was at the top of the stairs. The door didn't have a lock, so I sat with my back against it and cooked up.

I closed my eyes, wishing for a nod. The dope was good, but my tolerance was too high.

Dale opened the bathroom door twenty minutes later. I pretended to be asleep, and he carried me down the stairs and set me on the couch, grabbing my butt before pulling his hands away. I stayed like that for hours, lying on the couch so I wouldn't have to answer Lexy's questions.

They bickered over waking me up and going to the store for more booze, and Dale's parole officer testing him for alcohol. But their fighting didn't last long because Dale passed out in his chair. While he snored, Lexy made phone calls and painted her nails. She gossiped with a friend about Dustin and me, and then yelled at her mom. She asked for rent money and from the sounds of it, her mom said no.

Lexy went upstairs and returned with another bottle of liquor. She watched some shopping show that was selling jewelry and bought two rings and a necklace. She polished off that bottle just as the sun began to trickle through the blinds and then made coffee and fried up some eggs.

"Eat up," she said, slapping Dale on the back of the head.

He snorted and almost fell off his chair. "It's morning already?"

"You were supposed to be watching her and slept the whole damn night instead," she said.

"She's knocked out too, can't watch a sleeping person," he said.

Just as I was about to go to the bathroom and use, Dustin came through the front door. I jumped off the couch and hugged him. "What happened?" I asked.

My face hurt worse than it had last night, and I couldn't open my right eye.

"It's taken care of," he said.

He handed Lexy a small wad of cash. "Thanks for helping me out."

She had the money counted before Dustin had even said thanks.

"She slept the whole time," Lexy said. "You giving her some strong shit?"

"Don't worry about it," Dustin said.

"I've got a right to worry when she's doing that crap in my house."

"I just paid your rent," Dustin said, pointing to the cash she was scrunching in her hand. "So really it's my house."

We walked out the door and got into the waiting taxi.

"Did you find Renee?" I asked as the taxi drove towards the city.

Dustin was looking out his window. His knuckles were white from gripping the handle bar on the door.

"What about Jose—"

"Don't ever say his name to me again, or Raul or Que," he shouted.

How did he know about Raul and Que? I'd never told him that Raul and I were together. Actually, I hadn't told him anything about my past. He knew about Renee, but that was it.

"It's taken care of," he said. "That's all you need to know."

We pulled up to a hotel on Dorchester Avenue not too far from Richard's house, and Dustin paid the driver. He put his arm around my shoulder and led me through the front door. The man at the desk didn't look at us when we walked in. He sat behind the glass and watched his TV.

"We're living here from now on," he said when we got inside our room.

I was going to ask why, but then I saw all the trash bags. There were at least fifteen of them on the floor by the couch and they looked like the ones from Jose's basement.

"Are those—"

"Check the closet, it's full of clothes for you," he said.

I opened the closet. There was a mound of clothes on the floor— pants, shorts, and shirts. Shoes were on the top shelf.

"Thank you," I said.

I'd been wearing the same clothes since rehab, and my shirt and jeans were stained with blood.

"They're Renee's. She won't be needing them anymore."

He came up behind me and wrapped his hands around my chest, squeezing my tits like he was fist pumping for a vein. "Not a word of this, ever," he said. "Got it?"

The only thing that mattered was that Dustin hadn't gotten hurt. And with Jose taken care of, I didn't have to worry about running into him and his gang on the street. Dustin was good to me, and tonight was just another reason I wanted to be with him forever.

"Yeah, I got it," I said.

CHAPTER TWENTY

Renee had to be dead. Dustin never said he killed her, but why else wouldn't she need her clothes? That bitch had hurt me too many times. It was her fault Eric had died, she'd left me at McDonald's and at Jose's. Mason would never see his mom again, but Renee got what she deserved.

Since Dustin and I had moved to Dorchester, I hadn't spoken to Sunshine. But I wondered how much she knew about Renee. Was she there when Dustin took Renee's clothes? Had she come home to an empty hotel room and thought Renee had just taken off? Maybe Sunshine was dead too. I'd never know unless I called her. But she hadn't been a good friend to me either. She'd kicked me out of her bed when we'd both been dope sick and lied to me about Richard. She used me to get her drugs. I'd long paid her back for letting me stay with her for free. She could go to Roxbury and get her own damn drugs. I was done with her.

The only person I couldn't get out of my head was Richard. It had been months since I'd made the deal with him, and if it weren't for the fire, I would have already paid him back. I had this feeling he was going to say something to Dustin if I didn't pay up soon. So every day when Dustin left for his runs, I boosted. And at night, Dustin and I shot up and had sex. We talked about our future, how we were going to leave Boston and quit using and start a family. We both wanted that, but he'd also lost all the cash he'd saved in the fire, and our plans had to be pushed back. I was going to get my little girl. And this time I'd know the baby's daddy, and she wouldn't die from junk. But all that was going to take some time.

Dustin came home one night and said Heather was out of the loony bin and back with Richard. He told me he didn't have a run tomorrow and asked if I wanted to go see her. We'd stay for just a little while and get some dinner after. In the four months we'd been together, we'd never been on an actual date.

The timing was perfect. In the last week, I'd finally earned enough money to pay Richard. I'd thought about having Dustin give him the money. But then Dustin would ask questions and I'd have to lie, and Richard probably wouldn't back me up. Heather was crazy, and addicts couldn't be trusted to deliver money. There was no other way to get him the cash. I had to do it.

I told Dustin I was excited for tomorrow and we got into bed. He turned on the TV, and when I started kissing his neck, he told me to stop. The news was on, and he turned up the volume. Since everything had gone down with Jose and Renee, he'd been watching the news every night. I didn't know if Renee and Jose and his gang members were dead or had just left Boston but so far, the newscasters hadn't reported they were missing or that their bodies had been found.

When the weatherman came on to give the forecast, Dustin turned off the TV and kissed me back.

The next night, I hid the cash in my bra, and we walked to Richard's. Dustin held my hand, and when we got to the front door, he turned around at the top step and leaned down to kiss me.

"Happy birthday, baby," he said.

He opened the door, and everyone inside yelled, "Surprise."

The gang of squatters greeted me with hugs and wished me a happy birthday. Everyone except the twins and Richard. Sierra and Erin were on the couch looking sour, and Richard must have been in his bedroom.

I knew it was spring because the snow was melting and we'd turned off the heat in our hotel room. But that today was my twenty-fifth birthday—that came as a total surprise.

The birthday party Dustin put together was different than the ones I'd been to in the past. There weren't any balloons or streamers, any food or gifts. Besides Heather, everyone here was Dustin's friend, not mine. And once the surprise was over, they all went into the living room to shoot up, snort, and smoke their drugs.

Dustin had gotten me a cake, but no one sang, and there weren't any candles to blow out. I still made a wish. Before I took my first bite, I wished to move away from here. Maybe in a couple years when we had the money and we were ready to put this life behind us, I'd eat my birthday cake on a plate instead of a napkin and have a fork to feed myself with. But for now, my fingers worked just fine.

Heather and I sat alone in the living room. The guys had gone into Richard's bedroom to talk, and the twins had left to sell on the street. Besides the cast that ran from Heather's shoulder to her wrist, she looked good. Her hair was brushed, and she'd gained weight. Her face had a little color too.

"How's your arm?" I asked.

Her pupils were pinned and her movements were heavy. Heather was a tweaker, but tonight she'd shot up heroin instead of crystal meth.

"It's fucked, I cut through muscle and I'm gonna have to wear this thing for a while," she said. "Supposed to have another surgery soon, but you know…"

Her eyes got droopy.

That surgery would never happen. Addicts didn't go to the hospital unless they OD'd or got pregnant.

"This shit is good," she slurred.

She was still eating her cake, but that's not what she was talking about.

"You done with meth?" I asked.

"It made me too crazy, but dope, yeah, dope is all right," she said. "How you and Dustin doing?"

I told her about the fire and how we'd moved down the street from Richard's. I gave her the name of the hotel and asked her to come by. Her eyes were closed, and she was in a nod. She said something that sounded like, "Yeah."

When I first started using, it was so easy to find a vein on my unmarked skin, and the nod came as soon as the chamber emptied. That had all changed. Dope got me straight, not high, and I hadn't had a good nod since the night we left rehab. Especially one like Heather was having. Her face had fallen in her cake.

The guys came out of Richard's bedroom, and I could tell Dustin wasn't happy. He came over to the couch and kneeled in front of me. "Baby, I'm so sorry," he said. "There's a big run tonight, and the guys can't do it without me."

The cash was still in my bra. Dustin going on a run actually worked out perfectly.

I put on a sad face. "But you promised."

"I know, I'll make it up to you tomorrow night," he said. "Come on, I'll walk you home."

Before I cut the cake, I'd taken off my jacket and put it on the counter in the kitchen. And on the way out the door, I didn't grab it. If Dustin ever found out I came back to Richard's, I'd tell him I'd forgotten my jacket. But Dustin wouldn't find out. Besides Richard, Heather was the only squatter left in the house, and she was passed out on the couch.

Dustin said he was going to be home late because he and the guys still had to pack the van and get it all ready to be delivered. So I decided to wait a couple hours to make sure they were gone. To pass time, I shot up and watched TV, flipping between reruns of *The Cosby Show* and a movie about some girl training to be a boxer. When the movie was over, I walked back to Richard's.

My jacket was still in the kitchen, and I snagged it before going to his bedroom. His door was shut and I knocked once, opening it just a crack. Richard and Heather were fucking on the air mattress. I couldn't see her face, just her long brown hair spread over the white sheet, and Richard's backside moving up and down on top of her.

"Richard, I have something for you," I said, opening the door wider.

The smell of his room—rotten food and sweat—was worse than usual. I put my hand over my nose and breathed through my mouth.

He stopped humping and looked over his shoulder. "Come back," he said.

But I finally had the money and I didn't know when Dustin would bring me here again. Even though Richard had agreed to the new deal I'd come up with, he was sketchy. But with Heather in his bed, I didn't think he'd try to have sex with me.

"Heather, I'm sorry to interrupt you guys," I said. "But it'll just take a sec."

She didn't say anything.

Richard got off her and she stayed on her stomach. Her naked body lay uncovered and her casted arm was over her head. She didn't even roll over to say hello.

Richard moved to the center of the room. His dick was pointed at me, and I looked at my feet so I wouldn't be caught staring.

I reached inside my bra. "Here's the money I owe you," I said and placed it in his hand.

He counted the wad of bills and flung the cash on his desk.

"We're even now, right?" I asked.

He glanced at Heather and then back at me. His tongue circled his lips and his eyes were wide and fierce.

"We good?" I said.

"Yeah, we're good."

Heather still hadn't moved since Richard had gotten off her. I stepped over to the bed and touched her foot. "Come by the hotel tomorrow, okay?"

She didn't answer.

Her toes were purplish. I shook her heel and her ankle. "Heather?"

When I was in a nod, I could hear the people around me and feel their touch, and I'd respond to them. Something was wrong if she wasn't answering me.

I kneeled on the bed, inching closer. "Heather?"

I slowly rolled her over. Her body was heavy, and the smell was stronger than it had been in the doorway.

"Leave her alone," Richard said.

But I couldn't. She needed help.

The skin on her ear had a purplish tint. She had the same smell as the sumo dude at Abdul's hotel.

Sometime after Dustin had walked me back to the hotel, Heather had OD'd. And Richard was fucking her dead body.

I had to stay calm. If I freaked out, he'd do to me what he'd done to Sunshine.

I crawled backwards off the mattress, keeping my eyes on Heather. And at the edge of the bed, I pushed myself up.

Richard hadn't moved from the center of the room.

I took a step and another and was almost at the door.

He moved fast. I didn't hear him coming, but I felt his hands around my neck and his body against my back.

"Where do you think you're going?" he asked.

Stay calm.

"I'm going home," I said.

"Don't you owe me something first?"

"I already gave you the money."

He pushed his dick against my ass. "That's what you owe me."

"But you said we're good."

"I'm not going to let you renege on your promise."

I tried to rip his hands off my throat. "I can't, I have my period," I lied.

He laughed, and his body rumbled.

"A little blood won't kill me," he said.

His grip tightened and he pulled me back, my heels dragging on the carpet. There wasn't any of his skin near my mouth to bite. My hands thrashed, and my fingernails stabbed, but that didn't stop him.

He threw me on the bed and I fell sideways over Heather. My head landed on her chest. My legs dangled off the side of the bed, and he reached for the button and zipper on my jeans.

I slapped his face.

The corners of his lips pointed down, and he punched the same spot where Jose had hit me with his gun.

"Don't do this to me," I screamed. "Please."

"Shut up, you fucking whore," he said. "Act like you like it."

My jeans were pulled off and thrown to the floor. The crotch of my underwear was ripped open. I squeezed my legs together, trying to keep him out. But I didn't have his strength, and he spread them apart.

"Please..." I yelled.

He forced his dick into my body.

"Stop..."

"Say it louder, it turns me on," he said.

His breath smelled just like the death coming off Heather. His hands were oily, and his neck was caked with dirt.

I kicked my legs and dug my nails into his cheeks.

"I'm gonna fuck the Dustin out of you," he said and yanked my hair, pulling strands out of my head. "And when you're with him, you're going to think about my dick instead."

I held Heather's hand, squeezing her heavy fingers.

"No..." I cried.

But no matter how loud I yelled, Richard was the only one who could hear me.

His grip was too strong.

I had no fight left in me.

My head fell to the side. I couldn't look at the eyes of the man who was raping me.

Behind my lids, I saw my mom. The love on her face and tenderness of her touch when she kissed my burnt arm.

Richard moved in and out of my dry body.

I drove my nails into Heather's skin.

Would I be getting raped if I had listened to Walter and Sandra when they were trying to help me? And Kara who had tried to teach me the Twelve Steps? And Henry when he had told me to make Claire proud? And Dustin when he had said to stay away from this house? I should have listened to them.

Richard's breathing turned heavy. His strokes were rough and painful.

I focused on the needle.

My mom's face popped back in my mind, and I shook my head to get her out.

The needle. Its orange cap and clear chamber, filled with the sickest dope that would get me higher than I'd ever been.

I pulled Heather's hand to my face, and pushed her cold fingers against my cheek.

Richard moaned and his body wriggled on mine.

The warmness of heroin that would flow through my body. The tingling in each of my muscles and the beautiful nod that would follow.

He lay limp on top of me. His tongue circled my neck and his cum dripped from my crotch. "I'm done with you," he said. "You can go."

I slid out from under him, grabbed my jeans and jacket, and ran out the door.

When Dustin came home, I was in bed. I'd already showered and scrubbed every part of my body so he wouldn't smell Richard on me. My eye was a little red from where he'd punched me, but Dustin wouldn't notice because it was still bruised from when Jose had hit me with his gun.

He crawled on top of me and kissed my neck. His lips were on the same spot where Richard's tongue had circled.

"I've got bad news," he said.

I opened my eyes, meeting his stare.

"Heather died tonight," he said. "She OD'd at Richard's."

My tears tasted salty like Richard's skin.

Heather was dead, Eric too, and Richard had raped me.

"I know it hurts," he said. "I'm sad too."

Henry's ring was tucked under my fingers, and the metal band felt cool against my burning skin.

"This is a bad ending, but I still hope you had a good birthday, baby."

I squeezed the ring tighter, digging my nails into my palm.

Claire, you have to get me through this. Make me forget about the rape. Please, make me forget.

CHAPTER TWENTY-ONE

A t first, I was numb and empty. I knew what Richard was capable of and that I couldn't trust him. And I'd practically set myself up to be raped when I'd gone to his bedroom. I had no memory of the first rape that happened five years ago in college. But with Richard, I could see his face over mine, feel his touch, and hear his moans. He was right, all I could think about was his dick instead of Dustin's.

A few days passed. And then one morning as I was pulling out the needle, the numbness was gone. I realized the rape was just more unwanted sex. I was an ex-hooker who had years of unwanted sex. I gave Johns whatever they wanted and took their money. I'd taken Richard's too. So did it really matter that he'd raped me? He didn't take anything that hadn't already been taken from me or do anything that hadn't already been done.

But there was Dustin to worry about. He gave me everything I needed, all the dope I could shoot, a place to live, and money for food. And he'd only asked for two things in return—to stop hooking and to stay away from Richard. If he found out about Richard, he'd leave me for sure.

And he was going to find out. Richard would tell him. I guess stealing Dustin's girls was Richard's way of showing he was in control even though Dustin basically ran his business. But Richard wouldn't tell Dustin he'd raped me. He'd tell him some lie like I came to his bed and begged him to have sex with me. Dustin would be too mad to listen, and he'd never let me explain. Before any of that could happen, I had to get Dustin away from him.

But how could I make him want to leave so soon? He had a good thing in Boston. What could I say that would convince him to give it all up and choose to leave with me?

We'd talked about moving so many times before, but he wanted to save enough money first. We'd need a car to get away, and I didn't know if he had money for that. We could take a bus or hitchhike, and stay in hotels along the way. If we ran out of money, we could live on the streets. But I didn't have anything solid to make him want to leave now. Our move came down to money, and if Dustin didn't have enough, he wouldn't want to go.

A plan popped in my head. Dustin drove Richard's van to New York City every Thursday to drop off a shipment of dope. The delivery had to be worth thousands of dollars, plenty for us to live on. All I had to do was convince him to take me to New York, and once we got the money, I'd tell him my plan.

So when he got home from his run Wednesday night and climbed into bed, I straddled him. I peeled off his shirt and kissed his neck.

"I missed you too," he said and rubbed my thighs.

I licked his chest. "I have an idea," I said.

"I like it so far."

When I got to his pubes, I looked up. "I want to go to New York."

He pushed my head down.

"Will you take me with you tomorrow?" I asked.

He pushed down a little harder. "It's not safe," he said. "You know that."

I circled my tongue around his tip, thinking I could change his mind.

He moaned and scrunched his head into the pillow.

"So can I go?"

"No, but I like the effort you're putting in, just go a little deeper."

I wanted to bite down until he said yes, but I didn't. I moved to the other side of the bed and got under the covers.

"Tell me you're kidding," he said. "You're not going to leave me hard like this, are you?"

When I didn't answer, he got under the blanket and kissed my back and around to my stomach. He made it as far down as my belly button before I wriggled out of his arms and stood at the side of the bed.

"What's your problem?" he asked.

"I want to go to New York."

"If this is about your birthday then I'll take Friday off and have Tommy do my run."

He still hadn't taken me out to dinner. I didn't want him to take me out to celebrate, I wanted to forget my birthday had ever happened.

"I just want to see what you do every day," I said. "And get out of Boston for a little while."

"If you want to go to New York, I'll take you, but not tomorrow."

I walked over to the couch and lay across the cushions.

"Baby, come back."

The bed squeaked when he got up, and I felt his breath on my ear. "Friday, I'm all yours, okay?" He kissed my forehead.

He asked me to go to bed with him, and I said I'd be there in a little while.

I needed to think of a new plan. He didn't want me to go to New York because he couldn't protect me from the men he did business with. I couldn't be mad at him for that. But still, there had to be a way, a reason he'd have to take me or a way he couldn't stop me from going. I could bus it to New York in the morning and call him when I got there, and he could pick me up after his delivery. But I needed money for the ticket.

I waited until he was asleep and then tiptoed over to the dresser where he kept his wallet. There were a few hundred bucks inside. As I was about to pull out some of the cash, I saw his keys. Which meant the van was parked downstairs.

Dustin was snoring.

With the keys in hand, I threw on some clothes and snuck out of our room. In the parking lot, I found the van and glanced around to make sure no one was watching. There were two kids on skateboards just beyond the parking lot. I waited for them to turn the corner before unlocking the passenger side door so I could sneak into the van in the morning.

Back in our room, I climbed into bed and snuggled up to Dustin. This was going to be our last night living in Boston. I was going with him to New York, he just didn't know it yet.

Dustin got up around noon and went in the bathroom to get ready for his run. When I heard him turn on the shower, I threw off the covers and put on some clothes. I left a note on the bed, telling him I was going to the store and I'd see him when he got home. And after I packed my pockets with dope, rigs, and spoons, I went down to the parking lot.

The white van was an old, rusted clunker Richard had bought years ago from a chop shop. On the driver's side was a picture of a hand holding a paintbrush, and most of the letters above the logo were missing. But below was a phone number and the words "licensed and insured."

I climbed in through the passenger side and over the seat. In the back of the van were rows of shelves on both sides that held paint cans, and on the floor were five-gallon buckets. I crouched between the buckets and covered myself with a tarp.

When I heard the key go in the driver's side door, I held my breath and grabbed the buckets for support. The van shook when he slammed the door, and all the paint cans rattled. I knew he didn't see me because he started the engine and pulled out onto the street. I could finally breathe again.

"Hey Dad," he said. "Just leaving now."

I peeked out from under the tarp. Dustin was on his cell phone.

Dad had to be Richard.

"I'm going to stop and get something to eat and then head up to Mom's. Should be there in five or six hours," he said. "I'll call you on my way home."

He hung up and turned on the radio, tapping his fingers on the steering wheel.

Ten minutes later, I peeked out again, trying to see through the windshield. We weren't on the highway. We weren't in Dorchester or Boston either because I didn't recognize the street. But I knew we were on our way to pick up the shipment. That was what he meant when he told Richard he was going to stop and get something to eat.

I didn't know when I should come out from under the tarp. I could wait until he opened the back doors to load up, but surprising him then didn't seem like the best idea. I didn't want to scare him while he was driving and cause an accident. So when he stopped at a red light, I crawled up behind him and kissed him on the cheek.

He jumped in his seat. "What the hell?" he shouted.

"Surprise."

"What are you doing in here?"

His face was red.

"I'm coming to New York with you."

The light turned green, and he pulled into the nearest gas station and started to turn around in the parking lot.

"Where are you going?"

"I'm taking you home," he said.

I climbed into the passenger seat. "No—"

"Nicole, I can't protect you from these people."

I grabbed the steering wheel to stop him from turning and he jammed on the breaks. "Hear me out, okay?" I said.

I told him I didn't want to be alone. I said losing Heather had been really hard on me and I didn't feel like myself anymore.

The redness on his cheeks began to fade, and he rubbed my shoulder as I talked. I was getting somewhere.

I said just being with him during the long drive would make me feel better. I even offered to wait in a restaurant while he picked up the shipment and dropped it off. The begging helped my case. But the blowjob gave me the answer I was looking for. While I sucked, he put the van in drive and turned back onto the road. He even told me I could go with him to the supplier's place, but for the delivery I'd have to wait at a restaurant.

We pulled onto a back street that ran parallel to a shipyard. There was a strong smell of fish in the air, and seagulls were flying overhead.

I asked where we were, and he said Conley Terminal in Southie. He explained that boats, stacked full of containers, came into the harbor to import goods for Boston and the surrounding areas.

"The drugs are hidden in the containers?" I asked.

He nodded.

"And a container is going to fit in this van?"

The yard was still a few football fields away. Even so, the containers looked bigger than the van. There were guards and dogs walking through the yard and what looked to be a security check-in gate up ahead. I didn't know how we were going to get past the guard on our way out with a van full of dope.

"No baby, we buy the drugs from an importer who's already cleared customs," he said.

I didn't understand, but he told me it would all make sense in a couple of minutes.

Buildings ran along the side of the shipyard, and a few blocks before the security gate, he pulled down a long driveway.

The lot behind the building was empty. Dustin drove up to the garage door and honked three times. The garage door opened. He drove in and parked, and the door shut behind us.

"Stay here and don't come out until I tell you to," he said and he got out of the van.

The building was a massive warehouse, and on all three sides were wooden shelves that ran from the floor to the ceiling. On the shelves were couches and oversized chairs wrapped in layers of thick plastic.

Dustin stood by the front of the van, waiting for the man walking towards him. His orangey red hair was cut in a fade. They shook hands. Dustin handed him the envelope tucked in the waist of his jeans. The man opened it, and his mouth moved like he was counting whatever was inside. When the guy put the envelope in his jacket pocket, Dustin pointed at me. The man's eyes moved over the hood and through the windshield, meeting my stare. He then looked back at Dustin and shrugged his shoulders.

Dustin waved, signaling for me to come out.

"Séamus, this is Nicole, my girlfriend," Dustin said.

Séamus stuck out his freckled hand for me to shake. "Nicole," he said and dipped his head.

His accent sounded like he was from Ireland. Southie was full of Irish mobsters. I knew Dustin dealt with some rough men, but the mob? Damn. He was in deeper than I thought.

Another guy drove a forklift with a wooden pallet with two couches wrapped in plastic over to where we were standing.

"Honk when you're done," Séamus said, and both men went into the office by the back wall.

Dustin went to the front seat and came back with a knife, cutting the plastic off the furniture. When both couches were uncovered, he sliced each of the cushions, the armrests, and the back panels. Fluff stuck out from each gash.

"Start pulling," he said.

He was standing in front of the first couch, yanking out the fluff.

"What am I looking for?" I asked.

Once all the outer fluff was out, he held up a brick of heroin wrapped in more plastic and stamped with a skull and crossbones.

"How many are there?"

"A lot," he said.

We worked our way through all the cushions and the back panels of the couches, and piled all the bricks on the ground. By the time we were done, there had to be over a hundred of them, and we packed them into the paint cans. When those were full, we stuffed the buckets too. We covered the buckets with tarps, and on top we scattered paint trays, brushes, and edging tape.

I waited in the passenger seat while Dustin looked everything over to make sure it was all secure, and then he joined me in the front seat. He honked and we backed out through the open door.

New York City was a four-hour drive and that was a long time to go without using. My stomach was already queasy. I couldn't wait. I took out a rig, spoon, and bundle from my pocket.

"Put that shit away," he said. "You've got to wait until we're in New York."

"But I'm starting to feel sick."

He looked in the side mirrors and the rearview. "Then hurry up, I try to only break one law at a time."

"I love you so much," I said, next I could ask him to stop at a gas station to pee. Dustin only did runs with guys on board and they probably peed in a soda bottle. I should have worn a diaper.

He kept his eyes on the road, but he squeezed my leg. "I love you too, baby," he said. "And you did good back there, but promise me you'll never sneak into the van again?"

"Yeah—"

"No, I mean it, Séamus is cool cause he's family, but the other guys I deal with don't fuck around," he said. "I can't just bring someone new with me to the delivery. There's a code, and I've got to follow it."

I never thought about the risks involved when Dustin ran these drugs. It seemed so simple, pick-up, drive, and drop off. But the mobsters were probably strapped, and if they sensed something wasn't right they wouldn't hesitate to shoot.

"You and Séamus are related?" I asked.

The road was bumpy, and I really had to pee, so I was having a hard time keeping the spoon steady.

"Séamus and Richard are brothers," he said.

Brothers? Shit, what if Séamus called Richard and told him I'd been at the pick-up? Richard would know I was up to something and he'd figure out my plan—get Dustin out of Boston before he found out we'd had sex—and order one of his squatters to kill us. Someone could even be following us now.

"Does Richard have another van?" I asked.

There was a mini-van behind us and a black car behind them.

"No, just a car," he said.

"What color?"

"Black, I think."

Even if I was being paranoid, there could still be someone waiting for us in New York. I couldn't let Dustin deliver these drugs.

"How much can we get for this load on the street?" I asked.

He took his eyes off the road to look at me. "Why?"

The smack was bubbling in the spoon and I dipped the rig into the mixture, filling the chamber.

"I don't want to go back to Boston," I said. "Let's go somewhere, anywhere, maybe California and sell these drugs on the street. Just think how rich we'll be."

"You're crazy." He looked in his rearview mirror and turned on his blinker to merge when the street went from three lanes to two. "Is that why you wanted to come to New York?"

I flicked the chamber with my finger to get out the air bubbles. "We could do it, you know, and we'd make a good team," I said. "We could hustle together out on the streets in California."

"Do you know what would happen if I didn't drop off these drugs and return the money to Richard?"

"How would he find us in California?"

"Richard and Séamus and his guys wouldn't be the only ones looking for us. The Guidos who are supposed to get this shipment would be looking too," he said. "Nicole, they'd hunt us down and kill both of us."

"Not over one little shipment."

He laughed, but nervously.

"Then we'll go to Mexico," I said.

"We can't run for the rest of our lives."

I stuck the needle into the back of my hand and waited for the flash. "As long as I'm with you, running wouldn't be so bad."

His knuckles were white from gripping the steering wheel, and his leg was bouncing. He wasn't convinced. But there was one thing I could say that might change his mind.

"I think I'm pregnant," I said and emptied the dope into my vein.

I hated lying, but it was the only way. And once we got settled somewhere, I'd figure out how to tell him I'd gotten my period.

He looked at me again and I smiled. "I'm a couple days late, and I'm never late."

But maybe I wasn't lying. I hadn't kept track of the twenty-eight day thing since the abortion, so there was a chance I could be pregnant. And since we'd been together, he'd never worn a condom and pulled out when he was ready to come. But pulling out wasn't the best birth control.

His eyes went wide, and his mouth opened.

The car in front of us pulled over and double-parked. "Watch out," I yelled.

He braked hard and swerved to the left so he wouldn't hit the car.

He had the van under control, and his eyes were on the road, but his lips were moving and no words were coming out. He was talking to himself. Why wasn't he talking to me, saying how happy he was that he was going to be a dad?

"I'm sorry, I shouldn't have told you," I said.

"No baby, I'm glad you did," he said and put his hand on my stomach. "I just wanted to wait until I had enough money saved, that's all."

"Mexico sounds a whole lot better now, doesn't it?" I asked.

"Hell yeah, it does."

"So what do you think? Should we go?"

He was about to answer when I heard the siren. I looked in the side mirror and saw flashing blue lights.

"Fuck," he shouted and put on his blinker, pulling over to the side of the road.

"Were you speeding?"

"I think the cop saw me swerve back there."

The cop got out of his car and waited for the traffic to slow down so he could come over to the van.

"Get rid of all this crap," Dustin said, pointing to my lap.

I stuffed the rig, spoon, and bags into my pocket just before the cop tapped on Dustin's window.

Dustin rolled his window down, and the cop peered inside the van.

"Saw you swerve back there," the cop said. "You almost hit that Neon."

"Sorry officer, my girl here just told me she's pregnant. Shocked the hell out of me and I just took my eyes off the road for a second."

The cop was a big man, taller than the van with fingers the size of sausages.

"License and registration," the cop said.

I felt his eyes on us, watching Dustin's hand as he pulled out his wallet. And on mine when I took the registration out of the glove box.

"Are you insulin dependent?" the cop asked me.

"No, sir," I said.

I handed the registration to the cop, and that's when I saw the blood drips from the needle hole running down the back of my hand.

"I picked a scab," I said.

The heroin was causing my whole body to tingle.

"Then why is there a needle sticking out of your pocket?" the cop asked.

I looked down.

He was right. Not only was the orange cap sticking out, but half the chamber was too.

I was a little high and my brain wasn't working right.

"It's for bees," Dustin said. "She's allergic and she's always gotta carry around that medicine in case she gets stung."

The cop told us to wait in the van and he'd be back in a few minutes.

Once he was away from the window, Dustin punched the steering wheel.

"Don't worry," I said. "I think he bought the whole bee thing."

"Screw the bee thing, there's a warrant out for my arrest."

Richard would bail him out if he got arrested. But that would screw up my plan to go to Mexico, and then Dustin would definitely find out about Richard and me. If he got in trouble I didn't know what I'd do, where I'd live, and how I'd get dope.

"Do you know what that means?" he asked. "It gives them the right to search the van."

I turned around, glancing at all the brushes and trays and paint cans. It looked legit. Why would the cops even bother to search through it all?

Dustin sent a text message and then rested his head on the steering wheel. "We're fucked."

We? I'd get in trouble too? But Dustin had the warrant, not me. Why wouldn't they let me go after he was arrested?

"Don't say anything to the cops, not now or when you're in jail," he said.

Jail?

"Why would I get arrested too?" I asked.

"Nicole, I was arrested on a drug charge and never showed up to court," he said. "They're gonna search the van and when they find the drugs, you've got to keep your mouth shut. Richard will bail us out, just keep fucking quiet. Got it?"

Richard would bail me out too? But what if he didn't? I'd have to call Michael or my parents. I could just imagine their faces when I called them collect from jail. I'd left rehab and hadn't talked to them since the morning they'd dropped me off. They probably wouldn't bail me out either.

My armpits were soaked with sweat.

A second cruiser pulled up, and the cops talked behind the van. I couldn't hear what they were saying, but they were pointing to Dustin's side of the van and one of them was calling someone on their cell phone.

Sausage fingers came up to Dustin's window, and the other cop tapped on mine. I rolled down the window and the cop said, "Ma'am, please step out of the vehicle."

Once Dustin and I got out of the van, we were both handcuffed.

Dustin was told he was being arrested for his warrant, and the cop read him his rights as he shoved him in the back of the cruiser.

My cop backed me up against the hood of the other cruiser and stood in front of me. Sausage fingers joined him, and both cops towered over me.

"Are we going to find a warrant on you too?" one of them asked me.

"No, sir," I said, keeping my eyes on their feet. "I have a clean record."

"What about the van, is that clean too?"

Dustin had told me to keep my mouth shut, but what if I could get us out of this mess? Maybe if I said the right things, they wouldn't check the van and they'd let me go.

"It's my boyfriend's work van."

"He's a painter?"

I nodded. "We were just driving to a job."

"I called the number," one of the cops said, pointing to the lettering on the side of the van. "And the line has been disconnected. Why's that?"

"Money is tight, I must have forgotten to pay the bill," I said.

One cop stayed with me, and the other opened the back doors of the van. He picked up the brushes and paint trays and lifted the tarps. He tapped his wand on the tops and sides of the paint cans.

Slowly, he pulled the lid off one of the five-gallon buckets.

Dustin was right. We were fucked. I wanted to run, but I couldn't. I was cuffed, and the cop was standing next to me.

"Foster," the cop in the van said. "We got something big here." He was holding one of the bricks up in the air.

Foster grabbed the back of my arms and read me my rights before pushing me in the backseat of his cruiser.

Dustin was in the car in front of mine. He turned around, and I saw parts of his face through the plastic shield. I knew this was going to be the last time I'd ever see Dustin.

All the pee I'd been holding in was now running down my legs.

CHAPTER TWENTY-TWO

O nce I was booked at the police station, an officer brought me into a small room and pushed me down in a chair next to a double-sided mirror. He slammed the door behind him, leaving me alone. From the other side of the mirror, I felt different sets of eyes scanning my face and body. I couldn't hear their voices, but I knew they were talking about how they could get me to rat out Dustin.

The chair was metal and uncomfortable, and I could only sit on half of it with my hands cuffed behind me. I circled my thumbs, and to get my mind off the trouble I was in, I counted each time my nails touched. Sweat was still dripping down my back even though the room was freezing and the pee on my pants hadn't dried yet.

After what seemed like hours, two men came in and sat down. They were both dressed in dark suits and striped ties. The guy behind the desk introduced himself as Detective Shay, and the other guy's name I didn't catch.

I thought of all the people who had been in this room before me. Mobsters and murderers, serial rapists. And here I was, put in the same room like I'd done the same horrible shit.

Shay commented on my pee-stained jeans and swollen eyes. I'd sobbed the whole way to the police station, but my eyes were dry now. If he thought I was scared, he was right, but that didn't mean I was going to answer any of their questions. Dustin had told me to keep my mouth shut, so I did. I listened to him ask about my involvement with the heroin trafficking, where we picked up the drugs, and where we were taking them. He threatened a fifteen to twenty-year jail sentence. Still, I didn't say anything. I stared at his coffee cup and the folder with my name and booking ID number on the corner. The overhead light showed little gray hairs in Shay's black goatee, and there was a hole in the other guy's ear where an earring used to be.

I didn't know how all this worked—getting arrested, posting bail, going to court—but I'd seen enough movies to know I could ask for a lawyer. And so I did.

Shay stopped pacing the small space between the desk and me and looked into my eyes. I told him I wouldn't say a word unless it was to my lawyer, and both men left.

I was put in a holding cell where I'd stay until my arraignment the next morning. There were three other women I shared the cell with, but only one talked to me. Her name was Venus, and she wore a silver, low-cut fitted dress with black eye makeup that could hardly be seen over her dark skin. She mostly did escort work through the Internet so she could stay off the streets but said she knew Sunshine. She told me she hadn't seen Sunshine around lately and heard she was working at one of those massage parlors that gave happy endings. I had a hard time believing Sunshine would ever work for someone especially since it was almost summer and that meant hooking season was here.

An officer came by our cell to deliver dinner: a bologna sandwich, chips, and milk. I wasn't hungry. The shot I'd done in the van had long worn off, and I was starting to feel dope sick. A part of me, not looking forward to the withdrawal, wished I'd never tried heroin.

Lights out was at nine, and by then the other women looked like they were feeling as bad as I was. Sweaty, flushed skin, jittery arms and legs, and stomach cramps that made me double over. The only bed that wasn't taken was on the top bunk, but I didn't have enough energy to climb up. I couldn't even swallow my own spit without gagging.

I crouched in a ball in the corner of the cell by the toilet, which was right out in the open. Besides my mom, Sunshine had been the only other person who had ever seen me use the bathroom. And here the other women, both junkies and also dope sick, were squatting next to me on the metal rim when they had to go. Their smell made me feel worse, and so did their noises. Venus had said she didn't use drugs and slept through our noises and smells. Damn her. I never should have left rehab. Damn Dustin, too.

The police station was loud at night. Cops brought in more men and women for booking and processing. Their handcuffs clinked as they were escorted and locked into cells. The officers' boots pounded and squeaked on the linoleum floor, and doors banged as they slid shut. Everyone yelled out the same questions: why am I here, can I get some help, can I make a phone call, and can I get some medicine so I won't be sick? I cupped my palms like earmuffs and tried to block it all out.

I thought of Claire to keep my mind off being dope sick. The first time we'd met and the movie we'd watched together. How she'd shimmied her shoulders and smiled when she saw Marilyn on the TV screen. And Dustin, and how I felt the first time we'd kissed in rehab. I was never going to feel the softness of his lips ever again, but I didn't care. If he hadn't been so possessive, I would have been able to tell him the truth about the deal I'd made with Richard, and then I wouldn't have been raped. I snuck into the van, but this was his fault. If there hadn't been a warrant out for him, we wouldn't have gotten arrested.

My stomach flipped, and I leaned over to puke.

How was I going to make it through court tomorrow when I couldn't get my face out of the toilet?

An officer came to our cell early the next morning and said my court-appointed attorney was here. He told me to stick my hands through the meal slot so he could cuff me, and then he led me to a private room. My attorney didn't look that much older than me. But where I was dressed in a blue jumpsuit with unwashed hair, she was in a suit and heels with beige nails, and flower-smelling perfume.

The guard sat me in the seat across from her. Before he left, he told her he'd be right outside the door in case she needed him.

My hands were shackled behind my back. Did he think I was going to hurt her?

"My name is Melissa Davidson," she said.   "And I'll be representing you."

She had a pad of paper, a leather folder, and a shiny silver pen and was reading from a printout. She never looked up at me, even when I'd come into the room. I wanted to see her eyes. I'd always been able to tell how rough a John was going to be by his eyes. There was something about them—the size of the pupil and how he looked at me with either big open lids or squinted ones—that told me what kind of person he was. But so far, I couldn't get a vibe from Melissa.

"Do you understand the charges that have been brought against you?" she asked. She flipped to the next page and continued to read.

Could I trust her? I didn't know if I could trust anyone. I'd never been in trouble before. Was I supposed to tell her the truth or play dumb?

"I think so," I said. "I mean, the cops think the drugs in the van were ours and we were delivering them to someone."

"When you said 'our,' you were referring to yourself and Mr. Dustin Howard?"

"Yeah."

She still hadn't looked up. She was holding the silver pen and was writing on the pad of paper.

"And what's your affiliation to Mr. Howard?" she asked.

My affiliation? Why was she talking so fancy?

I didn't want to do this here. Especially not in handcuffs, half-sitting on the chair. Not without seeing her eyes. And most importantly, not without hitting the needle first.

I leaned forward, resting my forehead on my knees. The movement made me dizzy. I still hadn't eaten, and my stomach was churning.

"Ms. Brown, I hope you understand the seriousness of these charges and how you're facing up to twenty years in jail?"

I wasn't an idiot. I understood the jail time the detectives had threatened me with. But maybe I was. I'd always ripped on Henry and my roommate in rehab because they'd been stupid enough to get busted.

"But if you talk to the detectives," she said, "I can get your sentence significantly reduced."

She meant if I ratted everyone out. Richard and his gang. Séamus and his.

"You're going to be bused to the courthouse in an hour, and I want you to plead not guilty to the judge," she said. "I'll come here tomorrow or if you get released on bail, I want you to come by my office so we can discuss your case in more detail."

I sat up in the chair. "Is someone going to bail me out?"

She slid her business card across the table. "I don't know."

I didn't have a hand to grab the card, but her office was in downtown Boston and I knew the building. I said if I were released, I'd come by her office in the morning.

I had a lot to think about—how much I was going to tell her, and if I should rat out Richard and Séamus. I needed time to figure this all out before I'd say anymore.

She looked up from the sheet of paper and straight into my eyes. "I'll see you in court."

Her eyes were thin slits and almost squinty, the color of mud, and cold like snow. She gave me the same stare I'd given to Richard after he'd raped me. I needed a new attorney. Even if it was her job to defend me, Melissa wasn't on my side.

An hour later, I was handcuffed again and put on a full bus. When we got to the courthouse, we were all seated on benches inside the courtroom. The judge faced us, sitting behind a huge desk on a raised platform.

When it was my turn, a guard brought me through a wooden gate and up to one of the two tables only feet away from the judge's desk. Melissa stood next to me, holding the same leather folder in front of her. The judge read my charges. Possession of less than one gram of a class A substance. Distribution, intent to distribute, and trafficking of over two hundred grams of a class A substance.

I wanted to throw up, but I had nothing left in my stomach.

"How do you plead?" the judge asked.

I looked at Melissa and she nodded.

"Not guilty," I said. I sounded like a boy going through puberty.

And I wasn't guilty. Maybe I was guilty of the possession charge. The cop had found heroin and paraphernalia in my pockets before he put me in the back of his cruiser. But the rest was bullshit.

The judge said my court date was scheduled for the first Monday in July. That was two months away. Then he set my bail at ten thousand dollars.

I was bused to the Nashua Street jail and put in a cell with a nineteen-year-old named Shelby. She had been arrested for forgery and robbery and hadn't posted bail, so she was waiting for her trial. With her rosy cheeks and big oval eyes, she looked like the Raggedy Ann doll my parents had given me for my fourth birthday.

Venus had been arrested for prostitution, but she was escorting to support her four kids. Shelby had stolen checks out of mailboxes and cashed them at banks to feed her eight brothers and sisters back in Alabama.

Shelby and Venus looked better than I did. But did I look like someone who would traffic two hundred grams of heroin? Maybe on the outside—track marks all over my arms and legs, rail-thin body, sunken eyes—and yet on the inside, I felt innocent. I was guilty of being a junkie, of stealing and hooking to support my addiction, but I wasn't being charged with those crimes. All I'd done was sneak into Dustin's van and help him load up the heroin. Since I'd messed up so bad my parents weren't going to help me, I'd be stuck with Melissa and probably get the whole sentence. Twenty years in jail with no smack? I was as good as dead.

After lunch, a corrections officer came to my cell and said I'd posted bail. He brought me to registration, and once I signed all the forms and changed into my clothes, they let me leave the jail. I hoped to see Michael or my parents when I walked out the front door. But instead, Tweaker Tommy was waiting for me on the steps of the jail.

So Richard had paid to bail me out. I didn't know if that was good or not.

"Where's Dustin?" I asked, looking around the steps and on the sidewalk.

"The judge didn't set bail," he said. "Dustin's too much of a flight risk, I guess."

I walked down the steps and turned in the direction of the train station. Tommy was behind me, and over my shoulder I said, "Tell Richard I said thanks for getting me out."

He grabbed the back of my arm. "Not so fast," he said. "Richard wants to talk to you. You're coming with me."

Of course Richard wanted to talk. He wanted to know what I'd said to the cops and what I was going to say during my trial.

His fingers clamped my wrist, and he dragged me to the street where his car was parked. A black Toyota, just like Dustin said. He put me in the passenger seat and went around to the driver's side. My stomach churned, not just from being dope sick and from the thought of seeing Richard, but from the scent of the car too. The odor was a mix of bong water and cat piss. I rolled down the window, and he told me to put it back up.

"Do you have any dope?" I asked.

Tommy only used meth, but he might be carrying some smack since he'd know how sick I'd be when I got out.

"I'll get you some once we get to Richard's," he said.

Richard's house was the one place I didn't want to go. He knew I hadn't ratted him out. If I had, the police would have already raided his house. But how was he going to make sure I wouldn't talk? He'd probably make me stay at his house until the trial to make sure I didn't meet with any detectives behind his back. I'd be locked in one of the bedrooms or worse, the basement. And he'd rape me again, or he might just have one of his squatters kill me instead.

I didn't know what Richard was going to do, but I knew I had to get out of this car. The jail wasn't too far from his house. If I was going to escape, I had to do it soon.

The road went from three lanes to two, and Tommy stayed to the right. I checked the lock and it was up. He didn't expect me to bolt from the car.

I waited for him to speed up after stopping at a red light and when the gauge hit fifteen miles per hour, I opened the door.

Tommy shouted, "What the fuck are you doing?"

He reached for my arm, but I moved away just in time, rolling out of the seat and onto the pavement. My shoulder slammed onto the road first, and then the side of my stomach hit and my thigh. I felt the sting immediately, my skin scraping against the street.

The car behind Tommy's slammed on its breaks. Tommy did too, but I was already up and running. I ached, and blood oozed from my cuts, but I only ran faster.

I sprinted down side streets and through alleys, looking over my shoulder to make sure he wasn't following. After a few more blocks, I came to a music store. I went inside and headed towards the back of the store, pretending to look through the racks of CD's while keeping my eyes locked on the front of the building.

One of the sales clerks came over and asked if she could help me. I told her I was just checking out the new music. She looked at me like I was still wearing my blue jumpsuit and handcuffs and at any minute I was going to pull out a gun.

I didn't need a mirror to know how bad I looked. My fingertips were black from when the cops took my prints, and my clothes were covered with blood from the jump.

She said the new releases were in the front of the store and I was in the oldies section. She also said my appearance was bothering the other customers and she asked me to leave. Enough time had passed and I knew I'd lost Tommy, so it was safe to go back on the street. But I had to be careful. Richard and his whole gang would be looking for me, and I had to stick to places outside Dorchester and spots in Boston where they wouldn't check.

I apologized to the clerk and left the store.

On the way to the train station, I stopped by a Goodwill drop box. There was a trash bag full of clothes that hadn't made it inside. I found jeans and a t-shirt that looked like they'd fit, along with a winter hat and scarf, and changed in a McDonald's bathroom. Outside the train station, I panhandled, and when I collected enough money, I rode to Roxbury and scored a few bags and a rig.

When I finally made it to the park, I curled up in the small space between the slide and monkey bars and shot up. My stomach pains went away, but I didn't get high. I didn't have enough money to get high, and the dope was cut and not that strong.

I didn't know what to do. On the way to the park I'd stopped at a newspaper stand and saw Dustin's mug shot along with mine had made the front page of the *Boston Globe* under the headline "Boston Police Make Decades-Largest Heroin Bust." I was sure Michael read the paper and had told my parents the news.

If I decided to go to court, I wouldn't be able to stay sober until my trial, so in prison I'd have to detox all over again. And if I didn't talk to the police, I'd rot in that cell for at least fifteen years. When I got out, I'd be forty, and half my life would be over. Even if I ratted everyone out, I was still going to jail, and any amount of time was too long. The only thing I could do was live on the streets until I figured out a plan.

When I was a kid and imagined my life, this wasn't what I dreamed of: addicted to heroin, getting arrested and living on the streets. My friends and I talked trash about the kids we grew up with who turned into oxy-heads and went to Acadia Hospital for rehab. And now I was one of those fucked up kids too. But I didn't want to be.

I put on the winter hat and pulled it down past my eyebrows, covered the bottom of my face with the scarf, and set out to boost in the morning. It wasn't exactly hat and scarf weather, but I couldn't take the chance of being recognized by any of the store clerks. Boosting gave me enough money to buy dope. And later tonight I'd trick, buy food, and rent a hotel room.

But by midnight, I'd only been hired by one John, and he only paid me ten bucks for the blowjob. Johns were driving up and down the track looking to hire and all the other hoes on the street were getting picked up. My clothes weren't sexy, and they were covered in filth from sleeping in the park. I'd tucked the bottom of my t-shirt under my bra to show off my caved-in stomach, but even that didn't help. My face was dirty. My hair was greasy and tangled, and I didn't have an elastic to tie it back.

The hookers around me were charging eighty for sex. When a trick pulled over to negotiate a price with one of the girls, I went up to the driver's side window and offered to do him for twenty instead. He turned me down.

I moved further down the street and took off my t-shirt, standing at the corner in my bra. A car pulled up, and as I was telling him my fee, a cop turned down the street and drove towards us with its blue lights on. I took off running and cut through an alley, hiding next to a dumpster. The cop didn't follow me, but I wasn't going to risk going back out onto the track.

There were some Styrofoam take-out boxes in front of the dumpster. Most of the food inside was rotten except for a few chunks of bread. Once I picked off the green fuzz, I ate the bread, and when I had to go to the bathroom, I squatted on the opposite side of the dumpster. I watched my river of pee spread into the middle of the alley and a rat scurry through it.

How much longer could I do this—sleep in an alley without any food and water and barely have enough smack to keep me straight? I kept reminding myself that this was better than jail. Anything was better than being locked up and sober, being wakened every night by nightmares. This time, they'd be filled with visions of Richard raping me.

But life on the street only got worse. My clothes got dirtier, and my stomach got hungrier. The food I was eating out of the trash bins, moldy and mushy, was making me sick. Maybe I was sick because I wasn't shooting enough dope. Either way, I was throwing up every few hours. I went from getting one or two Johns a night to none. I stole CD's and electronics out of the cars parked on the streets, but I ran out of energy after a couple hours and would collapse, dizzy and puking, on a bench. The pawnshops were ripping me off too and only giving me half of what the electronics were worth. I didn't have enough money to buy clean rigs, and the one I had was dull, and an abscess was forming on my arm.

I hadn't seen Sunshine on the track all week, so I stopped by our old hotel to see if she'd let me move in with her. Lucchi, the owner, said she didn't live there anymore. I called her cell phone and it was disconnected.

I had to talk to Michael and beg him to help me. Even if he'd only give me food, at least that would give me some more energy so I could steal for longer without getting sick.

When I knew he'd be home from work, I walked to his apartment. His doorman, a different guy than before, told me to wait on the sidewalk while he called him. Michael came outside. He smelled so clean, like the hospital room when I'd overdosed. How long ago was that? Six months?

Michael didn't say anything. He just stood against the building with his arms crossed.

"I need help," I said. "I'm starving."

His eyes didn't move from mine. His posture didn't shift, and his expression didn't soften. He still didn't say anything.

"Please, Michael, I need your help."

"I'll only help you if you're willing to help yourself."

Help myself? Did he mean tell the cops the truth and take the plea bargain, go to jail and get sober? If he thought I was going to do that, he was fucking crazy.

"Can I have some food?" I asked.

He covered his face with his hands. "As much as I want to feed you," he said from behind his fingers, "I can't until you get clean."

"All I need is some food, and I promise I won't ask for anything else ever again."

He shook his head and reached for the door.

"You can't leave me like this," I shouted. "I'm starving."

The door slammed in my face. I banged on the glass, leaving smudge marks and prints. "I'm your sister," I yelled.

He got into the elevator.

"Please," I screamed. My foot slipped, and I fell to my ass on the hard pavement.

The doorman said if I didn't leave, he'd call the police.

I looked up at him from the ground. "Michael won't let you call the cops on me, I'm his sister—"

"He's already given me his permission," the doorman said. "Now leave."

Michael was done with me, and that meant my parents were too. Screw them. I didn't need their help anyway. I'd done just fine without them for years.

I walked down the sidewalk and sat in the park. I didn't have any dope. I couldn't steal until after sunset, but that was only a few hours away.

CHAPTER TWENTY-THREE

The street wasn't a kind place to live. Business people wouldn't spare much change, car doors were locked more often than not, and dealers wouldn't let me pay them with sex. Every time I went to the shelter to sleep, it was full, and the soup kitchen was always running out of food. They'd give me fruit or granola bars and say to come back in a couple hours when they restocked. I never did, it was too far of a walk. I was surviving, but barely.

And then I met Big Teddy. I was lying on the sidewalk, dope sick and starving, and days had passed since I'd eaten or shot up. Big Teddy kneeled down in front of me wearing a black velour tracksuit and overgrown cornrows hidden behind a bandana. His skin was so dark the only part of his face I could see were his gold teeth.

"Come work for me," he said. "I'll watch your back and give you what you need." He pulled my arm away from my body and turned it over, eyeing my track marks. "I've got some real tight shit too, no street grade junk for my girls."

I needed to get well again. I had nothing more to lose.

"You in?" he asked.

"Yeah, I'm in," I said.

He picked me up in his arms and put me in the passenger seat of his van, and we drove to his house in Roxbury. Compared to the streets, any place would have been luxurious, but his place really was. There was leather furniture and a big-screen TV on the living room wall.

Big Teddy introduced me to Emma, the girl sitting on one of the couches, and to Suzette, the housemother, who was in the kitchen. Suzette told me to call her Mama. She was a hefty woman, fat like

Big Teddy and over six feet tall with blond hair teased like a beehive. Big Teddy said Suzette would take good care of me and left the house.

Suzette brought me over to the kitchen table and helped me sit down. She made me a sandwich and sat across from me, watching me chew and swallow. The sandwich was the first real meal I'd eaten since the day before Dustin and I had been arrested, and it tasted as good as lobster.

After I polished off a bag of chips, she brought me to a room upstairs, which she told me I'd be sharing with two other girls. On the bed, she placed cotton shorts and a t-shirt and a bundle of junk. I asked for a rig and she told me she didn't allow her girls to shoot dope because her clients got turned off by track marks.

"But—"

"No back talking," she snapped. "Snort it like all the other girls do. We're nice enough to even supply you with that shit."

She had seemed so nice when I was eating my sandwich and had even asked if I wanted dessert.

She took me into the bathroom where she gave me a razor, my own bar of soap, and a towel.

"Strip," she said.

"Right here?"

She closed the bathroom door. "Hurry up, I don't have all night."

I took off everything I was wearing, and she looked me all over, inspecting every inch of my body and mouth. I hadn't showered in weeks, and I'd thrown up on myself that morning. My smell was too much for even me, but she didn't seem bothered by it.

When she was done examining me, she told me to sit on the toilet and spread my legs. She put on a pair of rubber gloves and combed my pubes with her fingers. I'd spread my legs for Johns, but this was different. She was crouched down in front of me, her face inches from my crotch. This was like when the nurses had checked the dirty kids at school for lice.

When I asked what she was looking for, she said warts and crabs. "Big Teddy can't get a rep for giving the crawlies to his clients."

The Johns I was used to doing on the streets never asked if I had any STDs. Big Teddy must have some big paying clients.

She threw the gloves in the trash, and I crossed my legs and cupped my tits with my hands.

"I'm going to give you the night off so you can get yourself cleaned up," she said. "But you're working tomorrow night."

Once she left the bathroom, I snorted a few bags and got in the shower. I scrubbed the dirt off my skin and washed my hair twice. I didn't think I'd be able to get the street smell off me, but I did. I put on the shorts and t-shirt and went downstairs, taking a seat next to Emma on the couch.

The TV volume was really low, and Suzette was in the kitchen, answering the non-stop phone calls and typing on her computer. I whispered to Emma, "Taking the night off?"

She had short, black, choppy hair with eyelashes so long they curled up to her eyebrows.

"I'm on the rag," she said. "That's the only time we're allowed to take off."

"You like working for Big Teddy?"

She shrugged her shoulders. "Better than being on the streets, I guess."

I agreed. Suzette was a little bitchy, but the house was nice, and the dope she'd given me was better than the dirt I bought from the dealers in Roxbury.

"How long have you worked for him?" I asked.

"About a year," she said. "I want to go back home to New Hampshire, but I don't have the money for a bus ticket."

Didn't she just say she worked every night except for when she had her period? If Big Teddy supplied food and drugs, then why didn't she have fifty bucks for a bus ticket?

"Does he charge you rent or something?"

She'd been staring at the TV, but she finally looked over at me. "Once you start working, you'll catch on real quick."

"What do you mean? Do you—"

"Nicole," Suzette said from the kitchen. "Come in here now."

Emma took off down the hall, and I went to the kitchen. Suzette, still typing, asked me to pour her a glass of gin. I filled the glass with ice and booze and set it in front of her.

As I was about to walk away, she grabbed my wrist. "If you've got questions, you ask me, not Emma."

"I wasn't—"

"This isn't the streets, you do as I say and don't you ever talk to the other girls. Got it?"

Her fingers tightened around my wrist.

I nodded.

Suzette reminded me of Miss Piggy, but her voice was deep and her face wasn't cute.

"I know all about you," she said. "All it would take is one phone call, and your ass would be back in jail."

With my mug shot being on the front page of the paper, I guess I was kind of famous now. But couldn't I say the same thing to her? She ran a whorehouse and handed out drugs to her hookers. I decided to keep my mouth shut. I went to my room, sniffed a bag, and got into bed.

After everything Sunshine had taught me about pimps, I never thought I'd be working for one, living in a whorehouse and taking orders from a madam. But Emma was right. This was better than being on the streets. I could hide out here and skip my court date and avoid Richard and jail while I saved some money and came up with a plan. And even later that night when Big Teddy climbed on top of me and humped me until my crotch felt raw, I still thought living here was the best place for me.

Suzette came into my room the next night and told me to get ready for work. She was going to start me on the street, and if I hustled and impressed her and Big Teddy, she'd promote me to an escort where I'd work in hotels. She gave me an outfit and makeup and products to do my hair. When all the girls and I were ready, we got into Big Teddy's van, and he drove us to the track. The girls got out and went to their spots, and Big Teddy pulled me aside. He handed me condoms and told me where to stand and how much to charge. He said I wasn't to take anything less than the prices he set or I'd owe him the difference.

I did what I was told, standing at the corner with my skirt hiked high and my boobs spilling out of my tank top and waving at the cars driving by. It didn't take long before a white pickup pulled over and the John rolled down his window. He had golden skin and talked with a Spanish accent, asking how much I charged for a blowjob. Big Teddy was standing not too far behind me, and I could feel his eyes on my back while I leaned into the window. I told the John forty bucks, and he said to get in. He drove to a side street and parked in the lot behind a hair salon. I asked for the money up front, and when both twenties were tucked inside my bra, I put on the condom and sucked as hard and as fast as I could.

Sunshine and I had only charged twenty for head. But even though I was charging forty, I was still making the same because I had to give Big Teddy his cut. At least that was how I thought it worked.

The John held my hair with one hand and my boob with his other. While I was bobbing on his dick, he made these weird cough-like noises, and when he came he neighed like a horse. I got out of the truck and Big Teddy met me at the corner.

He stuck out his hand and I pulled out one of the twenties from my bra and put it on his palm.

"You only charged twenty for head?" he asked.

"No, forty like you said."

"Then where's the rest of my damn money?"

His money? I pointed at my bra.

"Give it to me," he said.

"I thought I got half?"

"You thought wrong. Hand it over now."

Just because he put me up and fed me didn't mean he deserved all the money I made. Twenty bucks was my cut, and I wasn't going to give it to him.

"No," I said.

He grabbed my arms and threw me against the brick building. "I'm only going to tell you this once, you keep five bucks from every trick you turn, and I keep the rest. There's no negotiating."

"That's not fair," I said.

He released one of my arms and slapped me across the face with the back of his hand.

I tasted blood on my lip.

I didn't care how much dope Big Teddy gave me. I didn't need him. I'd find another pimp who would take care of me and let me keep half my earnings.

"I'm not giving you shit, and I'm not working for you anymore either," I said.

His knuckles slammed into my jaw, and my head bounced against the brick before I fell to the ground.

He stood over me and pointed with his finger. "It doesn't work like that, once you're mine you're mine until I let you go." He kicked my side with his black shiny shoe. And then he kicked me again. I rolled onto my stomach and dug my nails against the pavement, trying to crawl away from him.

A red car pulled up to the curb a few feet away and the door opened. From the corner of my eye, a pair of sneakers was moving over to me. I lifted my head to see who it was, and Big Teddy stomped on my back.

I screamed from the pain.

"Touch her again and I'm calling the police," a man said from behind me.

His voice sounded familiar. But my back hurt too much to turn around and see who it was.

Big Teddy laughed. "She's my whore and I'll touch her whenever I damn well please."

Someone's fingers grazed the skin on my throat and I winced, waiting for them to hurt me. But they didn't hurt me, they checked my pulse. "Cole, I'll get you out of here in a second."

Cole? Michael was here? Michael's fingers were touching me?

I rolled over to my back, and Michael was crouched next to me.

"Are you okay?" he asked.

I nodded.

"Just hang tight," Michael said.

"Get your fucking hands off her," Big Teddy said.

"She's coming with me," Michael said.

Big Teddy reached his hand into his jacket, and the head of his gun poked out from his inside pocket.

"Michael, watch out," I shouted. "He's got a gun."

Michael reacted fast, drew back his arm and clocked Big Teddy in the nose. Big Teddy staggered back a few steps, and blood dripped down his mouth and onto his jacket. Michael punched him again, but this time his fist landed on Big Teddy's stomach. Big Teddy leaned over like he was trying to catch his breath, and his hand disappeared into his pocket again. He pulled out the gun and stood up straight, aiming it at Michael. And as Michael tried to grab the gun from his hand, it went off. The bang echoed in my ears. Michael collapsed, falling over on top of my legs. Blood soaked through his shirt and pooled onto my jeans and the pavement.

Big Teddy reached for me. "You're coming with me," he said. He yanked at my arm, trying to pull me out from under Michael's heavy body.

"Leave me alone," I screamed. I bit his hand, sinking my teeth deep into his flesh.

He kicked me so I'd unclamp his fingers from my mouth and said, "Come with me or I'll kill you too."

I released his hand and he looked around at the crowd that was gathering behind us. "Get in the van now," he said.

"Call the police," I yelled at the people around us.

Big Teddy pushed through the crowd, waddling over to his van and driving away.

I pulled my legs out from under Michael and sat behind him with his head on my lap. "You're going to be okay," I said. "Does anyone have a cell phone?"

No one answered and they all started to move away from Michael and me.

I searched Michael's pockets and found his cell, calling 9-1-1. I told the operator my brother had been shot and he was losing a lot of blood and gave him our location.

As I hung up, Michael's eyes were closing, and I shook his head. "Michael, open your eyes." His eyes opened and closed and opened again. I knew the pain he was feeling. I'd been shot in the chest too.

"Just wanted... help you..." he said.

I put my ear closer to his mouth so I could hear him and cradled his chest in my arms. "I know you did."

"I left you. Outside. Starving." Blood came out of his mouth. "Sorry, Cole."

"I'm fine, Michael, you did the right thing. Do you hear me? I'm just fine."

His eyes closed again and I shook him so he'd stay awake. "You're going to be okay," I said. "You just need to stay with me and keep your eyes open."

The sirens from the ambulance got louder and louder, and when it pulled up next to us I had to cover my ears. The shrieking sound and all the blood was just too much.

The paramedics lifted Michael from my arms and put him on a stretcher which they put in the back of the ambulance. I jumped inside and sat next to him. The paramedic moved quickly, hooking him up to machines and an IV.

I held Michael's other hand.

"Is he going to be okay?" I asked the medic.

He was speaking to the driver, using medical words I didn't understand.

"He's coding," he said to the driver.

He put a balloon-like machine in Michael's mouth and pumped it. Then he started pushing on Michael's chest. "One, two, three," he counted and squeezed the balloon.

"What's going on?" I asked.

"One, two, three," he said and pumped the balloon again.

I'd seen CPR done only once before and that was when I was a kid, swimming at the lake and a lifeguard had saved a little boy from drowning. But the little boy hadn't made it. He died on the beach in front of his whole family.

"Is he going to be okay?" I shouted.

"What's the ETA?" he asked the driver.

"Thirty seconds," the driver said.

"One, two, three," he said again and pumped.

"Please, answer me," I said. But he didn't. I kept squeezing Michael's hand.

At the ER entrance, the driver opened the back door and pulled the stretcher onto the ground where a group of nurses was waiting. They wheeled Michael into the ER, and I followed until a nurse stopped me. She put on a pair of gloves and held my face with her hands, checking out my busted lip and bruised jaw. She said she'd get a doctor to check me out, and I told her I was fine, and I just wanted to see Michael. She told me to sit in the waiting room and they'd keep me updated.

I still had Michael's cell phone and dialed my parents' number. It was after midnight and when mom answered, she sounded like I'd woken her. "Is everything alright, honey?"

"It's Nicole."

"Why are you calling from Michael's phone? What's going on?"

After all these months of not talking, I could only imagine how strange it was for her to hear my voice.

She asked again if everything was okay. She had to know something was up.

"You need to drive down here and hurry," I said.

"What are you talking about?"

"Michael's been shot."

"Steve, wake up," Mom screamed. "Michael's hurt."

"Give me the phone," Dad said in the background. "Who is this?"

"It's Nicole."

"Where is he?"

"We're at Boston Medical," I said.

He told me they'd be here as soon as they could and hung up.

I watched the clock in the waiting room. Every time the second hand moved, there was a loud ticking noise, the same noise as when Big Teddy cocked his gun. The sound made my skin hurt.

Michael was going to be fine.

The doctor rounded the corner of the waiting room. He moved slowly and with no expression on his face.

"Are you related to Michael Brown?" the doctor asked.

I moved to the edge of my seat. "Yes."

"I'm sorry," he said. "Michael didn't survive..." The doctor continued to talk, but I didn't hear anything else he said.

My brother was dead. It didn't seem real.

I squeezed my hands together and pierced my skin with my nails. I was totally numb and couldn't feel anything. I felt like I was outside my body, looking at myself.

Heroin. This was all the heroin's fault. But it was my fault too, my fault for trying it and continuing to use, not letting my parents take me to rehab at Eric's funeral, or Michael when he found me in the bar and all the times I'd gone to his apartment for money. It was my fault for leaving rehab with Dustin, getting arrested, skipping my court date, and agreeing to work for Big Teddy. I'd gotten Michael killed. And Michael wasn't the only person I'd lost from this drug. Eric and Claire and Heather were dead too. Raul had gone to jail and so had Dustin. Smack had affected everyone around me. It had ruined me, destroyed my body, killed my baby and now my poor Michael too.

I wasn't the same person anymore. I'd stopped caring about everything and everyone. My beliefs—being a good person, treating people with respect, and standing on the right side of the law—had been thrown away when dope had entered my life. I'd stolen from innocent people, I'd lied to my family, I'd sold my body.

I had to take back the control I'd lost. I had to come clean for Michael. And for me too. I had to fess up to my crimes and tell the police everything I knew about Richard, Séamus, and Dustin, and Big Teddy to make this right.

My parents ran into the ER entrance and up to the nurses' station.

"Mom," I yelled.

Mom and Dad ran over to me. I stood and met them half way.

"How is he? Can we see him?" Mom asked.

I shook my head and looked down at my hands. I'd washed them several times in the bathroom, but Michael's blood was still caked under my fingernails. His blood was on my tank top and skirt too.

"Nicole? Say something," Dad said.

"The bullet was too close to his heart," I said. I looked up and into their eyes. "He's dead."

Mom dropped to her knees and clung to dad's leg. I'd seen my mom cry before, but this wasn't crying. Her whole body convulsed, and screams poured from her mouth. Dad, always the stronger of the two, rubbed the top of Mom's head and then crouched down next to her and rocked her in his arms. His face was red, and the lines of his wrinkles sunk even deeper as they were filled with tears.

I didn't know what to say. I was covered in their son's blood. But they deserved to know the truth. They needed to hate me and blame me because Michael had died for me.

I sat on the floor and they both looked over at me. I started with when I had gone to Michael's apartment and asked him for food and how he wanted me to help myself before he'd help me. I told them how I'd gotten picked up by Big Teddy and worked for him on the street. I explained the fight I'd had with him over money and how Michael had somehow found me and tried to stop Big Teddy from beating me to death. And finally how Big Teddy had pulled out his gun and shot Michael in the chest.

Not too long into my confession, they stopped looking at me. And I understood. I didn't want to look at me either. Hell, I didn't want to be me.

"You already ruined this family," Mom shouted. "And now you've gotten your brother killed. I can't even stand being in the same room as you."

Dad stood and helped Mom to her feet. He wrapped his arm around her shoulder, and they began to walk away.

"Dad, Mom, I'm sorry," I said.

Neither of them turned around. I didn't expect them to, but I wanted them to know I was sorry. And that I was going to do right.

They went to the nurses' station, and one of the nurses took them through the double doors, the same doors the paramedics had wheeled Michael through.

Once they were out of sight, I asked a nurse if the hospital had any extra clothes I could change into. She gave me a pair of sweatpants and a sweatshirt, and I put them on in the bathroom and left the hospital.

It was five in the morning and the streets were chilly and dark. I walked and looked at everything around me like it was the first time I'd ever seen trees and sidewalks and stores. The leaves looked green under the streetlamps, and the storefronts were bright with neon signs. Chewed-up gum, in a rainbow of colors, was stuck to the sidewalk. In my head, I made shapes out of the gum like I did when I looked at clouds.

There was something beautiful about Boston. Maybe it was because the heroin had worn off and I was seeing things more clearly. There had to be beauty outside of Boston too, things I'd never seen before and places I'd never been. Twenty-five was too young to die. I didn't want to die like Michael had, getting murdered or overdosing on junk. I wanted to live and be the girl I was in college before I'd gotten raped. In order for that to happen, I had to fess up to my crimes. And I had to quit smack.

The police had come to the hospital right after the doctor had given me the news and wanted a statement from me. At the time, I wasn't ready to talk and I didn't give them any information. But I was ready now. I called Jesse, Michael's boyfriend, told him what happened and which hospital he was at. Then I walked to the police station and told the officer about Big Teddy, where he lived, and about the gun he shot Michael with.

By the time I left the police station, the sun was lighting up the sky, the sidewalks packed with pedestrians and the streets jammed with cars. I decided not to take the train. I wanted to walk and look at the city because it was going to be the last time I'd see it for a while.

I walked straight to downtown and entered the building on Federal Street. I took the elevator up to Melissa's office.

CHAPTER TWENTY-FOUR

My cell in the South Bay House of Corrections was dark. There was a small, barred window, but the sky was too cloudy for stars, and I was on the top floor far from the streetlamps. The only things I could see around me were the shiny metal toilet and sink, and the side rails of the bunk bed on top of mine. My celly, Devry, was snoring. Her snores had been keeping me awake every night for the last two months.

I was familiar with the South Bay House of Corrections; actually, it was the same jail Henry was in. I never thought I'd be living four floors above him. I guess that was what happened when you were stupid enough to get caught. But this time I wasn't stupid; I'd done the right thing for once. I'd met with Melissa, and she set up a meeting with the detectives and the DA. I told them everything I knew about Richard and Séamus and Dustin. When the DA presented me with a plea bargain of two-and-a-half years in jail, I took it and stood in front of the judge and plead guilty.

Dustin's trial was set to begin in a few months, and I knew my testimony was going to get him a sentence of at least twenty years, plus the time he'd get for his previous arrest. He deserved twenty years for trafficking heroin to dealers who got people strung out and killed on that shit. I deserved my two-and-a-half year sentence too because my involvement with the run was just as wrong.

During the months that followed Renee and Jose's death, I'd been too addicted and in love to care about what Dustin had done to them. At the time, I thought Renee should be punished for letting Eric die, and Jose too for threatening my life and hitting me with his gun. I thought Dustin was a hero. But he was a murderer. No one deserved to die. Eric had been dead for three years, and it had taken me all this time to grasp how much I missed him. I missed Claire, too.

This morning, I enrolled in the jail's ninety-day substance abuse program. I thought being in prison would be enough to keep me sober, but drugs floated around in here, and if I had the money, I could buy them. I hadn't yet. But I was tempted, and that made me realize I needed help. Just like when I was in rehab, the counselor wrote the Twelve Steps on the board while all of us addicts sat at desks with notebooks and pencils in hand. In my head, I recited Step One: We admitted we were powerless over our addiction – that our lives had become unmanageable.

Before I came to prison, I'd lost all power and control, and my life had definitely become unmanageable. Today was only my first day and I'd already graduated Step One. I was doing a lot better than I'd done during my one week in rehab.

I listened to the other women tell their stories, how drugs had affected their lives, and then I told mine. What I didn't want was sad faces looking back at me and pity in their eyes while I confessed all the mistakes I'd made. I'd chosen to use heroin, and everything that had happened to me was my fault. I didn't deserve sympathy. And I didn't receive any of that. The women told me my heroin cravings would start to subside and achieving sobriety, even after all the bad shit I'd done, would happen in time. I thought about Michael every day. I didn't think I'd ever get over his death and I'd want to use just to block it out, but I trusted my counselors and the women who were in my group. Trust was part of sobriety, so I was working on that too.

I hadn't spoken to my parents since they left me in the waiting room at the hospital. But I got a letter from them, written in mom's handwriting. She wrote that they had buried Michael in the Mount Hope Cemetery in Bangor and they visited him every day. She said she was proud of me for turning myself in to the police and giving them all the information on my dealers so the cops could take them down too. I guess she had followed my case. She wrote that she'd lost one child and didn't want to lose another and hoped I was getting help and starting the process of recovery. She ended the letter by saying she'd like to see me, and she and dad would be coming to visit at some point, but they weren't ready for that yet. She didn't say anything about forgiving me. I knew that would take time. I hadn't forgiven myself, and I wasn't sure if I ever would.

While in prison, I realized what heroin really was. Like the cop had said during my fifth grade D.A.R.E. class, heroin was a terrorist. And it had destroyed me. But I wasn't dead and with time and help from my counselors, I had a chance to mend everything I'd broken. I didn't know how that was possible, how I could live a normal life without being filled with anxiety, haunted by my past, and not reach for a needle to erase those memories. But I guess I had two years and four months to figure all that out.

The only thing I brought with me to prison was Henry's gold band. Like me, it had survived living on the streets, and I hadn't lost it like everything else in my life.

I leaned off the bed and grabbed the ring off the sink, where I'd kept it since coming to prison, and rolled it around in my palm. I hadn't put it on yet because I didn't want to disrespect Claire. The ring was for sobriety.

I pictured my life in ten years. With a felony on my record, teaching at a school was no longer an option. During the day, I'd work at a rehab center, helping kids with their own addiction. At night, I'd come home to my loft in the South End. My children would be home from school and I'd help them with their reading, vocabulary, and math. From all the damage I'd done to my body, being able to bear children would be a gift in itself. After dinner, Pork Chop, our Boston terrier, would need to be walked, and the kids and I would take him to the park. On my ring finger would be Henry's gold band, and I'd never take it off. Not even to shower.

I placed the ring back on the sink. For now, that was the perfect place for it.

I heard for some people there was life after heroin. At least that was what the other inmates said during chow and my counselors made us believe during my drug classes. All the junkies I knew were either dead or in jail. And if they weren't in either of those places, their story wasn't a happy one.

Mine wasn't either.

My memoir is no damn fairytale. But my story isn't over yet.

More Great Reads from Booktrope Editions

Riversong by Tess Hardwick (Contemporary Romance) Sometimes we must face our deepest fears to find hope again. A redemptive story of forgiveness and friendship.

Sweet Song, by Terry Persun (Historical Fiction) This tale of a mixed race man passing as white in post-Civil War America speaks from the heart about where we've come from and who we are.

Wolf's Rite, by Terry Persun (Adventure) _A ruthless big city ad exec is captured by mystical Native Americans who send him on a spirit walk, where he discovers love and violence at the edges of sanity.

Throwaway by Heather Huffman (Romantic Suspense) A prostitute and a police detective fall in love, proving it's never too late to change your destiny and seek happiness. That is, if she can take care of herself when the mob has a different idea.

Jailbird by Heather Huffman (Romantic Suspense) A woman running from the law makes a new life. Sometimes love, friendship and family bloom against all odds...especially if you make a tasty dandelion jam. (coming fall 2011)

Ring of Fire by Heather Huffman (Romantic Suspense) Wealth, beauty and power are somehow not enough. Maybe if you add in smuggling and rare diamonds? (coming December, 2011)

Don Juan in Hankey, PA by Gale Martin (Contemporary Fantasy) A fabulous mix of seduction, ghosts, humor, music and madness, as a rust-belt opera company stages Mozart's masterpiece. You needn't be an opera lover to enjoy this wonderful book.

... and many more!

Sample our books at www.booktrope.com

Learn more about our new approach to publishing at
www.booktropepublishing.com

Made in the USA
San Bernardino, CA
21 April 2014